Socialism

John Spargo

Contents

SOCIALISM

BY

John Spargo

To
ROBERT HUNTER
WITH ADMIRATION AND AFFECTION

PREFACE TO SECOND EDITION

A new edition of this little volume having been rendered necessary, I have availed myself of the opportunity thus afforded me by the publishers to revise it. Some slight revision was necessary to correct one or two errors which crept unavoidably into the earlier edition. By an oversight, an important typographical blunder went uncorrected into the former edition, making the date of the first use of the word "Socialism" 1835 instead of 1833. That error, I regret to say, has been subsequently copied into many important publications. Even more important were some errors in the biographical sketch of Marx, in Chapter III. These were not due to any carelessness upon the part of the present writer, but were reproduced from standard works, upon what seemed to be good authority-- that of his youngest daughter and his intimate friend, the late Wilhelm Liebknecht. It is now known with certainty that the father of Karl Marx embraced Christianity of his own free choice, and not in obedience to an official edict.

These and some other minor changes having to be made, I took the time to rewrite large parts of the volume, making such substantial changes in it as to constitute practically a new book. The chapter on Robert Owen has been recast and greater emphasis placed upon his American career and its influence; in Chapter IV the sketch of the Materialistic Conception of History has been enlarged somewhat, special attention being given to the bearing of the theory upon religion. All the rest of the book has been changed, partly to meet the requirements of many students and others who have written to me in reference to various points of difficulty, and partly also to state some of my own ideas more successfully. I venture to hope that the brief chapter on "Means of Realization," which has been added to the book by way of postscript, will, in spite of its brevity, and the fact that it was not written for inclusion in this volume, prove helpful to some who read the book.

The thanks of the writer are due to all those friends--Socialists and others-- whose kindly efforts made the earlier edition of the book a success.

YONKERS, N.Y.,   December, 1908.

CHAPTER I
INTRODUCTION

I

It is not a long time since the kindest estimate of Socialism by the average man was that expressed by Ebenezer Elliott, "the Corn-Law Rhymer," in the once familiar cynical doggerel:--

"What is a Socialist? One who is willing
 To give up his penny and pocket your shilling."

There was another view, brutally unjust and unkind, expressed in blood-curdling cartoons representing the Socialist as a bomb-throwing assassin. According to the one view, Socialists were all sordid, envious creatures, yearning for the
 "Equal division of unequal earnings,"
while the other view represented them as ready to enforce this selfish demand by means of the cowardly weapons of the assassin.

Both these views are now, happily, well-nigh extinct. There is still a great deal of misconception of the meaning of Socialism; the ignorance concerning it which is manifested upon every hand is often disheartening, but neither of these puerile misrepresentations is commonly encountered in serious discussion. It is true that the average newspaper editorial confounds Socialism with Anarchism, often enlisting the prejudice which exists against the most violent forms of Anarchism in attacking Socialism, though the two systems of thought are fundamentally opposed to each other; it is likewise true that Socialists are not infrequently asked to explain their supposed intention to have a great general "dividing-up day" for the equal distribution of all the wealth of the nation. The Chancellor of a great American university returns from a sojourn in Norway, and naively hastens to inform the world that he has "refuted" Socialism by asking the members of some poor, struggling sect of Communists what would happen to their scheme of equality if babies should be born after midnight of the day of the equal division of wealth!

Recognizing it to be the supreme issue of the age, the Republican Party, in its national platform,[1] defines Socialism as meaning equality of ownership as against equality of opportunity, notwithstanding the fact that every recognized exponent of Socialism would deny that Socialism means equality of ownership, or that it goes beyond equality of opportunity; that the voluminous literature of Socialism teems with unequivocal and unmistakable disavowals of any desire for the periodic divisions of property and wealth which alone could make equality of ownership possible for brief periods.

Still, when all this has been said, it must be added that these criticisms do not represent the attitude of the mass of people toward the Socialist movement to the same extent as they once did. In serious discussions of the subject among thinking people it is becoming quite rare to encounter either of the two criticisms named. Most of those who seriously and honestly discuss the subject know that modern Socialism comprehends neither assassination nor the equal division of wealth. The enormous interest manifested in Socialism during recent years and the steady growth of the Socialist vote throughout the world bear witness to the fact that the views expressed in the satirical distich of the poet's fancy and the blood-curdling cartoon of the artist's invention are no longer the potent appeals to prejudice they once were.

The reason for the changed attitude of the public toward the Socialist movement and the Socialist ideal lies in the growth of the movement itself. There are many who would change the order of this proposition and say that the growth of the Socialist movement is a result of the changed attitude of the public mind toward it. In a sense, both views are right. Obviously, if the public mind had not revised its judgments somewhat, we should not have attained our present strength and development; but it is equally obvious that if we had not grown, if we had remained the small and feeble band we once were, the public mind would not have revised its judgments much, if at all. It is easy to enlist prejudice against a small body of men and women when they have no powerful influence, and to misrepresent and vilify them.

But it is otherwise when that small body has grown into a great body with far-reaching influence and power. So long as the Socialist movement in America consisted of a few poor workingmen in two or three of the largest cities, most of them foreigners, it was very easy for the average man to accept as true the wildest charges brought against them. But when the movement grew and developed a powerful organization, with branches in almost every city, and a well-conducted press of its own, it became a very different matter. The sixteen years from 1888 to 1904 saw the Socialist vote in the United States grow steadily from 2068 in the former year to 442,402 in the latter. Europe and America together had in 1870 only about 30,000 votes, but by 1906 the number had risen to considerably over 7,000,000. These figures constitute a vital challenge to the thoughtful and earnest men and women of the world.

It is manifestly impossible for a great world-wide movement, numbering its adherent by millions, and having for its advocates many of the foremost thinkers, artists, and poets of the world, to be based upon either sordid selfishness or murderous hate and envy. If that were true, if it were possible for such a thing to be true, the most gloomy forebodings of the pessimist would fall far short of the real measure of Humanity's impending doom. It is estimated that no less than thirty million adults are at present enrolled in the ranks of the Socialists throughout the world, and the number is constantly increasing. This vast army, drawn from every part of the civilized world, comprising men and women of all races and creeds, is not motivated by hate or envy, but by a consciousness that in their hands and the hands of their fellows rests the power to win greater happiness for themselves. Incidentally, their unity for this purpose is perhaps the greatest force in the world to-day making for international peace.

Still, notwithstanding the millions enlisted under the banner of Socialism, the word is spoken by many with the pallid lips of fear, the scowl of hate, or the amused shrug of contempt; while in the same land, people of the same race, facing the same problems and perils, speak it with glad voices and hopelit eyes. Many a mother crooning over her babe prays that it may be saved from the Socialism to which another, with equal mother love, looks as her child's heritage and hope. And with scholars and statesmen it is much the same. With wonderful unanimity agreeing that, in the words of Herbert Spencer, "Socialism will come inevitably, in spite of all opposition," they yet differ in their estimates of its character and probable effects upon the race quite as much as the unlearned. One welcomes and another fears; one envies the unborn generations, another pities. To one the coming of Socialism means the coming of Human Brotherhood, the long, long quest of Humanity's choicest spirits; to another it means the enslavement of the world through fear.

Many years ago Herbert Spencer wrote an article on "The Coming Slavery," which conveyed the impression that the great thinker saw what he thought to be signs of the inevitable triumph of Socialism. All over the world Socialists were cheered by this admission from their implacable enemy. In this connection it is worthy of note that Spencer continued to believe in the inevitability of Socialism. In October, 1905, a well-known Frenchman, M. G. Davenay, visited Mr. Spencer and had a long conversation with him on several subjects, Socialism among them. Soon after his return, he received a letter on the subject from Mr. Spencer, written in French, which was published in the Paris *Figaro* a few days after Mr. Spencer's death in December, 1905, two months or thereabouts from the time of the interview which called it forth.[2] After some brief reference to his health, Mr. Spencer wrote: "The opinions I have delivered here before you, and which you have the liberty to publish, are briefly these: (1) Socialism will triumph inevitably, in spite of all opposition; (2) its establishment will be the greatest disaster which the world has ever known; (3) sooner or later, it will be brought to an end by a military despotism."

Anything more terrible than this black pessimism which clouded the latter part of the life of the great thinker, it would be difficult to imagine. After living his long life of splendid service to the cause of intellectual progress, and studying as few men have ever done the history of the race, he went down to his grave fully believing that the world was doomed to inevitable disaster. How different from the confidence of the poet,[3] foretelling:--

"A wonderful day a-coming when all shall be better than well."

The last words of the great French Utopist, Saint-Simon, were, "The future is ours!" And thousands of times his words have been echoed by those who, believing equally with Herbert Spencer that Socialism must come, have seen in the prospect only the fulfillment of the age-long dream of Human Brotherhood. Men as profound as Spencer, and as sincere, rejoice at the very thing which blanched his cheeks and filled his heart with fear.

There is, then, a widespread conviction that Socialism will come and, in coming, vitally affect for good or ill every life. Millions of earnest men and women have enlisted themselves beneath its banner in various lands, and their number is steadily growing. In this country, as in Europe, the spread of Socialism is one of the most evident facts of the age, and its study is therefore most important. What does it mean, and what does it promise or threaten, are questions which civic duty prompts. The day is not far distant when ignorance of Socialism will be regarded as a disgrace, and neglect of it a civic wrong. No man can faithfully discharge the responsibilities of his citizenship until he is able to give an answer to these questions, to meet intelligently the challenge of Socialism to the age.

II

The word "Socialism" is admittedly one of the noblest and most inspiring words ever born of human speech. Whatever may be thought of the principles for which it is the accepted name, or of the political parties which contend for those principles, no one can dispute the beauty and moral grandeur of the word itself. I refer not merely, of course, to its etymology, but rather to its spiritual import. Derived from the Latin word, ***socius***, meaning a comrade, it is, like the word "mother," for instance, one of those great universal speech symbols which find their way into every language.

Signifying as it does faith in the comradeship of man as the basis of social existence, prefiguring a social state in which there shall be no strife of man against man, or nation against nation, it is a verbal expression of a great ideal, man's loftiest aspirations crystallized into a single word. The old Hebrew prophet's dream of a world-righteousness that shall give peace, when nations "shall beat their swords into plowshares, and their spears into pruning-hooks,"[4] and the Angel-song of Peace and Goodwill in the legend of the Nativity, mean no more than the word "Socialism" in its best usage means. Plato, spiritual son of the Socrates who for truth's sake drained the hemlock cup to its dregs, dreamed of such social peace and unity, and the line of those who have seen the same vision of a love-welded world has never been broken: More and Campanella, Saint-Simon and Owen, Marx and Engels, Morris and Bellamy--and the end of the prophetic line is not yet.

But if the dream, the hope itself, is old, the word is comparatively new. It is hard to realize that the word which means so much to countless millions of human beings, and which plays such a part in the vital discussions of the world, in every civilized country, is no older than many of those whose lips speak it with reverence and hope. Yet such is the fact. Because it will help us to a clearer understanding of modern Socialism, and because, too, it is little known, notwithstanding its intensely interesting character, let us linger awhile over that page of history which records the origin of this noble word.

Some years ago, anxious to settle, if possible, the vexed question of the origin and first use of the word "Socialism," the present writer devoted a good deal of time to an investigation of the subject, spending much of it in a careful survey of all the early nineteenth-century radical literature. It soon appeared that the generally accepted account of its introduction, by the French writer, L. Reybaud, in 1840, was wrong. Indeed, when once fairly started on the investigation, it seemed rather surprising that the account should have been accepted, practically without challenge, for so long. Finally the conclusion was reached that an anonymous writer in an English paper was the first to use the word in print, the date being August 24, 1833. [5] Since that time an investigation of a commendably thorough nature has been made by three students of the University of Wisconsin,[6] with the result that they have been unable to find any earlier use of the word. It is somewhat disappointing that after thus tracing the word back to what may well be its first appearance in print, it should be impossible to identify its creator.

The letter in which the term is first used is signed "A Socialist," and it is quite evident that the writer uses it as a synonym for the commonly used term "Owenite," by which the disciples of Robert Owen were known. It is most probable that Owen himself had used the word, and, to some extent, made it popular; and that the writer of the letter had heard "our dear social father," as Owen was called, use it, either in some of his speeches or in conversation. This is the more likely as Owen was fond of inventing new words. At any rate, one of Owen's associates, now dead, told the present writer that Owen often specifically claimed to have used the word at least ten years before it was adopted by any other writer.

The word gradually became more familiar in England. Throughout the years 1835-1836, in the pages of Owen's paper, ***The New Moral World***, there are many instances of the word occurring. The French writer, Reybaud, in his "Reformateurs Modernes," published in 1840, made the term equally familiar to the reading public of Continental Europe. By him it was used to designate the teachings not merely of Owen and his followers, but those of all social reformers and visionaries--Saint-Simon, Charles Fourier, Louis Blanc, and others. By an easy transition, it soon came into general use as designating all altruistic visions, theories, and experiments, from the "Republic" of Plato onward through the centuries.

In this way much confusion arose. The word became too vague and indefinite to be distinctive. It was applied--frequently as an epithet--indiscriminately to persons of widely differing, and often conflicting, views. Every one who complained of social inequalities, every dreamer of social Utopias, was called a Socialist. The enthusiastic Christian, pleading for a return to the faith and practices of primitive Christianity, and the aggressive atheist, proclaiming religion to be the bulwark of the world's wrongs; the State worshiper, who would extol Law, and spread the net of government over the whole of life, and the iconoclastic Anarchist, who would destroy all forms of social authority, have all alike been dubbed Socialists, by their friends no less than by their opponents.

The confusion thus introduced has had the effect of seriously complicating the study of Socialism from the historical point of view. Much that one finds bearing the name of Socialism in the literature of the middle of the nineteenth century, for example, is not at all related to Socialism as that term is understood to-day. Thus the Socialists of the present day, who do not advocate Communism, regard as a classic presentation of their views the famous pamphlet by Karl Marx and Friederich Engels, ***The Communist Manifesto***. They have circulated it by millions of copies in practically all the languages of the civilized world. Yet throughout it speaks of "Socialists" with ill-concealed disdain, and always in favor of Communism and the Communist Party. The reason for this is clearly explained by Engels himself in the preface written by him for the English edition, but that has not prevented many an unscrupulous opponent of Socialism from quoting the ***Communist Manifesto*** of Marx and Engels against the Socialists of the Marx-Engels school.[7] In like manner, the utterances and ideas of many of those who formerly called themselves Socialists have been quoted against the Socialists of to-day, notwithstanding that it was precisely on account of their desire to repudiate all connection with, and responsibility for, such ideas that the founders of the modern Socialist movement took the name "Communists."

Nothing could be clearer than the language in which Engels explains why the name Communist was chosen, and the name Socialist discarded. He says: "Yet, when it (the ***Manifesto***) was written, we could not have called it a ***Socialist Manifesto***. By Socialists, in 1847, were understood, on the one hand, the adherents of the various Utopian systems: Owenites in England, Fourierists in France, both of these already reduced to the position of mere sects, and gradually dying out; on the other hand, the most multifarious social quacks, who, by all manner of tinkering, professed to redress, without any danger to capital and profit, all sorts of social grievances; in both cases men outside of the working-class movement, and looking rather to the 'educated' classes for support. Whatever portion of the working class had become convinced of the insufficiency of mere political revolution and had proclaimed the necessity of a total social change, that portion, then, called itself Communist. It was a crude, rough-hewn, purely instinctive sort of Communism; still, it touched the cardinal point and was powerful enough among the working class to produce the Utopian Communism, in France, of Cabet, and in Germany, of Weitling. Thus Socialism was, in 1847, a middle-class movement; Communism a working-class movement. Socialism was, on the Continent at least, 'respectable'; Communism was the very opposite. And as our notion, from the very beginning, was that the 'emancipation of the working class must be the act of the working class itself,' there could be no doubt as to which of the names we must take. Moreover, we have ever since been far from regretting it."[8]

There is still, unfortunately, much misuse of the word "Socialism," even by some accredited Socialist exponents. Writers like Tolstoy, Ibsen, Zola, and many others, are constantly referred to as Socialists, when, in fact, they are nothing of the sort. Still, the word is now pretty generally understood as defined by the Socialists--not the "Socialists" of sixty years ago, who were mostly Communists, but the Socialists of to-day, whose principles find classic expression in the ***Communist Manifesto***, and to the attainment of which they have directed their political parties and programmes. In the words of Professor Thorstein Veblen: "The Socialism that inspires hopes and fears to-day is of the school of Marx. No one is seriously apprehensive of any other so-called Socialistic movement, and no one is seriously concerned to criticise or refute the doctrines set forth by any other school of 'Socialists.'"[9]

NOTES:
[1] Republican National Platform, 1908.
[2] I quote the English translation from the London ***Clarion***, December 18, 1905.
[3] William Morris.
[4] Isaiah ii. 4.
[5] See ***Socialism and Social Democracy***, by John Spargo. ***The Comrade***, Vol. II, No. 6, March, 1903.
[6] In ***The International Socialist Review***, Vol. VI, No. 1, July, 1905.
[7] As an instance of this I note the following example: "No severer critic of Socialists ever lived than Karl Marx. No one more bitterly attacked them and their policy toward the trade unions than he.... And yet Socialists regard him as their patron saint." Mr. Samuel Gompers, in ***The American Federationist***, August, 1905.
[8] Preface to ***The Communist Manifesto***, by F. Engels, Kerr edition, page 7.
[9] ***Quarterly Journal of Economics.***

CHAPTER II
ROBERT OWEN AND THE UTOPIAN SPIRIT

I

As a background to modern, or scientific, Socialism there is the Socialism of the Utopians, which the authors of the *Manifesto* so severely criticised. It is impossible to understand the modern Socialist movement, the Socialism which is rapidly becoming the dominant issue in the thought and politics of the world, without distinguishing sharply between it and the Utopian visions which preceded it. Failure to make this distinction is responsible for the complete misunderstanding of the Socialism of to-day by many earnest and intelligent persons.

It is not necessary that we study the Utopian movements which flourished and declined prior to the rise of scientific Socialism in detail. It will be sufficient if we consider the Utopian Socialism of Owen, which is Utopian Socialism at its best and nearest approach to the modern movement. Thus we shall get a clear view of the point of departure which marked the rise of the later scientific movement with its revolutionary political programmes. Incidentally, also, we shall get a view of the great and good Robert Owen, whom Liebknecht, greatest political leader of the movement, has called, "By far the most embracing, penetrating, and practical of all the harbingers of scientific Socialism."[10]

Friederich Engels, a man not given to praising overmuch, has spoken of Owen with an enthusiasm which he rarely showed in his descriptions of men. He calls him, "A man of almost sublime and childlike simplicity of character," and declares, "Every social movement, every real advance in England on behalf of the workers, links itself on to the name of Robert Owen."[11] And even this high praise from the part-author of **The Communist Manifesto** who for so many years was called the "Nestor of the Socialist movement," falls short, because it does not recognize the great influence of the man in the United States at a most important period of our history.

Robert Owen was born of humble parentage, in a little town in North Wales, on the fourteenth day of May, 1771. A most precocious child, at seven years of age, so he tells us in his "Autobiography," he had familiarized himself with Milton's "Paradise Lost," and by the time he was ten years old he had grappled with the ages-old problems of Whence and Whither and become a skeptic! It is doubtful whether his "skepticism" really consisted of anything more than the consciousness that there were apparent contradictions in the Bible, a discovery which many a precocious lad has made at quite as early an age, and the failure of the usual theological subterfuges to satisfy a boy's frank spirit. Still, it is worthy of note as indicating his inquiring spirit.

The great dream of his childhood was that he might become an educated man. He thirsted for knowledge and wanted above all things a university education. A passion for knowledge was the controlling force of his life. But his parents were too poor to gratify his desire for an extensive education. He was barely ten years old when his scanty schooling ended, and he set out to fight the battle of life for himself in London.

He was apprenticed to a draper, named McGuffeg, who seems to have been a rather superior type of man. From a small peddling business he had built up one of the largest and wealthiest establishments in that part of London, catering to the wealthy and the titled nobility. Above all, McGuffeg was a man of books, and in his well-stocked library young Owen could read several hours each day, and thus make up in a measure for his early lack of educational opportunities. During the three years of his apprenticeship he read prodigiously, and laid the foundations of that literary culture which characterized his whole life and added tremendously to his power.

This is not in any sense a biographical sketch of Robert Owen.[12] If it were, the story of the rise of this poor, strange, strong lad, from poverty to the very pinnacle of industrial and commercial power and fame, as one of the leading manufacturers of his day, would lead through pathways of romance as wonderful as any in our biographical literature. We are concerned, however, only with his career as a social reformer and the forces which molded it. And that, too, has its romantic side.

II

The closing years of the eighteenth century marked the beginning of a great and far-reaching industrial revolution. The introduction of new mechanical inventions enormously increased the productive powers of England. In 1770 Hargreaves patented his "spinning jenny," and in the following year Arkwright invented his "water frame," a patent spinning machine which derived its name from the fact that it was worked by water power. Later, in 1779, Crompton invented the "mule," which was really a combination of the principles of both machines. This was a long step forward, and greatly facilitated the spinning of the raw material into yarn. The invention was, in fact, a revolution in itself. Like so many other great inventors, Crompton died in poverty.

Even now, however, the actual weaving had to be done by hand. Not until 1785, when Dr. Cartwright, a parson, invented a "power loom," was it deemed possible to weave by machinery. Cartwright's invention, coming in the same year as the general introduction of Watt's steam engine in the cotton industry, made the industrial revolution. Had the revolution come slowly, had the inventors of the new industrial processes been able to accomplish that, it is most probable that much of the misery of the period would have been avoided. As it was, terrible poverty and hardship attended the birth of the new industrial order. Owing to the expense of introducing the machines, and the impossibility of competing with them by the old methods of production, the small manufacturers themselves were forced to the wall, and their misery, compelling them to become wage-workers in competition with other already far too numerous wage-workers, added greatly to the woe of the time. William Morris's fine lines, written a hundred years later, express vividly what many a manufacturer must have felt at that time:--

"Fast and faster our iron master,   The thing we made, forever drives."

But perhaps the worst of all the results of the new regime was the destruction of the personal relations which had hitherto existed between the employers and their employees. No attention was paid to the interests of the latter. The personal relation was forever gone, and only a hard, cold cash nexus remained. Wages went down at an alarming rate, as might be expected; the housing conditions became simply inhuman. Now it was discovered that a child at one of the new looms could do more than a dozen men had done under the old conditions, and a tremendous demand for child workers was the result. At first, as H. de B. Gibbins[13] tells us, there was a strong repugnance on the part of parents to sending their children into the factories. It was, in fact, considered a disgrace to do so. The term "factory girl" was an insulting epithet, and it was impossible for a girl who had been employed in a factory to obtain other employment. She could not look forward to marriage with any but the very lowest of men, so degrading was factory employment considered to be. But the manufacturers had to get children somehow, and they got them. They got them from the workhouses. Pretending that they were going to apprentice them to a trade, they arranged with the overseers of the poor regular days for the inspection of these workhouse children. Those chosen were conveyed to their destination, packed in wagons or canal boats, and from that moment were doomed to the most awful form of slavery.

"Sometimes regular traffickers would take the place of the manufacturer," says Gibbins,[14] "and transfer a number of children to a factory district, and there keep them, generally in some dark cellar, till they could hand them over to a mill owner in want of hands, who would come and examine their height, strength, and bodily capacities, exactly as did the slave owners in the American markets. After that the children were simply at the mercy of their owners, nominally as apprentices, but in reality as mere slaves, who got no wages and whom it was not worth while even to feed and clothe properly, because they were so cheap and their places could be so easily supplied. It was often arranged by the parish authorities, in order to get rid of imbeciles, that one idiot should be taken by the mill owner with every twenty sane children. The fate of these unhappy idiots was even worse than that of the others. The secret of their final end has never been disclosed, but we can form some idea of their awful sufferings from the hardships of the other victims to capitalist greed and cruelty. The hours of their labor were only limited by exhaustion, after many modes of torture had been unavailingly applied to force continued work. Children were often worked sixteen hours a day, by day and by night."

Terrible as this summary is, it does not equal in horror the account given by "Alfred,"[15] in his "History of the Factory System": "In stench, in heated rooms, amid the constant whirl of a thousand wheels, little fingers and little feet were kept in ceaseless action, forced into unnatural activity by blows from the heavy hands and feet of the merciless overlooker, and the infliction of bodily pain by instruments of punishment invented by the sharpened ingenuity of insatiable selfishness." The children were fed upon the cheapest and coarsest food, often the same as that served to their master's pigs. They slept by turns, and in relays, in filthy beds that were never cool. There was often no discrimination between the sexes, and disease, misery, and vice flourished. Some of these miserable creatures would try to run away, and to prevent them, those suspected had irons riveted on their ankles, with long links reaching up to the hips, and were compelled to sleep and work with them on, young women and girls, as well as boys, suffering this brutal treatment. The number of deaths was so great that burials took place secretly, at night, lest an outcry should be raised. Many of the children committed suicide.

These statements are so appalling that, as Mr. R. W. Cooke-Taylor says,[16] they would be "absolutely incredible" were they not fully borne out by evidence from other sources. It is not contended, of course, that conditions in all factories were as bad as those described. But it must be said emphatically that there were worse horrors than any here quoted, and equally emphatically that the very best factories were only a little better than those described. Take, for instance, the account given by Robert Owen of the conditions which obtained in the "model factory" of the time, the establishment at New Lanark, Scotland, owned by Mr. David Dale, where Owen himself was destined to introduce so many striking reforms. Owen assumed control of the New Lanark mills on the first day of the year 1800. In his "Autobiography,"[17] he gives some account of the conditions which he found there, in the "best regulated factory in the world," at that time. There were, says Owen, about five hundred children employed, who "were received as early as six years old, the pauper authorities declining to send them at any later age." They worked from six in the morning until seven in the evening, and ***then their education began***. They hated their slavery, and many absconded. Many were dwarfed and stunted in stature, and when they were through their "apprenticeship," at thirteen or fifteen years of age, they commonly went off to Glasgow or Edinburgh, with no guardians, ignorant and ready--"admirably suited," is Owen's phrase--to swell the great mass of vice and misery in the towns. The people in New Lanark lived "almost without control, in habits of vice, idleness, poverty, debt, and destitution. Thieving was general." With such conditions existing in a model factory, under a master whose benevolence was celebrated everywhere, it can be very readily believed that conditions elsewhere must have been abominable.

As a result of the appalling poverty which developed, it soon became necessary for poor parents to permit their children to go into the factories. The mighty machines were far too powerful for the prejudices of parental hearts. Child wage-workers became common. They were subjected to little better conditions than the parish apprentices had been; in fact, they were often employed alongside of them. Fathers were unemployed and frequently took meals to their little ones who were at work--a condition which sometimes obtains in some parts of the United States even to this day. Michael Sadler, a member of the House of Commons and a fearless champion of the rights of the poor and oppressed, described this aspect of the evil in touching verse.[18]

During all this time, let it be remembered, the English philanthropists, and among them many capitalists, were agitating against negro slavery in Africa and elsewhere, and raising funds for the emancipation of the slaves. Says Gibbins,[19] "The spectacle of England buying the freedom of black slaves by riches drawn from the labor of her white ones affords an interesting study for the cynical philosopher."

As we read the accounts of the distress which followed upon the introduction of the new mechanical inventions, it is impossible to regard with surprise or with condemnatory feelings, the riots of the misguided "Luddites" who went about destroying machinery in their blind desperation. Ned Lud, after whom the Luddites were named, was an idiot, but wiser men, finding themselves reduced to abject poverty through the introduction of the giant machines, could see no further than he. It was not to be expected that the masses should understand that it was not the machines, but the institution of their private ownership, and use for private gain, that was wrong. And just as we cannot regard with surprise the action of the Luddites in destroying machinery, it is easy to understand how the social unrest of the time produced Utopian movements with numerous and enthusiastic adherents.

The Luddites were not the first to make war upon machinery. In 1758, for example, Everet's first machine for dressing wool, an ingenious contrivance worked by water power, was set upon by a mob and reduced to ashes. From that time on similar outbreaks occurred with more or less frequency; but it was not until 1810 that the organized bodies of Luddites went from town to town, sacking factories and destroying the machines in their blind revolt. The contest between the capitalist and the wage-worker, which, as Karl Marx says, dates back to the very origin of capital, took on a new form when machinery was introduced. Henceforth, the worker fights not only, nor even mainly, against the capitalist, but against the machine, as the material basis of capitalist exploitation. This is a distinct phase of the struggle of the proletariat everywhere.

In the sixteenth century the ribbon loom, a machine for weaving ribbon, was invented in Germany. Marx quotes an Italian traveler, Abbe Lancellotti, who wrote in 1579, as follows: "Anthony Mueller, of Danzig, saw about fifty years ago, in that town, a very ingenious machine, which weaves four to six pieces at once. But the mayor, being apprehensive that this invention might throw a large number of workmen on the streets, caused the inventor to be secretly strangled or drowned."[20] In 1629 this ribbon loom was introduced into Leyden, where the riots of the ribbon weavers forced the town council to prohibit it. In 1676 its use was prohibited in Cologne, at the same time that its introduction was causing serious disturbances in England. "By an imperial Edict of the 19th of February, 1685, its use was forbidden throughout all Germany. In Hamburg it was burned in public, by order of the Senate. The Emperor Charles VI, on the 9th of February, 1719, renewed the Edict of 1685, and not till 1765 was its use openly allowed in the Electorate of Saxony. This machine, which shook all Europe to its foundations, was in fact the precursor of the mule and power loom, and of the industrial revolution of the eighteenth century. It enabled a totally inexperienced boy to set the whole loom, with all its shuttles, in motion by simply moving a rod backward and forward, and in its improved form produced from forty to fifty pieces at once."[21]

The introduction of machinery has universally caused the workers to revolt. Much futile denunciation has been poured upon the blind, stupid resistance of the workers, but in view of the misery and poverty which they have suffered, it is impossible to judge them harshly. Their passionate, futile resistance to the irresistible moves to pity rather than to condemnation. As Marx justly says, "It took both time and experience before the work people learned to distinguish between machinery and its employment by capital, and to direct their attacks, not against the material instruments of production, but against the mode in which they are used."[22]

III

Under the new industrial regime, Robert Owen, erstwhile a poor draper's apprentice, soon became one of the most successful manufacturers in England. At eighteen years of age we find him entering into the manufacture of the new cotton-spinning machines, with a borrowed capital of $500. His partner was a man named Jones, and though the enterprise was successful from a financial point of view, the partnership proved to be most disagreeable. Accordingly it was dissolved, Owen taking three of the "mules" which they were making as a reimbursement for his investment. With these and some other machinery, Owen entered the cotton manufacturing industry, employing at first only three men. He made $1500 as his first year's profit.

Erelong Owen ceased manufacturing upon his own account, and became superintendent of a Manchester cotton mill, owned by a Mr. Drinkwater, and employing some five hundred work people. A most progressive man, in his new position Owen was always ready to introduce new machinery, and to embark upon experiments, with a view to improving the quality of the product of the factory. [23] In this he was so successful that the goods manufactured at the Drinkwater mill soon commanded a fifty per cent advance above the regular market prices. Drinkwater, delighted at results like these, made Owen his partner. Thus when he was barely twenty years of age Owen had secured an eminent position among the cotton manufacturers of the time. It is interesting to recall that Owen, in that same year, 1791, used the first cotton ever brought into England from the United States. "American sea island cotton," as it was called from the fact that it was then grown only upon the islands near the southern coast of the United States, was not believed to be of any value for manufacture on account, chiefly, of its poor color. But when a cotton broker named Spear received three hundred pounds of it from an American planter, with the request that he get some competent spinner to test it, Owen, with characteristic readiness, undertook the test and succeeded in making a much finer product than had hitherto been made from the French cotton, though inferior to it in color. That was the first introduction of American cotton, destined soon to furnish English cotton mills with the greater part of their raw material.

Owen did not long remain with Mr. Drinkwater. He accepted another profitable partnership in Manchester, and it was at this time that he became active in social reform work. As a member of an important literary and philosophical society, he was thrown much into the company of men distinguished in all walks of life, one of his friends and admirers being the poet Coleridge. Here he began that agitation which led to the passing of the very first factory act of Sir Robert Peel, in 1802. The suffering of the children moved his great humane heart to pity. He well knew that his own wealth and the wealth of his fellow-capitalists had been purchased at a terrible cost in child life. He was only a philanthropist as yet; he saw only the pitiful waste of life involved, and sought to impress men of wealth with what he felt. His mind was constantly occupied with plans for practical, constructive philanthropy upon a scale never before attempted.

On the first day of the nineteenth century, Owen entered upon the wonderful philanthropic career at New Lanark, which attracted universal attention, and ultimately led him to those social experiments and theories which won for him the title of "Father of Modern Socialism." We have already seen what the conditions were in the "model factory" when Owen assumed control. His influence was at once directed to the task of ameliorating the condition of the work people. He shortened the hours of labor, introduced sanitary reforms, protected the people against the exploitation of traders through a vicious credit system, opening a store and supplying them with goods at cost, and established infant schools, the first of their kind, for the care and education of children from two years of age and upward. Still, the workers themselves were suspicious of this man who, so different from other employers, was zealous in doing things for them. He really knew nothing of the working class, and it had never occurred to him that they might do anything for themselves. New Lanark under Owen was, to use the phrase which Mr. Ghent has adopted from Fourier, "a benevolent feudalism." Owen complains pathetically, "Yet the work people were systematically opposed to every change which I proposed, and did whatever they could to frustrate my object."[24]

Opportunity to win the affection and confidence of his employees came to Owen at last, and he was not slow to embrace it. In 1806 the United States, in consequence of a diplomatic rupture with England, placed an embargo upon the shipment of raw cotton to that country. Everywhere mills were shut down, and there was the utmost distress in consequence. The New Lanark mills, in common with most others, were shut down for four months, during which time Owen paid every worker his or her wages in full, at a cost of over $35,000. Forever afterward he enjoyed the love and trust of his work people. In spite of all his seemingly reckless expenditure upon purely philanthropic work, the mills yielded an enormous profit. But Owen was constantly in conflict with his business associates, who sought to restrict his philanthropic expenditures, with the result that he was compelled again and again to change partners, always securing their interests and returning them big profits upon their investments, until finally, in 1829, he left New Lanark altogether.

During twenty-nine years he had carried on the business with splendid commercial success and at the same time attracted universal attention to New Lanark as the theater of the greatest experiments in social regeneration the modern world had known. Every year thousands of persons from all parts of the world, many of them statesmen and representatives of the crowned heads of Europe, visited New Lanark to study these experiments, and never were they seriously criticised or their success challenged. It was a wonderful achievement. Had Owen's life ended in 1829, he must have taken rank in history as one of the truly great men of the nineteenth century.

IV

Let us now consider briefly the forces which led this gentle philanthropist onward to the goal of Communism. His experiences at New Lanark had convinced him that human character depends in large part upon, and is shaped by, environment. Others before Owen had perceived this, but he must ever be regarded as one of the pioneers in the spread of the idea, one of the first to give it definite form and to demonstrate its truth upon a large scale. In the first of those keen "Essays on the Formation of Human Character," in which he recounts the results of his New Lanark system of education, Owen says, "Any general character from the best to the worst, from the most ignorant to the most enlightened, may be given to any community, even to the world at large, by the application of proper means; which means are to a great extent at the command and under the control of those who have influence in the affairs of men."

We may admit that there is a good deal of overemphasis in this statement, but the doctrine itself does not seem strange or sensational to-day. It might be promulgated in any fashionable church, or in any ministerial conference, without exciting more than a languid, passing interest. But in Owen's time it was far otherwise. Such a doctrine struck at the very roots of current theology and all that organized Christianity consciously stood for. It denied the doctrine of the freedom of the will, upon which the elaborate theology of the church rested. No wonder, then, that it brought much bitter denunciation upon the heads of its promulgators. A poet of the period, in a poem dedicated to Owen, aptly expresses the doctrine in somewhat prosaic verse:--

> "We are the creatures of external things,
> Acting on inward organs, and are made
> To think and do whate'er our tutors please.
> What folly, then, to punish or reward
> For deeds o'er which we never held a curb!
> What woeful ignorance, to teach the crime
> And then chastise the pupil for his guilt!"[25]

Owen learned other things at New Lanark besides the truth that character is formed largely by environment. Starting out with no other purpose than to ameliorate the conditions of his work people, he realized before many years had passed that he could never do for them the one essential thing--secure their real liberty. "The people were slaves of my mercy," he writes.[26] He saw, though but dimly at first, that no man could be free who depended upon another for the right to earn his bread, no matter how good the bread-master might be. The hopelessness of expecting reform from the manufacturers themselves was painfully forced upon him. First of all, there was the bitter hostility of those of his class who had no sympathy with his philanthropic ideas, manifested from the beginning of his agitation at Manchester. Then there was the incessant conflict with his own associates, who, though they represented the noblest and best elements of the manufacturing class, constantly opposed him and regarded as dangerous and immoral his belief in the inherent right of every child to the opportunities of sound physical, mental, and moral culture. Class consciousness had not yet become a recognized term in sociological discussions, but class consciousness, the instinctive conformity of thought and action with class interests, was a fact which confronted Owen at every step.

The Luddite riots of 1810-1811 awakened England to the importance of the labor question, and Owen, who since 1805 had been devoting much time to its study, secured a wider audience and a much more serious hearing than ever before. Then came the frightful misery of 1815, due to the crisis which the end of the great war produced. Every one seemed to think that when the war was over and peace restored, there would be a tremendous increase in prosperity. What happened was precisely the opposite; for a time at least things were immeasurably worse than before. Peace did not bring with it plenty, but penury.

Owen, more clearly than any other man of the time, explained the real nature of the crisis. The war had given an important spur to industry and encouraged many new inventions and chemical discoveries. "The war was the great and most extravagant customer of farmers, manufacturers, and other producers of wealth, and many during this period became very wealthy.... And on the day on which peace was signed, the great customer of the producers died, and prices fell as the demand diminished, until the prime cost of the articles required for war could not be obtained.... Barns and farmyards were full, warehouses loaded, and such was our artificial state of society that this very superabundance of wealth was the sole cause of the existing distress. ***Burn the stock in the farmyards and warehouses, and prosperity would immediately recommence, in the same manner as if the war had continued.*** This want of demand at remunerating prices compelled the master producers to consider what they could do to diminish the amount of their productions and the cost of producing until these surplus stocks could be taken out of the market. To effect these results, every economy in producing was resorted to, and men being more expensive machines for producing than mechanical and chemical inventions and discoveries so extensively brought into action during the war, the men were discharged and the machines were made to supersede them--while the numbers of the unemployed were increased by the discharge of men from the army and navy. Hence the great distress for want of work among all classes whose labor was so much in demand while the war continued. This increase of mechanical and chemical power was continually diminishing the demand for, and value of, manual labor, and would continue to do so, and would effect great changes throughout society."[27]

In this statement there are several points worthy of attention. In the first place, the analysis of the crisis of 1815 is very like the later analyses of commercial crises by the Marxists; secondly, the antagonism of class interests is clearly developed, so far as the basic interests of the employers and their employees are concerned. The former, in order to conserve their interests, have to dismiss the workers, thus forcing them into the direst poverty. Thirdly, the conflict between manual labor and machine production is frankly stated. Owen's studies were leading him from mere philanthropism to Socialism.

During the height of the distress of 1815, Owen called together a large number of cotton manufacturers at a conference, held in Glasgow, to consider the state of the cotton trade and the prevailing distress. He proposed (1) that they should petition Parliament for the repeal of the revenue tariff on raw cotton; (2) that they should call upon Parliament to shorten the hours of labor in the cotton mills by legislative enactment, and otherwise seek to improve the condition of the working people. The first proposition was carried with unanimity, but the second, and to Owen the more important, did not even secure a seconder.[28] The conference plainly showed the power of class interests. The spirit in which Owen faced his fellow-manufacturers is best seen in the following extract from the address delivered by him, with copies of which he afterward literally deluged the kingdom:--

"True, indeed, it is that the main pillar and prop of the political greatness and prosperity of our country is a manufacture which, as now carried on, is destructive of the health, morals, and social comfort of the mass of people engaged in it. It is only since the introduction of the cotton trade that children, at an age before they had acquired strength or mental instruction, have been forced into cotton mills,--those receptacles, in too many instances, for living human skeletons, almost disrobed of intellect, where, as the business is often now conducted, they linger out a few years of miserable existence, acquiring every bad habit which they may disseminate throughout society. It is only since the introduction of this trade that children and even grown people were required to labor more than twelve hours in a day, not including the time allotted for meals. It is only since the introduction of this trade that the sole recreation of the laborer is to be found in the pot-house or ginshop, and it is only since the introduction of this baneful trade that poverty, crime, and misery have made rapid and fearful strides throughout the community.

"Shall we then go unblushingly and ask the legislators of our country to pass legislative acts to sanction and increase this trade--to sign the death warrants of the strength, morals, and happiness of thousands of our fellow-creatures, and not attempt to propose corrections for the evils which it creates? If such shall be your determination, I, for one, will not join in the application,--no, I will, with all the faculties I possess, oppose every attempt made to extend the trade that, except in name, is more injurious to those employed in it than is the slavery in the West Indies to the poor negroes; for deeply as I am interested in the cotton manufacture, highly as I value the extended political power of my country, yet knowing as I do, from long experience both here and in England, the miseries which this trade, as it is now conducted, inflicts on those to whom it gives employment, I do not hesitate to say: ***Perish the cotton trade, perish even the political superiority of our country, if it depends on the cotton trade, rather than that they shall be upheld by the sacrifice of everything valuable in life.***"[29]

This conference doubtless had much to do with Owen's acceptance of a communistic ideal approaching that of modern Socialism in many important respects. It certainly intensified the hatred and fear of those manufacturers whose interests he had so courageously attacked. In 1817 we find him proposing to the British government the establishment of communistic villages, as the best means of remedying the terrible distress which prevailed at that time. From this time onward his interest in mere surface reforms such as he had been carrying on at New Lanark seemed to wane. He became at this juncture an apostle of Communism, or as he later preferred to say, Socialism. His ideal was a cooeperative world, with perfect equality between the sexes. He had completely demonstrated to his own mind that private property was incompatible with social well-being. Every month of his experience at New Lanark had deeply impressed him with the conviction that to make it possible for all people to live equally happy and moral lives they must have equal material resources and conditions of life, and he could not understand why it had never occurred to others before him.

Here we have the essential characteristic of Utopian Socialism as distinguished from modern, or scientific, Socialism. The Utopians regard human life as something plastic and capable of being shaped and molded according to systems and plans. All that is necessary is to take some abstract principle as a standard, and then prepare a plan for the reorganization of society in conformity with that principle. If the plan is perfect, it will be enough to demonstrate its advantages as one would demonstrate a sum in arithmetic. The scientific Socialists, on the other hand, are evolutionists. Society, they believe, cannot take leaps at will; social changes are products of the past and the present. They distrust social inventors and schemes. Socialism is not an ingenious plan for the realization of abstract Justice, or Brotherhood, but a necessary outgrowth of the centuries. Owen, then, was a Utopian. He regarded himself as one inspired, an inspired inventor of a new social system, and believed that it was only necessary for him to demonstrate the truth of his contentions and theories, by argument and practical experiment, to bring about the transformation of the world. He conducted a tremendous propaganda, by means of newspapers, pamphlets, lectures, and debates, and established various communities in England and this country. In face of a bitter opposition and repeated failure, he kept on with sublime faith and unbounded courage which nothing could shake.

In 1825 Owen began the greatest and most splendid of his social experiments in the village of Harmonie, Indiana, in the beautiful valley of the Wabash. The place had already been the theater of an interesting experiment in religious communism, Owen having bought the property from the Rappites. In February and March, 1825, the brave reformer addressed two of the most distinguished audiences ever gathered in the Hall of Representatives at the national capital. In the audiences were the President of the United States, the Judges of the Supreme Court, several members of the cabinet, and almost the entire membership of both houses of Congress. Owen explained his plans for the regeneration of society in detail, exhibiting a model of the buildings to be erected. It is almost impossible to realize at this day the tremendous interest which his appeal to Congress awakened. His vision of a re-created world caught the popular imagination.

Among those whose minds were fired was a boy of sixteen, tall, lank, uncouth, and poor. Word had come to him of Owen's splendid undertaking, and he had caught something of the enthusiasm of the great dreamer. Above all, it was said that New Harmony was to be a wonderful center of learning, that the foremost educators of the world would establish great schools there, fully equipped with books and all sorts of appliances. To be a scholar had been the boy's one great ambition, so he yearned wistfully for an opportunity to join the new community. But his father forbidding, claiming his services, the boy suffered grievous disappointment. One wonders what effect residence at New Harmony would have had upon the life of Abraham Lincoln, and upon the history of America! And how much, one wonders, was that splendid life influenced by that boyish interest in the regeneration of the world?

That the influence of New Harmony was felt by Lincoln we know. It was a child of New Harmony, Robert Dale Owen, son of Robert Owen, who, when emancipation seemed to hang in the balance, penned his remarkable letter to President Lincoln, dated September seventeenth, 1862. "Its perusal thrilled me like a trumpet call," said the great President. Five days after its receipt the Preliminary Proclamation was issued. "Your letter to the President had more influence on him than any other document which reached him on the subject--I think I might say than all others put together. I speak of that which I know from personal conference with him," wrote Salmon P. Chase, Secretary of the Treasury.

New Harmony failed. Other communities established by Owen failed, but the story of their failure is nevertheless full of inspiration. The world has long since written the word "Failure" as an epitaph for Robert Owen. But what a splendid failure that life was! Standing by his grave one day, in the picturesque little churchyard at Newton, by a bend of the winding river, not far from the ruins of the ancient castle home of the famous Deist, Lord Herbert, the writer said to an old Welsh laborer, "But his life was a failure, was it not?" The old man gazed awhile at the grave, and then with a voice of unforgettable reverence and love answered, "I suppose it was, sir, as the world goes; a failure like Jesus Christ's. But I don't call it failure, sir. He established infant schools; he founded the great cooeperative movement; he helped to make the trade unions;[30] he helped to give us the factory acts; he worked for peace between two great countries. His Socialism has not been realized yet, nor has Christ's--but it will come!"

V

Owen was not the only builder of Utopias in his time. In the same year that Owen launched his New Harmony venture, there died in Paris another dreamer of social millenniums, a gentle mystic, Henry de Saint-Simon, and in 1837, the year of Owen's third Socialist congress, another great Utopist died in the French capital, Charles Fourier. Each of these contributed something to the development of the theories of Socialism, each has a legitimate place in the history of the Socialist movement. But this little work is not intended to give the history of Socialism.[31] I have taken only one of the three great Utopists, as representative of them all: one who seems to me to be much nearer to the later scientific movement pioneered by Marx and Engels than any of the others. In the Socialism of Owen, we have Utopian Socialism at its best.

What distinguishes the Utopian Socialists from their scientific successors we have already noted. Engels expresses the principle very clearly in the following luminous passage: "One thing is common to all three. Not one of them appears as a representative of the interests of that proletariat which historical development had ... produced. Like the French philosophers,[32] they do not claim to emancipate a particular class to begin with, but all humanity at once. Like them, they wish to bring in the kingdom of reason and eternal justice, but this kingdom, as they see it, is as far as heaven from earth from that of the French philosophers.

"For, to our three social reformers, the bourgeois world, based upon the principles of these philosophers, is quite as irrational and unjust, and, therefore, finds its way to the dust hole quite as readily, as feudalism and all the earlier stages of society. If pure reason and justice had not, hitherto, ruled the world, this has been the case only because men have not rightly understood them. What was wanted was the individual man of genius, who has now arisen and who understands the truth. That he has now arisen, that the truth has now been clearly understood, is not an inevitable event, following of necessity in the chain of historical development, but a mere happy accident. He might just as well have been born five hundred years earlier, and might then have spared humanity five hundred years of error, strife, and suffering."[33]

Neither of these great Utopists had anything like the conception of social evolution, determined by economic conditions and the resulting conflicts of economic classes, which constitutes the base of the philosophy of the scientific Socialists. Each of them had some faint comprehension of isolated facts, but neither of them developed his knowledge very far, nor could the facts appear to them as correlated later by Marx. Saint-Simon, as we know, recognized the class struggle in the French Revolution, and saw in the Reign of Terror only the momentary reign of the non-possessing masses;[34] he saw, too, that the political question was fundamentally an economic question, declaring that politics is the science of production, and prophesying that politics would be absorbed by economics.[35] Fourier, we also know, applied the principle of evolution to society. He divided the history of society into four great epochs--savagery, barbarism, the patriarchate, and civilization. [36] But just as Saint-Simon failed to grasp the significance of the class conflict, and its relation to the fundamental character of economic institutions, which he dimly perceived, so Fourier failed to grasp the significance of the evolutionary process which he described, and, like Saint-Simon, he halted upon the brink, so to speak, of an important discovery. His concept of social evolution meant little to him and possessed only an academic interest. And Owen, in many respects the greatest of the three, realized in a practical manner that the industrial problem was a class conflict. Not only had he found in 1815 that pity was powerless to move the hearts of his fellow-manufacturers when their class interests were concerned, but later, in 1818, when he went to present his famous memorial to the Congress of Sovereigns at Aix-la-Chapelle, he had another lesson of the same kind. At Frankfort, Germany, he tarried on his way to the Congress, and was invited to attend a notable dinner to meet the Secretary of the Congress, M. Gentz, a famous diplomat of the day, "who enjoyed the full confidence of the leading despots of Europe." After Owen had outlined his schemes for social amelioration, M. Gentz was asked for his reply, and Owen tells us that the diplomat answered, "We know very well that what you say is true, but how could we govern the masses, if they were wealthy, and so, independent of us?"[37] Lord Lauderdale, too, had exclaimed on another occasion, "Nothing [i.e. than Owen's plans] could be more complete for the poor and working classes, but what will become of us?"[38] Scattered throughout Owen's writings and speeches are numerous evidences that he at times recognized the class antagonisms in industrial society as the heart of the industrial problem,[39] but to him, also, the germ of an important truth meant practically nothing. He saw only the facts in their isolation, and made no attempt to discover their meaning or to relate them to his teaching.

Each of the three men regarded himself as the discoverer of the truth which would redeem the world; each devoted himself with magnificent faith and heroic courage to his task; each failed to realize his hopes; and each left behind him faithful disciples and followers, confident that the day must come at last when the suffering and disinherited of earth will be able to say, in Owen's dying words, "Relief has come." Perhaps no better estimate of the value of the visions of these great Utopists has ever been penned than that by Emerson in the following tribute to Owen:[40]--

"Robert Owen of New Lanark came hither from England in 1845 to read lectures or hold conversations wherever he could find listeners--the most amiable, sanguine, and candid of men. He had not the least doubt that he had hit on the plan of right and perfect Socialism, or that mankind would adopt it. He was then seventy years old, and being asked, 'Well, Mr. Owen, who is your disciple? how many men are there possessed of your views who will remain after you are gone to put them in practice?' 'Not one,' was the reply. Robert Owen knew Fourier in his old age. He said that Fourier learned of him all the truth that he had. The rest of his system was imagination, and the imagination of a visionary. Owen made the best impression by his rare benevolence. His love of men made us forget his 'three errors.' His charitable construction of men and their actions was invariable. He was the better Christian in his controversies with Christians.

"And truly I honor the generous ideas of the Socialists, the magnificence of their theories, and the enthusiasm with which they have been urged. They appeared inspired men of their time. Mr. Owen preached his doctrine of labor and reward with the fidelity and devotion of a saint in the slow ears of his generation.

"One feels that these philosophers have skipped no fact but one, namely, life.

They treat man as a plastic thing, or something that may be put up or down, ripened or retarded, molded, polished, made into solid or fluid or gas at the will of the leader; or perhaps as a vegetable, from which, though now a very poor crab, a very good peach can by manure and exposure be in time produced--and skip the faculty of life which spawns and spurns systems and system makers; which eludes all conditions; which makes or supplants a thousand Phalanxes and New Harmonies with each pulsation....

"Yet, in a day of small, sour and fierce schemes, one is admonished and cheered by a project of such friendly aims, and of such bold and generous proportions; there is an intellectual courage and strength in it which is superior and commanding; it certifies the presence of so much truth in the theory, and in so far is destined to be fact.

"I regard these philanthropists as themselves the effects of the age in which they live, in common with so many other good facts the efflorescence of the period and predicting the good fruit that ripens. They were not the creators that they believed themselves to be; but they were unconscious prophets of the true state of society, one which the tendencies of nature lead unto, one which always establishes itself for the sane soul, though not in that manner in which they paint it."

> "Our visions have not come to naught,
> Who saw by lightning in the night;
> The deeds we dreamed are being wrought
> By those who work in clearer light;
> In other ways our fight is fought,
> And other forms fulfill our thought
> Made visible to all men's sight."[41]

NOTES:

[10] *Karl Marx: Biographical Memoirs*, by Wilhelm Liebknecht, page 101.

[11] *Socialism, Utopian and Scientific*, by F. Engels, London, 1892, pages 20-25.

[12] For good accounts of the life of Owen the reader is referred to the Biography, by Lloyd Jones, in *The Social Science Series*, 1890, published by Swan,

Sonnenschein & Co., London, and the *Life of Robert Owen*, by Frank Podmore, 2 vols., New York, 1907.

[13] *The Industrial History of England*, by H. de B. Gibbins, London, Methuen and Co.

[14] *Industrial History of England*, page 179.

[15] This anonymous historian is now known to have been Mr. Samuel Kydd, barrister-at-law (vide Cooke-Taylor).

[16] *The Factory System and the Factory Acts*, by R. W. Cooke-Taylor, London, 1894.

[17] In two volumes: London, Effingham Wilson, 1857 and 1858. Vol. I contains the Life; Vol. II is a Supplementary Appendix. Quotations are from Vol. I.

[18] See *Songs of Freedom*, by H. S. Salt, pages 81-83.

[19] *Industrial History of England*, page 181.

[20] *Capital*, by Karl Marx, Vol. I, page 467, Kerr edition.

[21] *Idem*, Vol. I, page 468.

[22] *Capital*, Vol. I, page 468.

[23] For instance, he so improved the machinery and increased the fineness of the threads that, instead of spinning seventy-five thousand yards of yarn to the pound of cotton, he spun two hundred and fifty thousand! At that time a pound of cotton, which in its raw state was worth $1.25, became worth $50 when spun.--Life of Robert Owen, Philadelphia, 1866.--Anonymous.

[24] *Autobiography.*

[25] *The Force of Circumstances*, a poem, by John Garwood, Birmingham, 1808.

[26] Quoted by Engels, *Socialism, Utopian and Scientific*, page 22 (English edition, 1892).

[27] Quoted by H. M. Hyndman, *The Economics of Socialism*, page 150.

[28] *The New Harmony Communities*, by George Browning Lockwood, page 71.

[29] Quoted by Lockwood, *The New Harmony Communities*, pages 71-72.

[30] Owen presided at the first organized Trade Union Congress in England.

[31] For the history of these and other Utopian Socialist schemes, the reader

is referred to Professor Ely's **French and German Socialism** (1883); Kirkup's **History of Socialism** (1900); and Hillquit's **History of Socialism in the United States** (1903).

[32] The Encyclopaedists.

[33] Engels, **Socialism, Utopian and Scientific**, pages 6-7.

[34] Engels, **Socialism, Utopian and Scientific**, page 15.

[35] **Idem.**

[36] **Idem**, page 18.

[37] **Autobiography.**

[38] **Idem.**

[39] See, for instance, **The Revolution in Mind and Practice**, by Robert Owen, pages 21-22.

[40] **Essay on Robert Owen.**

[41] Gerald Massey.

CHAPTER III
THE "COMMUNIST MANIFESTO" AND THE SCIENTIFIC SPIRIT

I

The ***Communist Manifesto*** has been called the birth-cry of the modern scientific Socialist movement. When it was written, at the end of 1847, little remained of those great movements which in the early part of the century had inspired millions with high hopes of social regeneration and rekindled the beacon fires of faith in the world. The Saint-Simonians had, as an organized body, disappeared; the Fourierists were a dwindling sect, discouraged by the failure of the one great trial of their system, the famous Brook Farm experiment, in the United States; the Owenite movement had never recovered from the failures of the experiments at New Harmony and elsewhere, and had lost much of its identity through the multiplicity of interests embraced in Owen's later propaganda. Chartism and Trade Unionism on the one hand, and the Cooeperative Societies on the other, had, between them, absorbed most of the vital elements of the Owenite movement.

There was a multitude of what Engels calls "social quacks," but the really great social movements, Owenism in England, and Fourierism in France, were utterly demoralized and rapidly dwindling away. One thing only served to keep the flame of hope alive--"the crude, rough-hewn, purely instinctive sort of Communism" of the workers. This Communism of the working class differed very essentially from the Socialism of Fourier and Owen. It was Utopian, being based, like all Utopian movements, upon abstract ideas. It differed from Fourierism and Owenism, however, in that instead of a universal appeal based upon Brotherhood, Justice, Order, and Economy, its appeal was, primarily, to the laborer. Its basis was the crude class doctrine of "the rights of Labor." The laborer was appealed to as one suffering from oppression and injustice. It was, therefore, distinctly a class movement, and its class-consciousness was sufficiently developed to keep its leaders from wasting their lives in abortive appeals to the master class. The leading exponents of this Communism of the workers were Wilhelm Weitling, in Germany, and Etienne Cabet, in France.

Weitling was a man of the people. He was born in Magdeburg, Germany, in 1808, the illegitimate child of a humble woman and her soldier lover. He became a tailor, and, as was the custom in Germany at that time, traveled extensively during his apprenticeship. In 1838 his first important work, "The World As It Is, and As It Might Be," appeared, published in Paris by a secret revolutionary society consisting of German workingmen of the "Young Germany" movement. In this work Weitling first expounded at length his communistic theories. It is claimed[42] that his conversion to Communism was the result of the chance placing of a Fourierist paper upon the table of a Berlin coffeehouse, by Albert Brisbane, the brilliant friend and disciple of Fourier, his first exponent in the English language. This may well be true, for, as we shall see, Weitling's views are mainly based upon those of the great French Utopist. In 1842 Weitling published his best-known work, the book upon which his literary fame chiefly rests, "The Guaranties of Harmony and Freedom." This work at once attracted wide attention, and gave Weitling a foremost place among the writers of the time in the affections of the educated workers. It was an elaboration of the theories contained in his earlier book. Morris Hillquit[43] thus describes Weitling's philosophy and method:--

"In his social philosophy, Weitling may be said to have been the connecting link between primitive and modern Socialism. In the main, he is still a Utopian, and his writings betray the unmistakable influence of the early French Socialists. In common with all Utopians, he bases his philosophy exclusively upon moral grounds. Misery and poverty are to him but the results of human malice, and his cry is for 'eternal justice' and for the 'absolute liberty and equality of all mankind.' In his criticism of the existing order, he leans closely on Fourier, from whom he also borrowed the division of labor into three classes of the Necessary, Useful, and Attractive, and the plan of organization of 'attractive industry.'

"His ideal of the future state of society reminds us of the Saint-Simonian government of scientists. The administration of affairs of the entire globe is to be in the hands of the three greatest authorities on 'philosophical medicine,' physics, and mechanics, who are to be reenforced by a number of subordinate committees. His state of the future is a highly centralized government, and is described by the author with the customary details. Where Weitling, to some extent, approaches the conception of modern Socialism, is in his recognition of class distinctions between employer and employee. This distinction never amounted to a conscious indorsement of the modern Socialist doctrine of the 'class struggle,' but his views on the antagonism between the 'poor' and the 'wealthy' came quite close to it. He was a firm believer in labor organizations as a factor in developing the administrative abilities of the working class; the creation of an independent labor party was one of his pet schemes, and his appeals were principally addressed to the workingmen."

Weitling visited the United States in 1846, a group of German exiles, identified with the Free Soil movement, having invited him to become the editor of a magazine, the ***Volkstribun***, devoted to the principles of the movement. By the time he reached America, however, the magazine had suspended publication. He stayed little more than a year, hastening back to the fatherland to share in the revolutionary activities of 1848. He returned to America again in 1849, after the failure of the "glorious revolution," and for many years thereafter was an active and tireless propagandist. He died in Brooklyn in 1871.

Etienne Cabet was, in many ways, a very different type of man from Weitling, but their ideas were not so dissimilar. Cabet, born in Dijon, France, in 1788, was the son of a fairly prosperous cooper, and received a good university education. He studied both medicine and law, adopting the profession of the latter and early achieving marked success in its practice. He took a leading part in the Revolution of 1830 as a member of the "Committee of Insurrection," and upon the accession of Louis Philippe was "rewarded" by being made Attorney-General for Corsica. There is no doubt that the government desired to remove Cabet from the political life of Paris, quite as much as to reward him for his services during the Revolution; his strong radicalism, combined with his sturdy independence of character, being rightly regarded as dangerous to Louis Philippe's regime. His reward, therefore, took the form of practical banishment. The wily advisers of Louis Philippe used the gloved hand. But the best-laid schemes of mice and courtiers "gang aft agley." Cabet, in Corsica, joined the radical anti-administration forces, and became a thorn in the side of the government. Removed from office, he returned to Paris, whereupon the citizens of Dijon, his native town, elected him as their deputy to the lower chamber in 1834. Here he continued his opposition to the administration, and was at last tried on a charge of *lese majeste*, and given the option of choosing between two years' imprisonment and five years' exile.

Cabet chose exile, and took up his residence in England, where he fell under the influence of Owen's agitation and became a convert to his Socialistic views. During this time of exile, too, he became acquainted with the "Utopia" of Sir Thomas More and was fascinated by it. The idea of writing a similar work of fiction to propagate his Socialist belief impressed itself upon his mind, and he wrote "a philosophical and social romance," entitled "Voyage to Icaria," which was published soon after his return to Paris, in 1839. In this novel Cabet follows closely the method of More, and describes "Icaria" as "a Promised Land, an Eden, an Elysium, a new terrestrial Paradise." The plot of the book is simple in the extreme, and its literary merit is not very great. The writer represents that he met, in London, a nobleman, Lord William Carisdall, who, having by chance heard of Icaria and the wonderful and strange customs and form of government of its inhabitants, visited the country. Lord William kept a diary in which he described all that he saw in this wonderland. This record, we are told, the traveler had permitted to be published through the medium of his friend, and under his editorial supervision. The first part of the book contains an attractive account of the cooeperative system of the Icarians, their communistic government, equality of the sexes, and high standard of morality. The second part is devoted to an account of the history of Icaria, prior to and succeeding the revolution of 1782, when the great national hero, Icar, established Communism.

The book created a tremendous furore in France. It appealed strongly to the discontented masses, and it is said that by 1847 Cabet had no less than four hundred thousand adherents among the workers of France. The numerical strength of revolutionary movements is almost invariably greatly exaggerated, however, and it is not likely that the figures cited are exceptional in this regard. It is possible, *cum grano salis*, to accept the figures only by remembering that a very infinitesimal proportion of these were adherents in the sense of being ready to follow Cabet's leadership, as subsequent events showed. When the clamor rose for a practical test of the theories set forth so alluringly, Cabet visited Robert Owen in England and sought advice as to the best site for such an experiment. Owen recommended Texas, then recently admitted into the union of states and anxious for settlers. Cabet accepted Owen's advice and called for volunteers to form the "advance guard" of settlers, the number responding being pitifully, almost ludicrously, small. Still, the effect of the book was very great, and it served to fire the flagging zeal of those workers for social regeneration whose hearts must otherwise have become deadly sick from long-deferred hopes.

The confluence of these two streams of Communist propaganda represented by Weitling and Cabet constituted the real Communist "movement" of 1840-1847. Its organized expression was the Communist League, a secret organization with its headquarters in London. The League was formed in Paris by German refugees and traveling workmen, and seems to have been an offspring of Mazzini's "Young Europe" agitation of 1834. At different times it bore the names, "League of the Just," "League of the Righteous," and, finally, "Communist League."[44] For many years it remained a mere conspiratory society, exclusively German, and existed mainly for the purpose of fostering the "Young Germany" ideas. Later it became an International Alliance with societies in many parts of Europe.

In 1847 Karl Marx was residing in Brussels. During a prior residence in Paris he had come into close association with the leaders of the League there, and had agreed to form a similar society in Brussels. Engels was in Paris in 1847, and it was probably due to his activities that the Paris League officially invited both him and Marx to join the international organization, promising that a congress should be convened in London at an early date. We may, in view of the after career of Engels as the politician of the movement, surmise so much. Be that how it may, the invitation, with its promise to call a congress in London, was extended and accepted. The reason for the step, the object of the proposed congress, is quite clear. Marx himself has placed it beyond dispute. During his stay in Paris he and Engels had discussed the position of the League with some of its leaders, and he had, later, criticised it in the most merciless manner in some of his pamphlets.[45] Marx desired a revolutionary working class political party with a definite aim and policy. Those leaders of the League who agreed with him in this were the prime movers for the congress, which was held in London, in November, 1847.

At the congress, Marx and Engels presented their views at great length, and outlined the principles and policy which their famous pamphlet later made familiar. Perhaps it was due to the very convincing manner in which they argued that the emancipation of the working class must be the work of that class itself, that there was some opposition to them, on the part of a few delegates, on the ground that they were "Intellectuals" and not members of the proletariat, a criticism which pursued them all through their lives. Their views found general favor, however, as might be expected from such an inchoate mass of men, revolutionaries to the core, and waiting only for effective leadership. A resolution was adopted requesting Marx and Engels to prepare "a complete theoretical and working programme" for the League. This they did. It took the form of the ***Communist Manifesto***, published in the early part of January, 1848.

II

The authors of the ***Manifesto*** were men of great intellectual gifts. Either of them alone must have won fame; together, they won immortality. Their lives, from the date of their first meeting in Paris, in 1844, to the death of Marx, almost forty years later, are inseparably interwoven. The friendship of Damon and Pythias was not more remarkable.

Karl Heinrich Marx was born on the fifth day of May, 1818, at Treves, the oldest town in Germany, dating back to Roman times. His parents were both people of remarkable character. His mother--nee Pressburg--was the descendant of Hungarian Jews who in the sixteenth century had settled in Holland. Many of her ancestors had been rabbis. Marx was passionately devoted to his mother, always speaking of her with reverent admiration. On his father's side, also, Marx boasted of a long line of rabbinical ancestors, and it has been suggested that he owed to this rabbinical ancestry some of his marvelous gift of luminous exposition. The true family name was Mordechia, but that was abandoned by his grandfather, who took the name of

Marx, which the grandson was destined to make famous. The father of Karl was a lawyer of some prominence and considerable learning, and a man of great force of character. In 1824, the boy Karl being then six years old, he renounced the Jewish religion and embraced Christianity, all the members of the family being baptized and received into the Church.

There is a familiar legend that this act was the result of compulsion, being taken in response to an official edict.[46] He held at the time the position of notary public at the county court, and it is claimed that the official edict in question required all Jews holding official positions to forego them, and to abandon the practice of law, or to accept the Christian faith. Many writers, including Liebknecht[47] and one of the daughters of Karl Marx,[48] have given this explanation of the renunciation of Judaism by the elder Marx. It seems certain, however, that the act was purely voluntary, and that there was no such edict.[49] It may be that social ambitions had something to do with it, that he hoped to attain, as a Christian, a measure of success not possible to an adherent of the Hebrew faith. Whatever the motive, the act was a voluntary one. A great admirer of the eighteenth-century "materialists," and a disciple of Voltaire, he believed in God, he said, as Newton, Locke, and Leibnitz had done before him. He discussed religious and philosophical questions very freely and frankly with his son, and read Voltaire and Racine with him. As for the mother of Marx, she also believed in God--"not for God's sake, but for my own," she explained when asked about it.

At the earnest behest of his father, Marx studied law at the universities of Bonn, Berlin, and Jena. But "to please himself" he studied history and philosophy, winning great distinction in these branches of learning. He graduated in 1841, as a Doctor of Philosophy, with an essay on the philosophy of Epicurus, and it was his purpose to settle at Bonn as a professor of philosophy. The plan was abandoned, partly because he had already discovered that his bent was toward political activity, and partly because the Prussian government had made scholastic independence impossible, thus destroying the attractiveness of an academic career. Accordingly, Marx accepted the editorship of a democratic paper, the ***Rhenish Gazette***, in which he waged bitter, relentless war upon the government. Time after time the censors interfered, but Marx was too brilliant a polemicist, even thus early in his career, and far too subtle for the censors. Finally, at the request of his managers, who hoped thus to avoid being compelled to suspend the publication, Marx retired from the editorship. This did not serve to save the paper, however, and it was suppressed by the government in March, 1843.

Soon after this Marx went to Paris, with his young bride of a few months, Jenny von Westphalen, the playmate of his childhood. The Von Westphalens were of the nobility, and a brother of Mrs. Marx afterward became a Prussian Minister of State. The elder Von Westphalen was half Scotch, related, on his maternal side, to the Argyles. He was a lineal descendant of the Duke of Argyle who was beheaded in the reign of James II. His daughter tells an amusing story of how Marx, many years later, having to pawn some of his wife's heirlooms, especially some heavy, antique silver spoons which bore the Argyle crest and motto, "Truth is my maxim," narrowly escaped arrest on suspicion of having robbed the Argyles![50] To Paris, then, Marx went, and there met, among others, Heinrich Heine, many of whose poems he suggested, Arnold Ruge, the poet, P. J. Proudhon, and Michael Bakunin, the Anarchist philosopher, and, above all, the man destined to be his very *alter ego*, Friedrich Engels, with whom he had already had some correspondence.[51]

The attainments of Engels have been somewhat overshadowed by those of his friend. Born at Barmen, in the province of the Rhine, November 28, 1820, he was educated in the gymnasium of that city, and after serving his period of military service, from 1837 to 1841, was sent, in the early part of 1842, to Manchester, England, to look after a cotton-spinning business of which his father was principal owner. Here he seems to have at once begun a thorough investigation of social and industrial conditions, the results of which are contained in a book, "The Condition of the Working Class in England in 1844," which remains to this day a classic presentation of the social and industrial life of the period. From the very first, already predisposed, as we know, he sympathized with the views of the Chartists and the Owenite Socialists. He became friendly with the Chartist leaders, notably with Feargus O'Connor, to whose paper, the *Northern Star*, he became a contributor. He also became friendly with Robert Owen, and wrote for his *New Moral World*.[52] His linguistic abilities were very great; it is said that he had thoroughly mastered no less than ten languages--a gift which helped him immensely in his literary and political associations with Marx.

When the two men met for the first time, in 1844, they were drawn together by an irresistible impulse. They were kindred spirits. Marx had gone to Paris mainly for the purpose of studying the Socialist movement of the time. During his editorship of the **Rhenish Gazette** several articles had appeared on the subject, and he had refused to attack the Socialists in any manner. He had gone to Paris with a considerable reputation already established as a leader of radical thought, and at once sought out the Saint-Simonians, under whose influence he was led to declare himself definitely a Socialist. At first this seems difficult to explain, so wide is the chasm which yawns between the "New Christianity" of Saint-Simon and the materialism of Marx. There seems to be no bond of sympathy between the religious mysticism of the French dreamer and the scientific thought of the German economist and philosopher.

Marx has been described as being "rigidly mathematical,"[53] and the picture of the man one gets from his writings is that of a cold, unemotional philosopher, dealing only with facts and caring nothing for idealism. But the real Marx was a very different sort of man. His life was itself a splendid example of noble idealism, and underlying all his materialism there was a great religious spirit, using the word "religious" in its noblest and best sense, quite independent of dogmatic theology. All his life he was a deep student of Dante, the **Divine Comedy** being his constant companion, so that he knew it almost completely by heart. Some of his attacks upon Christianity are very bitter, and have been much quoted against Socialism, but they are not one whit more bitter than the superb thunderbolts of invective which the ancient Hebrew prophets hurled against an unfaithful Church and priesthood. For the most part, they are attacks upon religious hypocrisy rather than upon Christianity. Marx was, of course, an agnostic, even an atheist, but he was full of sympathy with the underlying ethical principles of all the great religions. Always tolerant of the religious opinions of others, he had nothing but scorn and contempt for the blatant dogmatic atheism of his time, and vigorously opposed committing the Socialist movement to atheism as part of its programme.[54] In short, he was a man of fine spiritual instincts, splendidly religious in his irreligion.

This spiritual side of Marx must be considered if we would understand the man. It is not necessary, however, to ascribe the influence of Saint-Simonian thought upon him to a predisposing spiritual temperament. Marx, with his usual penetration, saw in Saint-Simonism the hidden germ of a great truth, the embryo of a profound social theory. Saint-Simon, as we have seen, had vaguely indicated the two ideas which were afterward to be cardinal doctrines of the Marx-Engels *Manifesto*--the antagonism of classes, and the economic foundation of political institutions. Not only so, but Saint-Simon's grasp of political questions, instanced by his advocacy, in 1815, of a triple alliance between England, France, and Germany,[55] appealed to Marx, and impressed him alike by its fine perspicacity and its splendid courage. Engels, in whom, as stated, the working-class spirit of Chartism and the ideals of Owenism were blended, found in Marx a twin spirit. They were, indeed,--

"Two souls with but a single thought,
Two hearts that beat as one."

III

The *Communist Manifesto* is the first declaration of an International Workingmen's Party. Its fine peroration is a call to the workers to transcend the petty divisions of nationalism and sectarianism: "The proletarians have nothing to lose but their chains. They have a world to win. Workingmen of all countries, unite!" These concluding phrases of the *Manifesto* have become the shibboleths of millions. They are repeated with fervor by the disinherited workers of all the lands. Even in China, lately so rudely awakened from the slumbering peace of the centuries, they are voiced by an ever increasing army of voices. No sentences ever coined in the mint of human speech have held such magic power over such large numbers of men and women of so many diverse races and creeds. As a literary production, the *Manifesto* bears the unmistakable stamp of genius.

But it is not as literature that we are to consider the historic document. Its importance for us lies, not in its form, but in its fundamental principle. And the fundamental principle, the essence or soul of the declaration, is contained in this pregnant summary by Engels:--

"In every historical epoch, the prevailing mode of economic production and exchange, and the *social organization necessarily following from it, form the basis upon which is built up, and from which alone can be explained, the politi-*

cal and intellectual history of that epoch, that consequently the whole history of mankind (since primitive tribal society holding land in common ownership) has been a history of class struggles, contests between exploiting and exploited, ruling and oppressed classes."[56]

Thus Engels summarizes the philosophy--as apart from the proposals of immediate measures to constitute the political programme of the party--of the *Manifesto*; the basis upon which the whole superstructure of modern, scientific Socialist theory rests. This is the materialistic, or economic, conception of history which distinguishes scientific Socialism from all the Utopian Socialisms which preceded it. Socialism is henceforth a theory of social evolution, not a scheme of world-building; a spirit, not a thing. Thus, twelve years before the appearance of "The Origin of Species," nearly twenty years after the death of Lamarck, the authors of the *Communist Manifesto* formulated a great theory of social evolution as the basis of the mightiest proletarian movement in history. Socialism had become a science instead of a dream.

IV

Naturally, in view of its historic role, the joint authorship of the *Manifesto* has been much discussed. What was the respective share of each of its creators? What did Marx contribute, and what Engels? It may be, as Liebknecht says, an idle question, but it is a perfectly natural one. The pamphlet itself does not assist us. There are no internal signs pointing now to the hand of the one, now to the hand of the other. We may hazard a guess that most of the programme of ameliorative measures was the work of Engels, and perhaps the final section. It was the work of Engels throughout his life to deal with present social and political problems in the light of the fundamental theories to the systematization and elucidation of which Marx was devoted.

Beyond this mere conjecture, we have the word of Engels with regard to the basal principle which he has summarized in the passage already quoted. "The *Manifesto* being our joint production," he says, "I consider myself bound to state that the fundamental proposition which forms its nucleus belongs to Marx.... This proposition, which, in my opinion, is destined to do for history what Darwin's theory has done for biology, we, both of us, had been gradually approaching for some years before 1845. How far I had progressed toward it is best shown by my 'Condition of the Working Class in England.'[57] But when I again met Marx at Brussels, in spring, 1845, he had it ready worked out, and put it before me in terms almost as clear as those in which I have stated it here."[58]

Engels has lifted the veil thus far, but the rest is hidden. Perhaps it is well that it should be; well that no man should be able to say which passages came from the mind of Marx and which from the mind of Engels. In life they were inseparable, and so they must be in the Valhalla of history. The greatest political pamphlet of all time must forever bear, with equal honor, the names of both. Their noble friendship unites them even beyond the tomb.

> "Twin Titans! Whom defeat ne'er bowed,
> Scarce breathing from the fray,
> Again they sound the war cry loud,
> Again is riven Labor's shroud,
> And life breathed in the clay.
> Their work? Look round--see Freedom proud
> And confident to-day."[59]

NOTES:

[42] Cf. *Social Democracy Red Book*, edited by Frederic Heath (1900), page 79.

[43] *History of Socialism in the United States*, by Morris Hillquit, pages 161-162.

[44] E. Belfort Bax, article on *Friederich Engels*, in *Justice* (London), No. 606, Vol. XII, August 24, 1895.

[45] *Disclosures about the Communists' Process, Herr Vogt*, etc.

[46] Cf. G. Adler, *Die Grundlagen der Karl Marx'schen Kritik der bestehenden Volkswirthschaft* (1887), page 226.

[47] *Karl Marx: Biographical Memoirs*, by Wilhelm Liebknecht, page 14.

[48] *Idem*, page 164.

[49] Cf. F. Mehring's *Aus dem literarischen Nachlass von Karl Marx, Friederich Engels, und Ferdinand Lassalle*, 1902; the *Neue Beitrage zur Biographie von Karl Marx und Friederich Engels, in Die Neue Zeit*, 1907, and Mehring's *Geschichte der deutschen Sozialdemokratie*, 1903.

[50] *Memoirs of Marx*, by Wilhelm Liebknecht, page 164.

[51] Karl Kautsky, article on F. Engels, *Austrian Labor Almanac*, 1887.

[52] E. Belfort Bax, article on *Friederich Engels*, in *Justice* (London), No. 606, Vol. XII, August 24, 1895.

[53] Cf. *Reminiscences of Karl Marx*, by W. Harrison Riley, in *The Comrade*, Vol. III, No. 1, pages 5-6.

[54] Marx opposed the "Alliance de la Democratic Socialiste," formed by Bakunin, with its headquarters at Geneva, almost as vigorously for its atheistic plank as for its denial of political methods. The first plank in the programme of the "Alliance" was as follows:--

"The Alliance declares itself Atheist; it demands the abolition of all worship, the substitution of science for faith, and of human justice for Divine justice; the abolition of marriage, so far as it is a political, religious, juridical, or civil institution."

This programme is frequently quoted against the Socialist propaganda,--as, for example, by George Brooks, in *God's England or the Devil's*?--in spite of the fact that the "Alliance" was an Anarchist organization, bitterly opposed by Marx, and, in turn, bitterly opposing him.

In this connection, it may be well to call attention to an alleged "quotation from Marx" which is frequently used by the opponents of Socialism. It appears in the work of Brooks, quoted above, and in Professor Peabody's *Jesus Christ and the Social Question* (1907), page 16. Used in a public discussion by a New York labor union official, in April, 1908, it was widely discussed by the press, and, according to that same press, drew from the President of the United States enthusiastic praise of the labor-union official in question. The passage reads: "The idea of God must be destroyed. It is the keystone of a perverted civilization. The true root of liberty, of equality, of culture, is Atheism. Nothing must restrain the spontaneity of the human mind." Had the opponents of Socialism been familiar with the teachings of Marx, they would have known that he could not have said anything like this, that it is absolutely at variance with all his teaching. The man who formulated the materialist conception of history could not by any possibility utter such balderdash. The fact is, the quotation is not from Karl Marx at all, but from a very different writer, an Anarchist, Wilhelm Marr, who was *a most bitter opponent of Socialism*. As given, the quotation is a free translation of a passage contained in Marr's *Das junge Deutschland in der Schweiz*, pages 131-134. Marr's programme, as given in the *Report of the Royal Commission on Labor* (Vol. V, Germany), was the abolition of Church, State, property, and marriage, with the one positive tenet of "a bloody and fearful revenge upon the rich and powerful."

[55] See F. Engels, *Socialism, Utopian and Scientific*, page 16 (London edition, 1892).

[56] F. Engels, Introduction to the *Communist Manifesto* (English translation, 1888). The italics are mine. J. S.

[57] F. Engels, *The Condition of the Working Class in England in 1844*. See, for instance, pages 79, 80, 82, etc.

[58] Introduction to the *Communist Manifesto* (English edition, 1888).

[59] From *Friederich Engels*, a poem by "J. L." (John Leslie), in *Justice* (London), August 17, 1895.

CHAPTER IV
THE MATERIALISTIC CONCEPTION OF HISTORY

I

Socialism, then, in the modern, scientific sense, is a theory of social evolution. Its hopes for the future rest, not upon the genius of some Utopia-builder, but upon the inherent forces of historical development. The Socialist state will never be realized except as the result of economic necessity, the culmination of successive epochs of industrial evolution. Thus the existing social system appears to the Socialist of to-day, not as it appeared to the Utopians and as it still must appear to mere ideologist reformers, as a triumph of ignorance or wickedness, the reign of false *ideas*, but as the result of an age-long evolutionary process, determined, not wholly indeed, but mainly, by certain methods of producing the necessities of life in the first place, and secondly, of effecting their exchange.

Not, let it be understood, that Socialism has become a mere mechanical theory of economic fatalism. The historical development, the social evolution, upon the laws of which the theories of Socialism are based, is a human process, involving all the complex feelings, emotions, aspirations, hopes, and fears common to man. To ignore this fundamental fact, as they must who interpret the Marx-Engels theory of history as a doctrine of economic fatalism, is to miss the profoundest significance of the theory. While it is true that the scientific spirit destroys the idea of romantic, magic transformations of the social system and the belief that the world may be re-created at will, rebuilt upon the plans of some Utopian architect, it still, as we shall see, leaves room for the human factor. Otherwise, indeed, it would only be a new kind of Utopianism. They who accept the theory that the production of the material necessities of life is the main impelling force, the ***geist***, of human evolution, may rightly protest against social injustice and wrong just as vehemently as any of the ideologists, and aspire just as fervently toward a nobler and better state. The Materialistic Conception of History does not involve the fatalist resignation summed up in the phrase, "Whatever is, is natural, and, therefore, right." It does not involve belief in man's helplessness to change conditions.

II

The idea of social evolution is admirably expressed in the fine phrase of Leibnitz, "The present is the child of the past, but it is the parent of the future."[60] The great seventeenth-century philosopher was not the first to postulate and apply to society that doctrine of flux, of continuity and unity, which we call evolution. In all ages of which record has been preserved to us, it has been sporadically, and more or less vaguely, expressed. Even savages seem to have dimly perceived it. The saying of the Bechuana chief, recorded by the missionary, Casalis, was probably, judging by its epigrammatic character, a proverb of his people. "One event is always the son of another," he said--a saying strikingly like that of Leibnitz.

Since the work of Lyell, Darwin, Wallace, Spencer, Huxley, Youmans, and their numerous followers--a brilliant school embracing the foremost historians and sociologists of Europe and America--the idea of evolution as a universal law has made rapid and certain progress. Everything changes; nothing is immutable or eternal. Whatever is, whether in geology, astronomy, biology, or sociology, is the result of numberless, inevitable, related changes. Only the law of change is changeless. The present is a phase only of a great transition process from what was, through what is, to what will be.

The Marx-Engels theory is an exploration of the laws governing this process of evolution in the domain of human relations: an attempt to provide a key to the hitherto mysterious succession of changes in the political, juridical, and social relations and institutions of mankind. Whence, for instance, arose the institution of chattel slavery, so repugnant to our modern ideas of right and wrong, and how shall we explain its defense and justification in the name of religion and morality? How account for the fact that what Yesterday regarded as righteous, To-day condemns as wrong; that what at one period of the world's history is regarded as perfectly natural and right--the practice of polygamy, for example--becomes abhorrent at another period; or that what is regarded with horror and disgust in one part of the world is sanctioned by the ethical codes, and freely practiced elsewhere? Ferri gives two examples of this kind: the cannibalism of Central African tribes, and the killing of parents, as a religious duty, in Sumatra.[61] To reply "custom" is to beg the whole question, for customs do not exist without reason, however difficult it may be to discern the reason for any particular custom. To reply that these things are mysteries, as the old theologians did when the doctrine of the Trinity was questioned, is to leave the question unanswered and to challenge doubt and investigation. The human mind abhors a mystery as nature abhors a vacuum. Despite Spencer, the human mind has never admitted the existence of the *Unknowable*. To explore the *Unknown* is man's universal impulse; and with each fresh discovery the *Unknown* is narrowed by the expansion of the *Known*.

The theory that ideas determine progress, that, in the words of Professor Richard T. Ely, "all that is significant in human history may be traced back to ideas,"[62] is only true in the sense that a half truth is true. It is true, nothing but the truth, but it is less than the whole truth. Truly all that is significant in human history may be traced back to ideas, but in like manner the ideas themselves can be traced back to material sources. For ideas have histories, too, and the causation of an idea must be understood before the idea itself can serve fully to explain anything. We must go back of the idea to the causes which gave it birth if we would interpret anything by it. We may trace the American Revolution, for example, back to the revolutionary ideas of the colonists, but that will not materially assist us to understand the Revolution. For that, it is necessary to trace the ideas themselves to their source, the economic discontent of an exploited people. This is the spirit which illumines the works of historians like Green, McMaster, Morse Stephens, and others of the modern school, who emphasize social forces rather than individual facts, and find the *geist* of history in social experiences and institutions.

What has been called the "Great Man theory," the theory according to which Luther created the Protestant Reformation, to quote only one example, and which ignored the great economic changes consequent upon the break-up of feudalism and the rise of a new industrial order, long dominated our histories. According to this theory, an idea, developed in the mind of Luther, independent of external circumstances, changed the political and social life of Europe. Had there been no Luther, there would have been no Reformation; or had Luther died before giving his idea to the world, the Reformation would have been averted. The student who seeks in the bulk of the histories written prior to, say, 1870, what he has a legitimate reason for seeking, namely, a picture of the actual life of the people at any period, will be sadly disappointed. He will find records of wars and treaties of peace, royal genealogies and gossip, wildernesses of names and dates. But he will not find such careful accounts of the jurisprudence of the period, nor any hint of the economical conditions of its development. He will find splendid accounts of court life, with its ceremonials, scandals, intrigues, and follies; but no such pictures of the lives of the people, their social conditions, and the methods of labor and commerce which obtained. He will be unable to visualize the life of the period. In other words, the histories lack realism; they are unreal, and, therefore, deceptive. The new spirit, in the development of which the materialist conception of Marx and Engels has been an important creative influence, is concerned less with the chronicle of notable events and dates than with their underlying causes and the manner of life of the people. Had it no other bearing, the Marx-Engels theory, considered solely as a contribution to the science of history, would have been one of the greatest intellectual achievements of the nineteenth century. By emphasizing the importance of the economic factors in social evolution, it has done much for economics and more for history.[63]

III

While the Materialistic Conception of History bears the names of Marx and Engels, as the theory of organic evolution bears the names of Darwin and Wallace, it is not claimed that the idea had never before been expressed. Just as thousands of years before Darwin and Wallace the theory which bears their names had been dimly perceived, so the idea that economic conditions dominate historical developments had its foreshadowings. The famous dictum of Aristotle, that only by the introduction of machines would the abolition of slavery ever be made possible, is a conspicuous example of many anticipations of the theory. It is true that "In dealing with speculations so remote, we have to guard against reading modern meanings into writings produced in ages whose limitations of knowledge were serious, whose temper and standpoint are wholly alien to our own,"[64] but the Aristotelian saying admits of no other interpretation. It is clearly a recognition of the fact that the supreme politico-social institution of the time depended upon hand labor.

In later times, the idea of a direct connection between economic conditions and legal and political institutions reappears in the works of various writers. Professor Seligman[65] quotes from Harrington's "Oceana" the argument that the prevailing form of government depends upon the conditions of land tenure, and the extent of its monopolization. Saint-Simon, too, as already stated, taught that political institutions depend upon economic conditions. But it is to Marx and Engels that we owe the first formulation into a definite theory of what had hitherto been but a suggestion, and the beginnings of a literature, now of considerable proportions, dealing with history from its standpoint. No more need be said concerning the "originality" of the theory.

A word as to the designation of the theory. Its authors gave it the name "historical materialism," and it has been urged that the name is, for many reasons, unfortunately chosen. Two of the leading exponents of the theory, Professor Seligman and Mr. Ghent, the former an opponent, the latter an advocate of Socialism, have expressed this conviction in very definite terms. The last-named writer bases his objection to the name on the ground that it is repellent to many persons who associate the word materialism with the philosophy "that matter is the only substance, and that matter and its motions constitute the universe."[66] That is an old objection, and undoubtedly contains much truth. It is interesting in connection therewith to read the sarcastic comment of Engels upon it in the introduction to his "Socialism, Utopian and Scientific." The objection of Professor Seligman is based upon another ground entirely. He impugns its accuracy. "The theory which ascribes all changes in society to the influence of climate, or to the character of the fauna and flora, is materialistic," he says, "and yet has little in common with the doctrine here discussed. The doctrine we have to deal with is not only materialistic, but also economic in character; and the better phrase is ... the 'economic interpretation' of history."[67]

For this reason he discards the name given to the theory by its authors and adopts the luminous phrase of Thorold Rogers, without credit to that writer.

By French and Italian writers the term "economic determinism" has long been used, and it has been adopted to some extent in this country by Socialist writers. But this term, as Professor Seligman points out, is objectionable, because it exaggerates the theory, and gives it, by implication, a fatalistic character, conveying the idea that economic influence is the *sole* determining factor--a view which its authors specifically repudiated. While the reasoning of Professor Seligman in the argument quoted against the name "historical materialism" is neither very profound nor conclusive, since climate and fauna and flora are included in the term "economic" as clearly as in the term "materialistic," much may be said in favor of his choice of the term he borrows from Thorold Rogers, and it is used by many Socialist writers in preference to that used by Marx and Engels.

Many persons have doubtless been deceived into believing that the theory involves the denial of all influence to idealistic or spiritual factors, and the assumption that economic forces *alone* determine the course of historical development. Much of the criticism of the theory, especially by the Germans, rests upon that assumption. The theory is attacked, also, as being sordid and brutal upon the same false assumption that it implies that men are governed solely by their economic *interests*, that individual conduct is never inspired by anything higher than the economic interest of the individual. These are misconceptions of the theory, due, no doubt, to the overemphasis placed upon it by its authors--a common experience of new doctrines--and, above all, the exaggerations of too zealous, unrestrained disciples. There is a wise saying of Schiller's which suggests the spirit in which these exaggerations of a great truth--exaggerations by which it becomes falsehood--should be regarded: "Rarely do we reach truth, except through extremes--we must have foolishness ... even to exhaustion, before we arrive at the beautiful goal of calm wisdom."[68] When it is contended that the "Civil War was at bottom a struggle between two economic principles,"[69] we have the presentation of an important truth, the key to the proper understanding of a great historical event. But when that important fact is exaggerated and torn from its legitimate place to suit the propaganda of a theory, and we are asked to believe that Garrison, Lovejoy, and other abolitionists were inspired solely by economic motives, that the urge and passion of human freedom did not enter into their souls, we are forced to reject it. But let it be clearly understood that it forms no part of the theory, that it is even expressly denied in the very terms in which Marx and Engels formulated the theory, and that its authors repudiated such perversions of it.

In no respect has the theory been more grossly exaggerated and misrepresented than in its application to religion. True philosopher that he was, Marx realized the absurdity of attempting "to abstract religious sentiment from the course of history, to place it by itself."[70] He recognized that all religion is, fundamentally, man's effort to put himself into harmonious relation with, and to discover an interpretation of, the forces of the universe. The more incomprehensible those forces, the greater man's need of an explanation of them. He could not fail to see that the religion of a people always bears a marked relation to their mental development and their special environment. He knew that at various stages the Yahve of the Hebrews represented very different conceptions, answering to changes in the social and political conditions of the people. To the primitive Israelitish tribes, Yahve was, as Professor Rauschenbusch remarks,[71] a tribal god, fortunately stronger than the gods of the neighboring tribes, but not fundamentally different from them, and the way to win his favor was to sacrifice abundantly. Later, with the development of a national spirit, the religious ideal became a theocracy, and Yahve became a King and Supreme Lord. In times of oppression and war Yahve was a God of War, but under other conditions he was a God of Peace. At every step the conception of Yahve bears a very definite relation to the material life.[72]

Marx knew that primitive religions have often a celestial pantheon fashioned after the existing social order, kings being gods, aristocrats being demigods, and common mortals occupying a celestial rank equal to their terrestrial one. The celestial hierarchy of the Chinese, for example, is an exact reproduction of the earthly hierarchy, and all the privileges of rank are observed celestially as on earth. So in India we find the religions reproducing in their concepts of heaven the degrees and divisions of the various castes,[73] while our own American Indian conceived of a celestial hunting ground, with abundant reward of game, as his Paradise. "The religious world is but the reflex of the real world," said Marx,[74] and the phrase has been used, both by disciples and critics, as an attack upon religion itself; as showing that the Marxian philosophy excludes the possibility of religious belief. Obviously, however, the passage will not bear such an interpretation. To say that "the religious world is but the reflex of the real world" is by no means to deny that men have been benefited by seeking an interpretation of the forces of the universe, or to assert that the quest for such an interpretation is incompatible with rational conduct. In his scorn for Bakunin's "Alliance" programme with its dogmatic atheism[75] Marx was perfectly consistent. The passage quoted simply lays down, in bare outline, a principle which, if well founded, enables us to study comparative religion from a new viewpoint.

It is not a denial of religion, then, which the famous utterance of Marx involves, but a recognition of the fact that, even as all religions may be traced to the same fundamental instinct in mankind, so the different forms which the religious conception assumes are, or may be, reflexes of the material life of those making them. Thus man makes religion for himself under the urge of his deepest instincts. The application of the theory to religion is analogous to its application to historical events. To say that a given religion assumes the form it does as an unconscious reflex of the environment in which it is produced, is no more a denial of that religion than to say that the Reformation arose out of economic and social conditions, and not out of an idea in Luther's mind, is a denial of the fact that there was a Reformation, or that the Reformation benefited the people. The value of the theory to the study of religions and religious movements is not less than to the study of history. Does anybody pretend that we can understand Christianity without taking into account the Roman Empire; or that we can understand Catholicism without knowing something of the economic life of medieval Europe; or Methodism without knowing the social condition of England in Wesley's day?[76]

In one of the very earliest of his writings upon the subject, some comments upon the philosophy of Ludwig Feuerbach, and intended to form the basis of a separate work, we find Marx insisting that man is not a mere automaton, driven irresistibly by blind economic forces. He says: "The materialistic doctrine, that men are the products of conditions and education, different men, therefore, the products of other conditions and changed education, *forgets that circumstances may be altered by men, and that the educator has himself to be educated*."[77] Thus early we see the master taking a position entirely at variance with those of his disciples who would claim that the human factor has no influence upon historical development, that man is without power over his own destiny. From that position Marx never departed. Both he and Engels recognized the human character of the problem, and the futility of attempting to reduce all the processes of history and human progress to one sole basic cause. And in no case, so far as I am aware, has either of them attempted to do this.

In another place, Marx contends that "men make their own history, but they make it not of their own accord or under self-chosen conditions, but under given and transmitted conditions. The tradition of all dead generations weighs like a mountain upon the brain of the living."[78] Here, again, the influence of the human will is not denied, though its limitations are indicated. This is the application to social man of the theory of limitations of the will commonly accepted as applying to individuals. Man is only a freewill agent within certain sharp and relatively narrow bounds. In a given contingency, I may be "free" to act in a certain manner, or to refrain from so acting. I may take my choice, in the one direction or the other, entirely free, to all appearances, from restraining or compelling influences. Thus, I have acted upon my "will." But what factors formed my will? What circumstances determined my decision? Perhaps fear, or shame, or pride; perhaps tendencies inherited from my ancestors.

Engels admits that the economic factor in evolution has sometimes been unduly emphasized. He says: "Marx and I are partly responsible for the fact that the younger men have sometimes laid more stress on the economic side than it deserves. In meeting the attacks of our opponents, it was necessary for us to emphasize the dominant principle denied by them; and we did not always have the time, place, or opportunity to let the other factors which were concerned in the mutual action and reaction get their deserts."[79] In another letter,[80] he says: "According to the materialistic view of history, the factor which is in *last instance* decisive in history is the production and reproduction of actual life. More than this neither Marx nor I have ever asserted. But when any one distorts this so as to read that the economic factor is the sole element, he converts the statement into a meaningless, abstract, absurd phrase. The economic condition is the basis; but the various elements of the superstructure,--the political forms of the class contests, and their results, the constitutions,--the legal forms, and also all the reflexes of these actual contests in the brains of the participants, the political, legal, philosophical theories, the *re-*

ligious views ... all these exert an influence on the development of the historical struggles, and, in many instances, determine their form."

It is evident, therefore, that the doctrine does not imply economic fatalism. It does not deny that ideals may influence historical developments and individual conduct. While, as we shall see in a later chapter, it is part of the doctrine that classes are formed upon a basis of unity of material interests, it does not deny that men may, and often do, act in accordance with the promptings of noble impulses and humanitarian ideals, when their material interests would lead them to do otherwise. We have a conspicuous example of this in the life of Marx himself; in his splendid devotion to the cause of the workers through years of terrible poverty and hardship when he might have chosen wealth and fame. It is known, for example, that Bismarck made the most extravagant offers to enlist the services of Marx, who declined them at the very time when he was suffering awful privations. Marx himself has noted more than one instance of individual idealism triumphing over material interests and class environment, and, by a perversity that is astonishing, and not wholly disingenuous, some of his critics, notably Ludwig Slonimski,[81] have used these instances as arguments against his theory, claiming that they disprove it! We are to understand the materialistic theory, then, as teaching, not that history is determined by economic forces only, but that in human evolution the chief factors are social factors, and that these factors in turn are *mainly* molded by economic circumstances.[82]

This, then, is the basis of the Socialist philosophy, which Engels regarded as "destined to do for history what Darwin's theory has done for biology." Marx himself made a similar comparison.[83] Marx was, so Liebknecht tells us, one of the first to recognize the importance of Darwin's investigations to sociology. His first important treatment of the materialistic theory, in "A Contribution to the Critique of Political Economy," appeared in 1859, the year in which "The Origin of Species" appeared. "We spoke for months of nothing else but Darwin, and the revolutionizing power of his scientific conquests,"[84] says Liebknecht. Darwin, however, had little knowledge of political economy, as he acknowledged in a letter to Marx, thanking the latter for a copy of "Das Kapital." "I heartily wish that I possessed a greater knowledge of the deep and important subject of economic questions, which would make me a more worthy recipient of your gift," he wrote.[85]

IV

The test of such a theory must lie in its application. Let us, then, apply the materialistic principle, first to a specific event, and then to the great sweep of the historic drama. Perhaps no single event has more profoundly impressed the imaginations of men, or filled a more important place in our histories, than the discovery of America by Columbus. In the schoolbooks, this great event figures as a splendid adventure, arising out of a romantic dream. But the facts are, as we know, far otherwise.[86] In the twelfth and thirteenth centuries there were numerous and well-frequented routes from Hindustan, that vast storehouse of treasure from which Europe drew its riches. Along these routes cities flourished. There were the great ports, Licia in the Levant, Trebizond on the Black Sea, and Alexandria. From these ports, Venetian and Genoese traders bore the produce over the passes of the Alps to the Upper Danube and the Rhine. Here it was a source of wealth to the cities along the waterways, from Ratisbon and Nuremburg, to Bruges and Antwerp. Even the slightest acquaintance with the history of the Middle Ages must suffice to give the student an idea of the importance of these cities.

When all these routes save the Egyptian were closed by the hordes of savages which infested Central Asia, it became an easy matter for the Moors in Africa and the Turks in Europe to exact immense revenues from the Eastern trade, solely through their monopoly of the route of transit. Thus there developed an economic parasitism which crippled the trade with the East. The Turks were securely seated at Constantinople, threatening to advance into the heart of Europe, and building up an immense military system out of the taxes imposed upon the trade of Europe with the East--a military power, which, in less than a quarter of a century, enabled Selim I to conquer Mesopotamia and the holy towns of Arabia, and to annex Egypt.[87] It became necessary, then, to find a new route to India; and it was this great economic necessity which set Columbus thinking of a pathway to India over the Western Sea. It was this same great problem which engaged the attention of all the navigators of the time; it was this economic necessity which induced Ferdinand and Isabella to support the adventurous plan of Columbus. In a word, without detracting in any manner from the splendid genius of Columbus, or from the romance of his great voyage of discovery, we see that, fundamentally, it was the economic interest of Europe which gave birth to the one and made the other possible. The same explanation applies to the voyage of Vasco da Gama, six years later, which resulted in finding a way to India over the southeast course by way of the Cape of Good Hope.

Kipling asks in his ballad, "The British Flag"--

"And what should they know of England, who only England know?"

There is a profound truth in the defiant line, a truth which applies equally to America or any other country. The present is inseparable from the past. We cannot understand one epoch without reference to its predecessors; we cannot understand the history of the United States unless we seek the key in the history of Europe-- of England and France in particular. At the very threshold, in order to understand how the heroic navigator came to discover the vast continent of which the United States is part, we must pause to study the economic conditions of Europe which impelled the adventurous voyage, and led to the discovery of a great continent stretching across the ocean path. Such a view of history does not rob it of its romance, but rather adds to it. Surely, the wonderful linking of circumstances--the demand for spices and silks to minister to the fine tastes of aristocratic Europe, the growth of the trade with the East Indies, the grasping greed of Moor and Turk--all playing a role in the great drama of which the discovery of America is but a scene, is infinitely more fascinating than the latter event detached from its historical setting!

It is not easy to give in the compass of a few pages an intelligent view of the main currents of history. The sketch here introduced--not without hesitation--is an endeavor to state the Socialist concept of the course of social evolution in a brief outline and to indicate the principal economic causes which have operated to determine that course.

It is now generally admitted that primitive man lived under Communism. Lewis H. Morgan[88] has calculated that if the life of the human race be assumed to have covered one hundred thousand years, at least ninety-five thousand years were spent in a crude, tribal Communism, in which private property was practically unknown, and in which the only ethic was devotion to tribal interests, and the only crime antagonism to tribal interests. Under this social system the means of making wealth were in the hands of the tribes, or **gens**, and distribution was likewise socially arranged. Between the different tribes warfare was constant, but in the tribe itself there was cooeperation and not struggle. This fact is of tremendous importance in view of the criticisms which have been directed against the Socialist philosophy from the so-called Darwinian point of view, according to which competition and struggle is the law of life; that what Professor Huxley calls "the Hobbesial war of each against all" is the normal state of existence.

This is described as "the so-called Darwinian" theory advisedly, for the struggle for existence as the law of evolution has been exaggerated out of all likeness to the conception of Darwin himself. In "The Descent of Man," for instance, Darwin raises the point under review, and shows how, in many animal societies, the **struggle** for existence is replaced by **cooeperation** for existence, and how that substitution results in the development of faculties which secure to the species the best conditions for survival. "Those communities," he says, "which included the greatest number of the most sympathetic members, would flourish best and rear the greatest number of offspring."[89] Despite these instances, and the warning of Darwin himself that the term "struggle for existence" should not be too narrowly interpreted or overrated, his followers, instead of broadening it according to the master's suggestions, narrowed it still more. Thus the theory has been exaggerated into a mere caricature of the truth. This is almost invariably the fate of theories which deal with human relations, perhaps it would be equally true to say of all theories. The exaggerations of Malthus's law of population is a case in point. The Marx-Engels theory of the materialistic conception of history is, as we have seen, another.

Kropotkin, among others, has developed the theory along the lines suggested by Darwin. He points out that "though there is an immense amount of warfare and extermination going on amidst various classes of animals, there is, at the same time, as much, or perhaps even more, of mutual support, mutual aid, mutual defense, amidst animals belonging to the same species or, at least, to the same society. Sociability is as much a law of nature as mutual struggle.... If we resort to an indirect test, and ask nature: 'Who are the fittest: those who are continually at war with each other, or those who support one another?' we at once see that those animals which acquire habits of mutual aid are undoubtedly the fittest. They have more chances to survive, and they attain, in their respective classes, the highest development of intelligence and bodily organization. If the numberless facts which can be brought forward to support this view are taken into account, we may safely say that mutual aid is as much a law of animal life as mutual struggle, but that, as a factor of evolution, it most probably has a far greater importance, inasmuch as it favors the development of such habits and characters as insure the maintenance and further development of the species, together with the greatest amount of welfare and enjoyment of life for the individual, with the least waste of energy."[90]

From the lowest forms of animal life up to the highest, man, this law proves to be operative. It is not denied that there is competition for food, for life, within the species, human and other. But that competition is not usual; it arises out of unusual and special conditions. There are instances of hunger-maddened mothers tearing away food from their children; men drifting at sea have fought for water and food as beasts fight, but these are not normal conditions of life. "Happily enough," says Kropotkin again, "competition is not the rule either in the animal world or in mankind. It is limited among animals to exceptional periods.... Better conditions are created by the ***elimination of competition*** by means of mutual aid and mutual support."[91] This is the voice of science now that we have passed through the extremes and arrived at the "beautiful goal of calm wisdom." Competition is not, in the verdict of modern science, the law of life, but of death. Strife is not nature's way of progress.

Anything more important to our present inquiry than this verdict of science it would be difficult to imagine. Men have for so long believed and declared struggle and competition to be the "law of nature," and opposed Socialism on the ground of its supposed antagonism to that law, that this new conception of nature's method comes as a vindication of the Socialist position. The naturalist testifies to the universality of the principle of coöperation throughout the animal world, and the historian and sociologist to its universality throughout the greatest part of man's history. Present economic tendencies toward combination and away from competition, in industry and commerce, appear as the fulfilling of a great universal law. And the vain efforts of men to stop that process, by legislation, boycotts, and divers other methods, appear as efforts to set aside immutable law. Like so many Canutes, they bid the tides halt, and, like Canute's, their commands are vain and mocked by the unheeding tides.

Under Communism, then, man lived for many thousands of years. As far back as we can go into the paleo-ethnology of mankind, we find evidences of this. All the great authorities, Morgan, Maine, Lubbock, Taylor, Bachofen, and many others, agree in this. And under this Communism all the great fundamental inventions were evolved, as Morgan and others have shown. The wheel, the potter's wheel, the lever, the stencil plate, the sail, the rudder, the loom, were all evolved under Communism in its various stages. So, too, the cultivation of cereals for food, the smelting of metals, the domestication of animals,--to which we owe so much, and on which we still so largely depend,--were all introduced under Communism. Even in our day there have been found many survivals of this Communism among primitive peoples. Mention need only be made here of the Bantu tribes of Africa, whose splendid organization astonished the British, and the Eskimos. It is now possible to trace with a fair amount of certainty the progress of mankind through various stages of Communism, from the unconscious Communism of the nomad to the consciously organized and directed Communism of the most highly developed tribes, right up to the threshold of civilization, when private property takes the place of common, tribal property, and economic classes appear.[92]

V

Private property, other than that personal ownership and use of things, such as weapons and tools, which involves no class or caste domination, and is an integral feature of all forms of Communism, first appears in the ownership of man by man. Slavery, strange as it may seem, is directly traceable to tribal Communism, and first appears as a tribal institution. When one tribe made war upon another, its efforts were directed to the killing of as many of its enemies as possible. Cannibal tribes killed their foes for food, rarely or never killing their fellow-tribesmen for that purpose. Non-cannibalistic tribes killed their foes merely to get rid of them. But when the power of mankind over the forces of external nature had reached that point in its development where it became relatively easy for a man to produce more than was necessary for his own maintenance, the custom arose of making captives of enemies and setting them to work. A foe captured had thus an economic value to the tribe. Either he could be set to work directly, his surplus product enriching the tribe, or he could be used to relieve some of his captors from other necessary duties, thus enabling them to produce more than would otherwise be possible, the effect being the same in the end. The property of the tribe at first, slaves become at a later stage private property--probably through the institution of the tribal distribution of wealth. Cruel, revolting, and vile as slavery appears to our modern sense,--especially the earlier forms of slavery before the body of legislation, and, not less important, sentiment, which surrounded it later arose,--it still was a step forward, a distinct advance upon the older customs of cannibalism and wholesale slaughter.

Nor was it a progressive step only on the humanitarian side. It had other, profounder consequences from the evolutionary point of view. It made a leisure class possible, and provided the only conditions under which art, philosophy, and jurisprudence could be evolved. The secret of Aristotle's saying, that only by the invention of machines would the abolition of slavery ever be made possible, lies in his recognition of the fact that the labor of slaves alone made possible the devotion of a class of men to the pursuit of knowledge instead of to the production of the primal necessities of life. The Athens of Pericles, for example, with all its varied forms of culture, its art and its philosophy, was a semi-communism of a caste above, resting upon a basis of slave labor underneath. Similar conditions prevailed in all the so-called ancient democracies of civilization.

The private ownership of wealth producers and their products made private exchange inevitable; individual ownership of land took the place of communal ownership, and a monetary system was invented. Here, then, in the private ownership of land and laborer, private production and exchange, we have the economic factors which caused the great revolts of antiquity, and led to that concentration of wealth into few hands, with its resulting mad luxury on the one hand and widespread proletarian misery upon the other, which conspired to the overthrow of Greek and Roman civilization. The study of those relentless economic forces which led to the break-up of Roman civilization is important as showing how chattel slavery became modified and the slave to be regarded as a serf, a servant bound to the soil. The lack of adequate production, the crippling of commerce by hordes of corrupt officials, the overburdening of the agricultural estates with slaves, so that agriculture became profitless, the crushing out of free labor by slave labor, and the rise of a wretched class of freemen proletarians, these, and other kindred causes, led to the breaking up of the great estates; the dismissal of superfluous slaves, in many cases, and the partial enfranchisement of others by making them hereditary tenants, paying a fixed share of their product as rent--here we have the embryonic stage of feudalism. It was a revolution, this transformation of the social system of Rome, of infinitely greater importance than the sporadic risings of a few thousand slaves. Yet, such is the lack of perspective which the historians have shown, it is given a far less important place in the histories than the risings in question. Slavery, chattel slavery, died because it had ceased to be profitable; serf labor arose because it was more profitable. Slave labor was economically impossible, and the labor of free men was morally impossible; it had, thanks to the slave system, come to be regarded as a degradation. In the words of Engels, "This brought the Roman world into a blind alley from which it could not escape.... There was no other help but a complete revolution."[93]

The invading barbarians made the revolution complete. By the poor freemen proletarians who had been selling their children into slavery, the barbarians were welcomed. Misery, like opulence, has no patriotism. Many of the proletarian freemen had fled to the districts of the barbarians, and feared nothing so much as a return to Roman rule. What, then, should the proletariat care for the overthrow of the Roman state by the barbarians? And how much less the slaves, whose condition, generally speaking, could not possibly change for the worse? The free proletarian and the slave could join in saying, as men have said thousands of times in circumstances of desperation:--

"Our fortunes may be better; they can be no worse."

VI

Feudalism is the essential politico-economic system of the Middle Ages. Obscure as its origin is, and indefinite as the date of its first appearances, there can be no doubt whatever that the break-up of the Roman system, and the modification of the existing form of slavery, constituted the most important of its sources. Whether, as some writers have contended, the feudal system of land tenure and serfdom is traceable to Asiatic origins, being adopted by the ruling class of Rome in the days of the economic disintegration of the empire, or whether it rose spontaneously out of the Roman conditions, matters little to us. Whatever its archaeological interest, it does not affect the narrower scope of our present inquiry whether economic necessity caused the adoption of an alien system of land tenure and agricultural production, or whether economic necessity caused the creation of a new system. The central fact is the same in either case.

That period of history which we call the Middle Ages covers a span of well-nigh a thousand years. If we arbitrarily date its beginning from the successful invasion of Rome by the barbarians in the early part of the fifth century, and its ending with the final development of the craft guilds in the middle of the fourteenth century, we have a sufficiently exact measure of the time during which feudalism developed, flourished, and declined. There are few things more difficult than the bounding of epochs in social evolution by exact dates. Just as the ripening of the wheat fields comes almost imperceptibly, so that the farmer can say when the wheat is ripe, yet cannot say when the ripening occurred, so with the epochs into which social history divides itself. There is the unripe state and the ripe, but no chasm yawns between them; they are merged together. We speak of the "end" of chattel slavery, and the "rise" of feudalism, therefore, in a wide, general sense. As a matter of fact, chattel slavery survived to some extent for centuries, existing alongside of the new form of servitude; and its disappearance took place, not simultaneously throughout the civilized world, but at varying intervals. Likewise, there is a vast difference between the first, crude, ill-defined forms of feudalism and its subsequent development.

The theory of feudalism is the "divine right of kings." God is the Supreme Lord of all the earth, the kings are His vice-regents, devolving their authority in turn upon whomsoever they will. All land is held as belonging to the king, God's chosen representative. He divides the realm among his barons, to rule over and defend. For this they pay tribute to the king--military service in times of war and, at a later period, money. In turn, the barons divide the land among the lesser nobility, receiving tribute from them. By these divided among the freemen, who also pay tribute, the land is tilled by the serfs, who pay service to the freeman, the lord of the manor.

The serf pays no tribute directly to the king, only to his liege lord; the liege lord pays to his superior, and so on, up to the king. This is the economic framework of feudalism; with its ecclesiastical side we are not here concerned.

At the base of the whole superstructure, then, was the serf, his relation to his lord differing only in degree, though in material degree, from that of the chattel slave. He might be, and often was, as brutally ill-treated as the slave before him had been; he might be ill-fed and ill-housed; his wife or daughters might be ravished by his master or his master's sons. Yet, withal, his condition was better than that of the slave. He could maintain his family life in an independent household; he possessed some rights, chief of which perhaps was the right to labor for himself. Having his own allotment of land, he was in a much larger sense a human being. Compelled to render so many days' service to his lord, tilling the soil, clearing the forest, quarrying stone, and doing domestic work, he was permitted to devote a certain, often an equal, number of days to work for his own benefit. Not only so, but the service the lord rendered him, in protecting him and his family from the lawless and violent robber hordes which infested the country, was considerable.

The feudal estate, or manor, was an industrial whole, self-dependent, and having few essential ties binding it to the outside world. The barons and their retainers, lords, thanes, and freemen, enjoyed a certain rude plenty, some of the richer barons enjoying a considerable amount of luxury and splendor. The *villein* and his sons tilled the soil, reaped the harvests, felled trees for fuel, built the houses, raised the necessary domestic animals, and killed the wild animals; his wife and daughters spun the flax, carded the wool, made the homespun clothing, brewed the mead, and gathered the grapes which they made into wine. There was little real dependence upon the outside world except for articles of luxury.

Such was the basic economic institution of feudalism. But alongside of the feudal estate with its serf labor, there were the free laborers, no longer regarding labor as shameful and degrading. These free laborers were the handicraftsmen and free peasants, the former soon organizing themselves into guilds. There was a specialization of labor, but, as yet, little division. Each man worked at a particular craft and exchanged his individual products. The free craftsman would exchange his product with the free peasant, and sometimes his trade extended to the feudal manor. The guild was at once his master and protector; rigid in its rules, strict in its surveillance of its members, it was strong and effective as a protector against the impositions and invasions of feudal barons and their retainers. Division of labor first appears in its simplest form, the association of independent individual workers for mutual advantage, sharing their products upon a basis of equality. This simple cooeeperation involved no fundamental, revolutionary change in society. That came later with the development of the workshop system, and the division of labor upon a definite, predetermined plan. Men specialized now in the making of *parts* of things; no man could say of a finished product, "This is *mine*, for I made it." Production had become a social function.

VII

At first, in its simple beginnings, the cooeeperation of many producers in one great workshop did not involve any general or far-reaching changes in the system of exchange. But as the new methods spread, and it became the custom for one or two wealthy individuals to provide the workshop and necessary tools and materials for production, the product of the combined laborers being appropriated in its entirety by the owners of the agencies of production, who paid the workers a money wage representing less than the actual value of their product, and based upon the cost of their subsistence, the whole economic system was once more revolutionized. The custom of working for wages, hitherto rare and exceptional, became general and customary; individual production for use, either directly or through the medium of personal exchange, was superseded by social production for private profit. The wholesale exchange of social products for private gain took the place of the personal exchange of commodities. The difference between the total cost of the production of commodities, including the wages of the producers, and their exchange value--determined at this stage by the cost of producing similar commodities by individual labor--constituted the share of the capitalist, his profit, and the objective of his investment.

The new system did not spring up spontaneously and full-fledged. Like feudalism, it was a growth, a development of existing forms. And just as chattel slavery lingered on after the rise of the feudal regime, so the old methods of individual production and direct exchange of commodities for personal use lingered on in places and isolated industries long after the rise of the system of wage-paid labor and production for profit. But the old methods of production and exchange gradually became rare and almost obsolete. In accordance with the stern economic law that Marx afterward developed so clearly, the man whose methods of production, including his tools, are less efficient and economical than those of his fellows, thereby making his labor more expensive, must either adapt himself to the new conditions or fall in the struggle which ensues. The triumph of the new system of capitalist production, with its far greater efficiency arising from associated production upon a plan of specialized division of labor, was, therefore, but a question of time. The class of wage-workers thus gradually increased in numbers; as men found that they were unable to compete with the new methods, they accepted the inevitable and adapted themselves to the new conditions. The industrial revolution which established capitalism was, like the great revolutions which ushered in preceding social epochs, the product of man's tools.

NOTES:

[60] Edward Clodd, ***Pioneers of Evolution from Thales to Huxley***, page 1.

[61] ***Socialism and Modern Science***, by Enrico Ferri, page 96.

[62] ***Studies in the Evolution of Industrial Society***, by R. T. Ely, page 3.

[63] Cf. Seligman, *The Economic Interpretation of History*.

[64] Clodd, ***Pioneers of Evolution from Thales to Huxley***, page 8.

[65] Seligman, *The Economic Interpretation of History*, page 50.

[66] ***Mass and Class***, by W. J. Ghent, page 9.

[67] Seligman, *The Economic Interpretation of History*, page 4.

[68] Schiller, ***Philosophical Letters***, Preamble.

[69] Seligman, *The Economic Interpretation of History*, page 86.

[70] Karl Marx, ***Notes on Feuerbach*** (written in 1845), published as an Appendix to ***Feuerbach, The Roots the Socialist Philosophy***, by Friederich Engels. English translation by Austin Lewis (1903).

[71] ***Christianity and the Social Crisis***, by Walter Rauschenbusch (1907), page 4.

[72] For a very scholarly discussion of this subject, the reader is referred to the series of articles by my friend, M. Beer, on *The Rise of Jewish Monotheism*, in the *Social Democrat* (London), 1908.

[73] Cf. *The Economic Foundations of Society*, by Achille Lorio, page 26.

[74] *Capital*, by Karl Marx (Kerr edition). Vol. I, page 91.

[75] Cf. *Karl Marx on Sectarianism and Dogmatism* (A letter written to his friend, Bolte), in the *International Socialist Review*, March, 1908, page 525.

[76] Very significant of the possibilities of a study of religious movements from this economic and social viewpoint is Professor Thomas C. Hall's little book, *The Social Meaning of Modern Religious Movements in England* (1900).

[77] Appendix to F. Engels' *Feuerbach, the Roots of the Socialist Philosophy*, translated by Austin Lewis, 1903.

[78] *The Eighteenth Brumaire.*

[79] Quoted from *The Sozialistische Akademiker*, 1895, by Seligman, *The Economic Interpretation of History*, page 142.

[80] *Idem*, page 143.

[81] *Karl Marx's Nationaloekonomische Irrlehren*, von Ludwig Slonimski, Berlin, 1897.

[82] I have not attempted to give a history of the development of the theory. For a more minute study of the theory, I must refer the reader to the writings of Engels, Seligman, Ferri, Ghent, Bax, and others quoted in these pages.

[83] *Capital*, Vol. I, page 406 n. (Kerr edition).

[84] Liebknecht, *Memoirs of Karl Marx*, page 91.

[85] *Charles Darwin and Karl Marx, A Comparison*, by Edward Aveling, London, 1897.

[86] See Thorold Rogers, *The Economic Interpretation of History*, second edition, 1891, pages 10-12.

[87] For various reasons, chief of which is that it would take me too far away from my present purpose, I do not attempt to develop the serious consequences of these events to Europe. See *The Economic Interpretation of History*, Chapter I, for a brief account of this.

[88] *Ancient Society, or Researches in the Lines of Human Progress from*

Savagery through Barbarism to Civilization, by Lewis H. Morgan. New edition, Chicago, 1907.

[89] Darwin, *The Descent of Man*, second edition, page 163.

[90] *Mutual Aid a Factor of Evolution*, by Peter Kropotkin, pages 5-6.

[91] *Idem*, page 74.

[92] Cf. *Ancient Society*, by Lewis H. Morgan, and *The Origins of the Family, Private Property, and the State*, by Friederich Engels.

[93] Engels, *Origin of the Family, Private Property, and the State*, p. 182.

CHAPTER V
CAPITALISM AND THE LAW
OF CONCENTRATION

I

Such was the mode of the development of capitalistic production in its first stage. In this stage a permanent wage-working class was formed, new markets were developed, many of them by colonial expansion and territorial conquest, and production for sale and profit became the rule, instead of the exception as formerly when men produced primarily for use and sold only their surplus products. A new form of class division thus arose out of this economic soil. Instead of being bound to the land as the serfs had been under feudalism, the wage-workers were bound to their tools. They were not bound to a single master, they were not branded on the cheek, but they were, nevertheless, dependent upon the industrial lords. Economic mastery gradually shifted from the land-owning class to the class of manufacturers. The political and social history of the Middle Ages is largely the record of the struggle for supremacy which was waged between these two classes. That struggle is the central fact of the Protestant Reformation and the Cromwellian Commonwealth.

The second stage of capitalism begins with the birth of the machine age; the introduction of the great mechanical inventions of the latter half of the seventeenth century, and the resulting industrial revolution, the salient features of which we have already traced. That revolution centered in England, whose proud but, from all other points of view than the commercial, foolish boast for a full century it was to be "the workshop of the world." The new methods of production, and the development of trade with India, and the colonies and the United States of America, providing a vast and apparently almost unlimited market, a tremendous rivalry was created among the people of England, tauntingly, but with less originality than bitterness, designated "a nation of shopkeepers" by Napoleon the First. Competition flourished and commerce grew under its mighty urge. Quite naturally, therefore, competition came to be regarded as "the life of trade," and the one supreme law of progress by British economists and statesmen. The economic conditions of the time fostered a sturdy individualism on the one hand, expressing itself in a policy of *laissez faire*, which, paradoxically, they as surely destroyed. The result was the paradox of a nation of theoretic individualists becoming, through its poor laws, and more especially through the vast body of industrial legislation which developed in spite of theories of *laissez faire*, a nation of practical collectivists.

The third and last stage of capitalism is characterized by new forms of industrial ownership, administration, and control. Concentration of industry and the elimination of competition are the distinguishing features of this stage. When, more than half a century ago, the Socialists predicted an era of industrial concentration and monopoly as the outcome of the competitive struggles of the time, their prophecies were mocked and derided. Yet, at this distance of time, it is easy to see what they were foresighted enough to envisage in the future; easy enough to see that competition carries in its bosom the germs of its own inevitable destruction. In words which, as Professor Ely says,[94] seem to many, even non-Socialists, like a prophecy, Karl Marx argued that the business units in production would continuously increase in magnitude, until at last monopoly emerged from the competitive struggle. This monopoly becoming a shackle upon the system under which it has grown up, and thus becoming incompatible with capitalist conditions, socialization must, according to Marx, naturally and necessarily follow.[95] In this as in all the utterances of Marx upon the subject we are reminded of the distinction which must be made between Socialism as he conceived it and the Socialism of the Utopians. We never get away from the law of economic interpretation. Socialism, according to Marx, will develop out of capitalist society, and follow capitalism necessarily and inevitably. It is not a plan to be adopted, but a stage of social development to be reached.

II

For the moment, we are not concerned with the prediction that Socialism must follow the full development of capitalism. The important point for our present study is the predicted growth of monopoly out of competition, and the manner in which that prediction has been realized. Concerning the manner and extent of the fulfillment of this prediction, there have been many keen controversies, both within and without the ranks of the followers of Marx. While Marx and Engels are properly regarded as the first scientific Socialists, having been the first to postulate Socialism as the outcome of evolution, and to explore the laws of that evolution, they were not wholly free from the failings of the Utopists. It would be unreasonable to expect them to be absolutely free from the spirit of their age and their associates. There is, doubtless, something Utopian in the very mechanical conception of capitalist concentration which Marx held; the process is too simple and sweeping, the revolution too imminent. Still, by followers and critics alike, it is generally conceded that the *control* of the means of production is being concentrated into the hands of small and ever smaller groups of capitalists. In recent years the increase in the number of industrial establishments has not kept pace with the increase in the number of workers employed, the increase of capital, or the value of the products manufactured. Not only do we find small groups of men controlling certain industries, but a selective process is clearly observable, giving to the same groups of men control of various industries otherwise utterly unrelated.

In the early stages of the movement toward concentration and trustification, it was possible to classify the leading capitalists according to the industries with which they were identified. One set of capitalists, "Oil Kings," controlled the oil industry; another set, "Steel Kings," controlled the iron and steel industry; another set, "Coal Barons," controlled the coal industry, and so on throughout the industrial and commercial life of the nation. To-day all this has been changed. An examination of the "Directory of Directors" shows that the same men control varied enterprises. The Oil King is at the same time a Steel King, a Coal Baron, a Railway Magnate, and so on. The men who comprise the Standard Oil group, for instance, are found to control hundreds of other companies. They include in the scope of their directorate, banking, insurance, milling, real estate, railroad and steamship lines, gas companies, sugar, coffee, cotton, and tobacco companies, and a heterogeneous host of other concerns. Not only so, but these same men are large holders of investments in all the great European countries, as well as India, Australia, Africa, Asia, and the South American countries, while foreign capitalists similarly, but to a less extent, hold large investments in American companies. Thus, the concentration of industrial control, through its finance, has become interindustrial and is rapidly becoming international. The predictions of Marx are being fulfilled, even though not in the precise manner anticipated by him.

III

During recent years there have been many criticisms of the Marxian theory, aiming to show that this concentration has been, and is, much more apparent than real. Some of the most important of these criticisms have come from within the ranks of the Socialist movement itself, and have been widely exploited as portending the disintegration of the Socialist movement. *Inter alia*, it may be remarked here that a certain fretfulness of temper characterizes most of the critics of Socialism. Strict adherence to the letter of Marx is pronounced as a sign of intellectual bondage of the movement and its leaders to the "Marxian fetish," and, on the other hand, every recognition of the human fallibility of Marx by a Socialist thinker is hailed as a sure portent of a split in the movement. Yet the most serious criticisms of Marx have come from the ranks of his followers--perhaps only another sign of the intellectual bankruptcy of the academic opposition to Socialism.

Of course, Marx was human and fallible. If "Capital" had never been written, there would still have been a Socialist movement, and if it could be destroyed by criticism, the Socialist movement would remain. Socialism is the product of economic conditions, not of a theory or a book. "Capital" is the intellectual explanation of the genesis of Socialism, and neither its cause nor an argument for it by which it must be judged. Hence the futility of such missions as that undertaken by Mr. W. H. Mallock, for example, based upon the assumption that attacks upon the text of Marx will serve to destroy or seriously hinder the living movement. Like a prophet's rebuke to these critics, as well as to those within the ranks of the Socialist movement who would make of the words of Marx and Engels fetters to bind the movement to a dogma, come the words of Engels, published recently, letters in which he writes vigorously to his friend Sorge concerning the working-class movement in England and America. Of his compatriots, the handful of German Socialist exiles in America, who sought to make the American workers swallow a mass of ill-digested Marxian theory, he writes, "The Germans have never understood how to apply themselves from their theory to the lever which could set the American masses in motion; to a great extent they do not understand the theory itself and treat it in a doctrinaire and dogmatic fashion.... It is a credo to them, not a guide to action." And again, "Our theory is not a dogma, but the exposition of a process of evolution, and that process involves several successive phases." Of the English movement he writes, "And here an instinctive Socialism is more and more taking possession of the masses which, ***fortunately***, is opposed to all distinct formulation according to the dogmas of one or the other so-called organizations," and again, he condemns "the bringing down of the Marxian theory of development to a rigid orthodoxy."[96] The critics who hope to destroy the Socialist movement of to-day by stringing together mistaken predictions of Marx and Engels, or who think that Socialism is losing its grip because it is adjusting its expressions to the changed conditions which the progress of fifty years has brought about, utterly mistake the character of the movement. In its abandonment of the errors of Marx it is most truly Marxian--because it is expressing life instead of repeating dogma.

Doubtless Marx anticipated a much more complete concentration of capital and industry than has yet taken place; doubtless, too, he underrated the powers of endurance of some petty industries, and saw the breakdown of capitalism in a cataclysm, whereas modern Socialists see its merging into a form of socialization. But, when all this is admitted, it cannot be fairly said that the sum of criticism has seriously affected the general Marxian theory, as apart from its particular exposition by Marx himself. So far as the criticism has touched the subject of capitalist concentration, it has been pitifully weak, and the furore it has created seems almost pathetic. The main results of this criticism may be briefly summarized as follows: First, in industry, the persistence, and, in some cases, even increase, of petty industries; second, in agriculture, the failure of large-scale farming, and the decrease of the average farm acreage; third, in retail trade, the persistence of the small stores, despite the growth in size and number of the great department stores; fourth, the fact that concentration of industry does not imply a like concentration of wealth, the number of shareholders in a great industrial combination being frequently greater than the number of owners in the units of industry prior to the combination. At first sight, and stated in this manner, it would seem as if these conclusions, if justified by the facts, involved a serious and far-reaching criticism of the Socialist theory of a universal tendency toward the concentration of industry and commerce into units of ever increasing magnitude.

But upon closer examination, these conclusions, their accuracy admitted, are seen to involve no very damaging criticism of the theory. To the superficial observer, the mere increase in the number of industrial establishments seems a much more important matter than to the careful student, who is not easily deceived by appearances. The student sees that while some petty industries undoubtedly do increase in number, the increase of large industries employing many more workers and much larger capitals is vastly greater. Furthermore, he sees what the superficial observer constantly overlooks, namely, that these petty industries are, for the most part, unstable and transient, being continually absorbed by the larger industrial combinations or crushed out of existence, as soon as they have obtained sufficient vitality and strength to make them worthy of notice, either as tributaries to be desired or potential competitors to be feared. Petty industries in a very large number of cases represent a stage in social descent, the wreckage of larger industries whose owners are economically as dependent as the ordinary wage-workers, or even poorer and more to be pitied. Where, on the contrary, it is a stage in social ascent, the petty industry is, paradoxical as the idea may appear, frequently part of the process of industrial concentration. By independent gleaning, it endeavors to find sufficient business to maintain its existence. If it fails in this, its owner falls back to the proletarian level from which, in most instances, he arose. If it succeeds only to a degree sufficient to maintain its owner at or near the average wage-earner's level of comfort, it may pass unnoticed and unmolested. If, on the other hand, it gleans sufficient business to make it desirable as a tributary, or potentially dangerous as a competitor, the petty business is pounced upon by its mightier rival and either absorbed or crushed, according to the temper or need of the latter. Critics of the Marxian theory have for the most part completely failed to recognize this significant aspect of the subject, and attached far too much importance to the continuance of petty industries.

IV

What is true of petty industry is true in even greater measure of retail trade. Nothing could well be further from the truth than the hasty generalization of some critics, that an increase in the number of retail business establishments invalidates the theory of a progressive concentration of capital. In the first place, many of these establishments have no independence whatsoever, but are merely agencies of larger enterprises. Mr. Macrosty has shown that in London the cheap restaurants are in the hands of four or five firms, and this is a branch of business which, because it calls for relatively small capital, shows in a marked manner the increase of establishments. Much the same conditions exist in connection with the trade in milk and bread. [97] Similar conditions prevail in almost all the large cities of this country. Single companies are known to control hundreds of saloons, restaurants, cigar stores, shoe stores, bake shops, coal depots, and the like. A multitude of other businesses are subject to this rule, and it is doubtful whether, after all, there has been the real increase of individual ownership which Mr. Ghent concedes.[98] However that may be, it is certain that a very large number of the business establishments which figure as statistical units in the argument against the Socialist theory of the concentration of capital might very properly be regarded as so many evidences in its favor.

A very large number of small businesses, moreover, are really manipulated by speculators, and serve only as a means of divesting prudent and thrifty artisans and others of their little savings. Whoever has lived in the poorer quarters of a great city, where small stores are most numerous, and has watched the changes constantly occurring in the stores of the neighborhood, will realize the significance of this observation. The writer has known stores on the upper East Side of New York, where for several years he resided, change hands as many as six or seven times in a single year. What happened was generally this: A workingman having been thrown out of employment, or forced to give up his work by reason of age, sickness, or accident, decided to attempt to make a living in "business." In a few weeks, or a few months at most, his small savings were swallowed up, and he had to leave the store, making place for the next victim. An acquaintance of the writer owns six tenement houses in different parts of New York City, the ground floors of which are occupied by small stores. These stores are rented by the month just as other portions of the buildings are, and the owner, on going over his books for a period of five years, found that the average duration of tenancy in them had been less than eight months.

During the past few years in the United States, as a result of the development of the many inventions for the production of "moving pictures," a new kind of cheap, popular theater has become common. Usually the charge of admission is five cents, whence the name "Nickelodeon"; the entertainment consists usually of a number of more or less dramatic incidents portrayed by means of the pictures, and a few songs, generally illustrated by pictures, and sung to the accompaniment of a mechanical piano. In almost every town in the United States these cheap pictorial theaters have appeared and their number will, doubtless, considerably swell the total of business establishments. In the small towns of the State of New York, the writer made an investigation and found that there were frequently several such places in the same town; that they were practically all built by the same persons, started by them, and then leased to others. These were generally people with small savings who, in the course of a few weeks, lost all their money and retired, their places being taken by other victims of the speculators. What seemed to the casual observer an admirable and conspicuous example of an increase in petty business, proved, upon closer study, to be a very striking example of concentration, disguised for purposes of speculation.

Thus reduced, the increase of small industries and retail establishments affects the contention that there is a general tendency to concentration very little. It does perhaps seriously weaken, or even destroy, some extreme statements of the theory, contending that the process of monopolization must be a direct, simple process of continuous absorption and elimination, leaving each year fewer small units than before. Small stores do exist; they have not been put out of existence by the big department stores as was at one time confidently predicted. They serve a real social need by supplying the minor commodities of everyday use in small quantities, just as the petty industries serve a real social need. Many of them are conducted by married women to supplement the earnings of their husbands, or by widows; others by men unable to work, whose income from them is less than the wages of artisans. Together, these probably constitute a majority of the small retail establishments which show any tendency to increase.[99]

The effect of this increase is still further lessened when it is remembered that only the critics of Socialism interpret the Marxian theory to mean that *all* petty industry and business must disappear, that all must be concentrated into large industrial and commercial units, to make Socialism possible. If we are to judge Marxism as the basis of the Socialist movement, we must judge it by the interpretation given to it by the Socialists, and not otherwise. There is no Socialist of note to-day who does not realize that many small industrial and business enterprises will continue to exist for a very long time, even continuing to exist under a Socialist regime. Kautsky, perhaps the ablest living exponent of the Marxian theories, leader of the "Orthodox" Marxists, admits this. He has very ably argued that the ripeness of society for Socialism, for social production and control, depends, not upon the number of little industries that still remain, but upon the number of great industries which already exist.[100] The ripeness of society for Socialism is not disproved by the number of ruins and relics abounding. "Without a developed great industry, Socialism is impossible," says this writer. "Where, however, a great industry exists to a considerable degree, it is easy for a Socialist society to ***concentrate production, and to quickly rid itself of the little industry***."[101] It is the increase of large industries, then, which Socialists regard as the essential preliminary condition of Socialism.

Far more important than the increase or decrease of the number of units is their relative significance in the total production, a phase of the subject which is rather disingenuously avoided by most critics of Marxism. Mr. Lucien Sanial, a Socialist statistician of repute, and one of the profoundest Marxian students in America, has shown this in a number of suggestive tables. For example, he takes twenty-seven typical manufacturing industries for the years 1880, 1900, and 1905, and compares the number of establishments in each year with the total amount of capital invested and workers employed. In 1880 the number of establishments was 63,233; in 1900 the number was 51,912, and in 1905 it was only 44,142. From 1880 to 1905 there had been a decrease in the number of establishments of 35.3 per cent, of which 15 per cent took place within the last five years. But within the same period there had been an increase in the amount of capital invested in these twenty-seven industries as follows: from $1,276,600,000 in 1880 to $3,324,500,000 in 1900 and to $4,628,800,000 in 1905--a total increase from 1880 to 1905 of 262.6 per cent. On the other hand, the number of wage-workers increased in the same period only 60.2 per cent, the number in 1905 being 1,731,500, as against 1,611,000 in 1900 and 1,080,200 in 1880.

In another table, forty-seven industries are taken. These forty-seven industries comprised 29,800 establishments in 1900; five years later there were but 26,182. In 1900 the total capital invested in these industries was $1,005,400,000, and in 1905 it had increased to $1,339,500,000. In the same five years the number of wage-workers increased only from 618,000 to 749,000. Thus, in the group of larger industries and the group of smaller ones we find the same evidences of concentration: less establishments, larger capitals, and an increase of wage-workers not equal to the increase in capitalization.[102]

In connection with these figures, the following table may be profitably studied, as showing the relative insignificance of the small producer in the total volume of manufacture. It will be seen that the two largest classes of establishments have only 24,163 establishments, 11.2 per cent of the total number. But they have $10,333,000,000, or 81.5 per cent of the total manufacturing capital, and employ 71.6 per cent of all wage-workers in manufacturing industries. It may be added that they turn out 79.3 per cent of the total product. Of the petty industries proper, those having a capital of less than $5000, it will be observed that they number 32.9 per cent of the total number of establishments, but employ only 1.3 per cent of the capital invested, and only 1.9 per cent of the wage-workers. It is clear, therefore, that our manufacturing industry in very highly concentrated, and that the petty industries are, despite their number, a very insignificant factor.

When we turn to agriculture, the criticisms of the Socialist theory appear more substantial and important. A few years ago we witnessed the rise and rapid growth of the great bonanza farms in this country. It was shown that the advantages of large capital and the consolidation of productive forces resulted, in farming as in manufacture, in greatly cheapened production.[104] The end of the small farm was declared to be imminent, and it seemed for a while that concentration in agriculture would even outrun concentration in manufacture. This predicted absorption of the small farms by the larger, and the average increase of farm acreage, has not, however, been fulfilled to any great degree. An increase in the number of small farms, and a decrease in the average acreage, is shown in almost all the states. The increase of great estates shown by the census figures probably bears little or no relation to real farming, consisting mainly of great stock grazing ranches in the West, and unproductive gentlemen's estates in the East.

Apparently, then, the Socialist theory that "the big fish eat up the little ones, and are in turn eaten by still bigger ones," is not applicable to agriculture. On the contrary, it seems that the great farms cannot compete successfully with the smaller farms. It is therefore not surprising that writers so sympathetic to Socialism as Professor Werner Sombart and Professor Richard T. Ely should claim that the Marxian system breaks down when it reaches the sphere of agricultural industry, and that it seems to be applicable only to manufacture. This position has been taken by a not inconsiderable body of Socialists in recent years, and is one of the tenets of that critical movement within the Socialist ranks which has come to be known as "Revisionism." Nothing is more delusive than statistical argument of this kind, and while these conclusions should be given due weight, they should not be too hastily accepted. An examination of the statistical basis of the argument is necessary.

In the first place, small agricultural holdings do not necessarily imply economic independence, any more than do petty industries or businesses. When we examine the census figures carefully, the first important fact which challenges attention is that, whereas of the farms in the United States in 1880, 71.6 per cent were operated by their owners, in 1900 the *proportion* had declined to 64.7 per cent. In 1900, of the 5,739,657 farms in the United States, no less than 2,026,286 were operated by tenants. Concerning the ownership of these rented farms little investigation has been made, and it is likely that careful inquiry would elicit the fact that this is a not unimportant phase of agricultural concentration, though not revealed by the figures in the census reports. It remains to be said concerning these figures, however, that they do not lend support to the theory that the small farms are being swallowed up by the larger ones, for in the same period there was a very decided increase in the *number* of farms operated by their owners. Thus we have the same set of figures used to support both sides of the controversy--one side calling attention to the decreased ***proportion*** of farms operated by their owners, the other to the increased ***number***.

A similar difficulty presents itself in connection with the subject of mortgaged farm holdings. In 1890, the mortgaged indebtedness of the farmers of the United States amounted to the immense sum of $1,085,995,960, a sum almost equal to the value of the entire wheat crop. Now, while a mortgage is certainly not suggestive of independence, it may be either a sign of decreasing or increasing independence. It may be a step toward the ultimate loss of one's farm or a step toward the ultimate ownership of one. Much that has been written by Populist and Socialist pamphleteers and editors upon this subject has been based upon the entirely erroneous assumption that a mortgaged farm meant loss of economic independence, whereas it often happens that it is a step toward it. The fact is that we know very little concerning the ownership of these mortgages, which is the crux of the question. It is known that many of the insurance, banking, and trust companies have invested largely in farm mortgages. This is another phase of concentration which the critics of the theory have overlooked almost entirely. One thing seems certain, namely, that farm ownership is not on the decline. It is not being supplanted by tenantry; the small farms are not being absorbed by larger ones. It seems a fair deduction from the facts, then, that the small farmer will continue to be an important factor--indeed, the most important factor--in American agriculture for a long time to come, perhaps permanently. If the Socialist movement is to succeed in America, it must recognize this fact in its propaganda.

V

Most of the criticism of the Marxian theory of concentration is based upon a very unsatisfactory definition of what is meant by concentration. The decrease of small units and their absorption or supercession by larger units is generally understood when concentration is spoken of. But concentration may take other, very different forms. There may be a concentration of ***control***, for example, without concentration of actual ownership, or there may be concentration of actual ownership disguised by mortgages, as already suggested. The sweated trades are a familiar example of the former method of concentration. It has been shown over and over again that while small establishments remain a necessary condition of sweated industry, there is almost always effective concentration of control. To all appearances an independent manufacturer on a small scale, the sweater is generally nothing more than the agent of some big establishment, which finds it more economical to let the work be done in sweatshops than in its own factories. The same thing holds good of the retail trades, many of the apparently independent retail stores being simply agencies for big wholesale houses, controlled by them in every way. In an even larger measure, agriculture is subject to a control that is quite independent of actual or even nominal ownership of the farm. Manifestly, therefore, we need a more accurate and comprehensive definition of concentration than the one generally accepted. Mr. A. M. Simons, in an admirable study of the agricultural question from the Socialist viewpoint, defines concentration as "a movement tending to give a continually diminishing minority of the persons engaged in any industry, a constantly increasing control over the essentials, and a continually increasing share of the total value of the returns of the industry."[105] It is no part of the purpose of this chapter to discuss this definition at length. It is sufficient to have thus emphasized that concentration may be quite as effective when it is limited to control as when it embraces ownership.

There are, then, other forms of concentration than the physical one, the amalgamation of smaller units to form larger ones, and very often these forms of concentration go on unperceived and unsuspected. There can be no doubt that this is especially true of agricultural industry. Many branches of farming, as the industry was carried on by our fathers and their fathers before them, have been transferred from the farmhouse to the factory. Butter and cheese making, for example, have largely passed out of the farm kitchen into the factory. The writer recalls a visit to a large farm in the Middle West. The sound of a churn is never heard there, notwithstanding that it is a "dairy farm," and all the butter and cheese consumed in that household is bought at the village store. Doubtless this farm but presented an exaggerated form of a condition that is becoming more and more common. The invention of labor-saving machinery and its application to agriculture leads to a division of the industry and the absorption by the factory of the parts most influenced by the new processes. When we remember the tremendous role which complex agencies outside of the farm play in modern agricultural industry, we see the subject of concentration as it applies to that industry in a new light. The grain elevators, cold-storage houses, creameries, and even railroads, are part of the necessary equipment of production, but they are owned and operated independently of the farm. There is a good deal of concentration of production in agriculture which takes the form of the absorption of some of its processes by factories instead of by other farms.

VI

We must also distinguish between the concentration of industry and the concentration of wealth. While there is a natural relation between these two phenomena, they are by no means identical. The trustification of a given industry may bring together a score of industrial units in one gigantic concern, so concentrating capital and production, but it is conceivable that every one of the owners of the units which compose the trust may have a share in it equal to the capital value of his particular unit, but more profitable. In that case, there can obviously be no concentration of wealth. What occurs is that all are benefited by certain economies, in exact proportion to their holdings in the capital stock. It may even happen that a larger number of persons participate, as shareholders, in the amalgamation than were formerly concerned in the ownership of the units of which the amalgamation is composed. Assuming, for the purposes of our argument, that these persons are represented by new capital, that the former owners of independent units share upon an equitable basis, there will be increased diffusion of wealth instead of its concentration. As Professor Ely says, "If the stock of the United States Steel Corporation were owned by individuals holding one share each, the concentration in industry would be just as great as it is now, but there would be a wide diffusion in the ownership of the wealth of the corporation."[106]

Obvious as this distinction may seem, it is very often lost sight of, and when recognized it presents difficulties which are almost insurmountable. It is well-nigh impossible to present statistically the relation of the concentration of capital to the concentration or diffusion of wealth, important as the point is in its bearings upon modern Socialist theory. While the distinction does not affect the argument that the concentration of capital and industry makes their socialization possible, it is nevertheless an important matter. If, as some writers, notably Bernstein,[107] the Socialist, have argued, the concentration of capital and industry really leads to the decentralization of wealth, and the diffusion of the advantages of concentration among the great mass of the people, especially by creating a new class of salaried dependents, then, instead of creating a class of exploiters ever becoming less numerous, and a class of proletarians ever becoming more numerous, the tendency of modern capitalism is to distribute the gains of industry over a widening area--a process of democratization in fact. It is very evident that if this contention is a correct one, there must be a softening rather than an intensifying of class antagonisms; a tendency away from class divisions, and to greater satisfaction with present conditions, rather than increasing discontent. If this theory can be sustained, the advocates of Socialism will be obliged to change the nature of their propaganda from an appeal to the economic interest of the proletariat to the general ethical sense of mankind. There can be no successful movement based upon the interests of one class if the tendency of modern capitalism is to democratize the life of the world and diffuse its wealth over larger social areas than ever before.

The exponents of this theory have based their arguments upon statistical data chiefly relating to: (1) The number of taxable incomes in countries where incomes are taxed; (2) the number of investors in industrial and commercial countries; (3) the number of savings bank deposits. As often happens when reliance is placed upon the direct statistical method, the result of all the discussion and controversy upon this subject is extremely disappointing and confusing. The same figures are used to support both sides of the argument with equal plausibility. The difficulty lies in the fact that the available statistics do not include all the facts essential to a scientific and conclusive result.

It is not intended here to add to the Babel of voices in this discussion, but to present the conclusions of two or three of the most careful investigators in this field. Professor Ely[108] quotes a table of incomes in the Grand Duchy of Baden, based upon the income tax returns of that country, which has formed the theme of much dispute. The table shows that in the two years, 1886 and 1896, less than one per cent of the incomes assessed were over 10,000 marks a year, and from this fact it has been argued that wealth in that country has not been concentrated to any very great extent. In like manner, the French economist, Leroy-Beaulieu, has argued that the fact that in 1896 only 2750 persons in Paris had incomes of over 100,000 francs a year betokens a wide diffusion of wealth and an absence of concentration. [109] But the important point of the discussion, the ***proportion of the total wealth owned by these classes***, is entirely lost sight of by those who argue in this manner. Further, it must always be borne in mind that there is a decided tendency in all income tax schedules to understate the amount of incomes above a certain size, the larger the income the more likelihood of its being understated in the returns. The psychology of this fact needs no elaborate demonstration. Taking the figures for the Grand Duchy of Baden as they are given, we have no particulars at all concerning the number of incomes under 500 marks, but of the persons assessed upon incomes of 500 marks and over, in 1886, the poorest two thirds had about one third of the total income, and the richest 0.69 per cent had 12.78 per cent of the total income. So far, the figures show a much greater concentration of wealth than appears from the simple fact that less than one per cent of the incomes assessed were over 10,000 marks a year.

Going further, we compare the two years, 1886 and 1896, and find that this concentration increased during the ten-year period as follows: In 1886, there were 2212 incomes of more than 10,000 marks assessed, being 0.69 per cent of the total number. In 1896, there were 3099 incomes of more than 10,000 marks assessed, being 0.78 per cent of the total number. In 1886, 0.69 per cent of the incomes assessed amounted to 51,403,000 marks, representing 12.77 per cent of the total assessed wealth; while in 1896, 0.78 per cent of the incomes assessed amounted to 81,986,000 marks, representing 15.02 per cent of the total wealth so assessed. In 1886 there were 18 incomes of over 200,000 marks a year, aggregating 6,864,000 marks, 1.70 per cent of the total value of all incomes assessed; in 1896, there were 28 such incomes, aggregating 12,481,000 marks, or 2.29 per cent of the total value of all incomes assessed. The increase of concentration shown by these figures is not disputable, it seems to the present writer, when they are thus carefully analyzed, notwithstanding the fact that the table from which they are drawn is sometimes used to support the opposite contention.

According to the late Professor Richmond Mayo-Smith,[110] seventy per cent of the population of Prussia have incomes below the income tax standard, their total income representing only one third of the total income of the population. An additional one fourth of the population enjoys one third of the total income, while the remaining one third goes to about four per cent of the people. The significance of these figures is clearly shown by the following diagram:--

In Saxony the statistics show that "two thirds of the population possess less than one third of the income, and that 3.5 per cent of the upper incomes receive more than 66 per cent at the lower end." From a table prepared by Sir Robert Giffen, a notoriously optimistic statistician, always the exponent of an ultra-roseate view of social conditions, Professor Mayo-Smith concludes that in England, "about ten per cent of the people receive nearly one half of the total income."[111] These figures are rather out of date, it is true, but they err in understating the amount of concentration rather than otherwise, as the researches of Mr. Chiozza Money, M.P., and others show.[112]

In this country, the absence of income tax figures makes it impossible to get direct statistical evidence as to the distribution of incomes. The most careful estimate of the distribution of wealth in the United States yet made is that by the late Dr. Charles B. Spahr.[113] Written in 1895, Dr. Spahr's book cannot be regarded as an accurate presentation of conditions as they exist at the present moment, yet here again there is every reason to believe that the process of concentration has gone on unchecked since he wrote. It is not necessary for our present purpose, however, to accept the estimate of Dr. Spahr as authoritative and conclusive. The figures are quoted here simply as the result reached by the most patient, conscientious, and scientific examination of the distribution of wealth in this country yet made. Dr. Spahr's conclusion was that in 1895 less than one half of the families in the United States were property-less; but that, nevertheless, seven eighths of the families owned only one eighth of the national wealth, while one per cent of the families owned more than the remaining ninety-nine per cent.

Mr. Lucien Sanial, in a most careful analysis of the census for 1900, shows that, classified according to occupations, 250,251 persons possessed $67,000,000,000, out of a total of $95,000,000,000 given as the national wealth; that is to say, 0.9 per cent of the total number in all occupations owned 70.5 per cent of the total national wealth. The middle class, consisting of 8,429,845 persons, being 29.0

per cent of the total number in all occupations, owned $24,000,000,000, or 25.3 per cent of the total national wealth. The lowest class, the proletariat, consisting of 20,393,137 persons, being 70.1 per cent of the total number in all occupations, owned but $4,000,000,000, or 4.2 per cent of the total wealth. To recapitulate: Of the 29,073,233 persons ten years old and over engaged in occupations,

0.9 per cent own	70.5 per cent of total wealth.
29.0 per cent own	25.3 per cent of total wealth.
70.1 per cent own	4.2 per cent of total wealth.

Startling as these figures are, it will be evident upon reflection that they do not adequately represent the amount of wealth concentration. The occupational basis is not quite satisfactory as applied to the richest class. It serves for the proletarian class, of course, and for a very large part of the middle class. In these classes, as a rule, the *occupied* persons represent wealth ownership. But this is by no means true of the richest class. In this class we have a very considerable proportion of the wealth owned by *unoccupied* persons, such as the wives rich in their own right, children and other unoccupied members of families rich by inheritance. Mr. Henry Laurens Call, in a paper read before the American Association for the Advancement of Science, at Columbia University, at the end of 1906, made these figures the basis of the startling estimate that one per cent of our population own not less than ninety per cent of our total wealth.

There is a peculiarity of modern capitalism which enables the great capitalists to control vastly more wealth than they own. Take any group of large capitalists, and it will be found that they *control* a much greater volume of capital than they *own*. The invested capital of a multitude of small investors is in their keeping, and they can and do use it for purposes of their own. Thus we have a concentration of capitalist control which goes far beyond the concentration of ownership. And this concentration of the essential control of the capital of a country becomes more and more important each year. It is recognized to-day that the most important capitalist is not he who himself owns the greatest amount of capital, but he who controls the greatest amount, quite irrespective of its ownership.

The growth of immense private fortunes is an indisputable evidence of the concentration of wealth. In 1854 there were not more than twenty-five millionaires in New York City, their total fortunes aggregating $43,000,000. There were not more than fifty millionaires in the whole of the United States, their aggregate fortunes not exceeding $80,000,000. To-day there are several individual fortunes of more than $80,000,000 each. New York City alone is said to have over two thousand millionaires, and the United States more than five thousand. By a curious mental process, the **New York World**, when the first edition of this little book appeared, sought to prove in a labored editorial that the increase of millionaires tended to prove an increasing diffusion of wealth rather than the contrary. It is hardly worth while, perhaps, making any reply to such puerility. Every student knows that the multimillionaire is only possible as a result of the concentration of wealth, that such fortunes are realized by the absorption of numerous smaller ones. Further, it is only necessary to add that all the millionaires of 1854, together with the half millionaires, owned not more than about $100,000,000 out of the total wealth, which was at that time something like $10,000,000,000. In other words, they owned not more than one per cent of the wealth of the country. In 1890, when the wealth of the country was slightly more than $65,000,000,000, Senator Ingalls could quote in the United States Senate a table showing that the millionaires and half millionaires of that time, 31,100 persons in all, owned $36,250,000,000, or just fifty-six per cent of the entire wealth of the United States.[114] Professor Ely accepts the logic of the statistical data gathered in Europe and the United States, and says "such statistics as we have ... all indicate a marked concentration of wealth, both in this country and Europe."[115]

VII

Summing up, we may state the argument of this chapter very briefly as follows: The Socialist theory is that competition is self-destructive, and that the inevitable result of the competitive process is to produce monopoly, either through the crushing out of the weak by the strong, or the combination of units as a result of a conscious recognition of the wastes of competition and the advantages of coöperation. The law of capitalist development, therefore, is from competition and division to combination and concentration. As this concentration proceeds, a large class of proletarians is formed on the one hand, and a small class of capitalist lords on the other, an essential antagonism of interests existing between the two classes. Petty industries may continue to exist, though, upon the whole, the tendency is toward their extinction. In certain industries, their number may even increase, but their relative importance is constantly decreasing. While Socialism does not preclude the continued existence of small private industry or business, it does require and depend upon the development of a large body of concentrated industry, monopolies which can be transformed into social monopolies whenever the people may decide so to transform them. These conditions are being fulfilled in the evolution of our economic system.

The interindustrial and international trustification of industry shows a remarkable fulfillment of the law of capitalist concentration which the Socialists were the first to formulate; the existence of petty industries and businesses, or their numerical increase even, being a relatively insignificant matter compared with the enormous increase in large industries and businesses, and their share in the total volume of industry and commerce. In agriculture, concentration, while it does not proceed so rapidly or directly as in manufacture and commerce, and while it takes directions and forms unforeseen by the Socialists of a generation ago, proceeds surely nevertheless. Along with this concentration of capital and industry proceeds the concentration of wealth into proportionately fewer hands. While a certain diffusion of wealth takes place through the mechanism of capitalist concentration, by developing a new class of highly salaried officials, and enabling numerous small investors to own shares in great industrial and commercial corporations, it is not sufficient to balance the expropriation which goes on in the competitive struggle, and it is true that a larger proportion of the national wealth is owned by a minority of the population than ever before, that minority being proportionately less numerous than ever before. Further, the peculiar financial organization of modern capitalist society enables the ruling capitalists to control and use to their own advantage the wealth of others invested in industrial and commercial corporations. Thus to the concentration of ownership must be added the concentration of control, which plays an increasingly important part in capitalist economics.

Whatever defects there may be in the Marxian theory, as outlined by Marx himself, and whatever modifications of his statement of it may be rendered necessary by changed conditions, in its main and essential features it has successfully withstood all the criticisms which have been directed against it. Economic literature is full of prophecies, but in its whole range there is not an instance of prophecy more literally and abundantly fulfilled than that which Marx made concerning the trend of capitalist development. And Karl Marx was not a prophet--he but read clearly the meaning of certain facts which others had not learned to read, the law of social dynamics. That is not prophecy, but science.

NOTES:

[94] *Studies in the Evolution of Industrial Society*, by R. T. Ely, page 95.

[95] *Capital*, Vol. I (Kerr edition), page 837.

[96] *Briefe und Auszuege aus Briefen von Joh. Phil. Becker, Jos. Dietzgen, Friederich Engels, Karl Marx u. A. an F. A. Sorge und Andere*, Stuttgart, 1906.

[97] H. W. Macrosty, *The Growth of Monopoly in English Industry* (Fabian Tract).

[98] *Our Benevolent Feudalism*, by W. J. Ghent, pages 17-21.

[99] A factor of tremendous importance in the maintenance of petty industries and business establishments in this country, which Marx could not have anticipated, has been the unprecedented volume of foreign immigration. Not only have some menial personal services--such as shoe cleaning, for example--been transformed into regular businesses by immigrants from certain countries, but the massing together of immigrants, aliens in language, customs, tastes, and manners, provides a very favorable soil for the development of small business enterprises.

[100] *The Social Revolution*, by Karl Kautsky, Part I, page 144. See also the argument by Paul Lafargue, Marx's son-in-law, that Socialism will not oppose petty agriculture by private individuals working their own farms.--Revue Politique et Parliamentaire, October, 1898, page 70.

[101] Kautsky, *The Social Revolution*, page 144.

[102] The figures are quoted from *Socialism Inevitable*, by Gaylord Wilshire, pages 325-326.

[103] The table is quoted from *Socialism Inevitable*, by Gaylord Wilshire,

page 326.

[104] The cost of raising wheat in California, where large farming has been most scientifically developed, is said to vary from 92.5 cents per 100 pounds on farms of 1000 acres to 40 cents on farms of 50,000 acres.

[105] *The American Farmer*, by A. M. Simons, page 97.

[106] *Studies in the Evolution of Industrial Society*, by Richard T. Ely, page 255.

[107] *Die Voraussetzungen des Sozialismus*, by Edward Bernstein, page 47.

[108] *Studies in the Evolution of Industrial Society*, by Richard T. Ely, pages 261-262.

[109] *Essai sur la repartition des richesses et sur la tendance a une moindre inegalite des conditions*, par Leroy-Beaulieu, page 564.

[110] *Statistics and Economics*, by Richmond Mayo-Smith, Book III, Distribution.

[111] *Statistics and Economics*, by Richmond Mayo-Smith, Book III, Distribution.

[112] Cf. *Riches and Poverty*, by Chiozza Money, M.P.; also, *Fabian Tract*, No. 5.

[113] *The Present Distribution of Wealth in the United States*, by Charles B. Spahr (1896).

[114] *Writings and Speeches of John J. Ingalls*, page 320.

[115] *Studies in the Evolution of Industrial Society*, page 265.

CHAPTER VI
THE CLASS STRUGGLE THEORY

I

No part of the theory of modern Socialism has called forth so much criticism and opposition as the doctrine of the class struggle. Many who are otherwise sympathetic to Socialism denounce this doctrine as narrow, brutal, and productive of antisocialistic feelings of class hatred. Upon all hands the doctrine is condemned as an un-American appeal to passion and a wicked exaggeration of social conditions. When President Roosevelt attacks the preachers of the doctrine, and wrathfully condemns class-consciousness as "a foul thing," he doubtless expresses the views of a majority of American citizens. The insistence of Socialists upon this aspect of their propaganda is undoubtedly responsible for keeping a great many outside of their movement who otherwise would be identified with it. If the Socialists would repudiate the doctrine that Socialism is a class movement, and make their appeal to the intelligence and conscience of all classes, instead of to the interests of a special class, they could probably double their numerical strength at once. To many, therefore, it seems a fatuous and quixotic policy to preach such a doctrine, and it is very often charitably ascribed to the peculiar intellectual and moral myopia of fanaticism.

Before accepting this conclusion, and before indorsing the Rooseveltian verdict, the reader is bound as a matter of common fairness, and of intellectual integrity, to consider the Socialist side of the argument. There is no greater fanaticism than that which condemns what it does not take the trouble to understand. The Socialists claim that the doctrine is misrepresented; that it does not produce class hatred; and that it is a vital and pivotal point of Socialist philosophy. The class struggle, says the Socialist, is a law of social development. We only recognize the law, and are no more responsible for its existence than for the law of gravitation. The name of Marx is associated with the law in just the same manner as the name of Newton is associated with the law of gravitation, but Marx is no more responsible for the social law he discovered than was Newton for the physical law he discovered. There were class struggles thousands of years before there was a Socialist movement, thousands of years before Marx was born, and it is therefore absurd to charge us with the creation of the class struggle, or class hatred. We realize perfectly well that if we ignored this law in our propaganda, making our appeal to a universal sense of abstract justice and truth, many who now hold aloof from us would join our movement. But we should not gain strength as a result of their accession to our ranks. We should be obliged to emasculate Socialism, to dilute it, in order to win a support of questionable value. History teems with examples of the disaster which inevitably attends such a course. We should be quixotic and fatuous indeed if we attempted anything of the kind. Such, briefly stated, are the main outlines of the reply which the average Socialist gives to the criticism of the class struggle doctrine described.

The class struggle theory is part of the economic interpretation of history. Since the dissolution of primitive tribal society, the modes of economic production and exchange have inevitably grouped men into economic classes. The theory is thus admirably stated by Engels in the Introduction to the **Communist Manifesto**:--

"In every historical epoch, the prevailing mode of economic production and exchange, and the social organization necessarily following from it, form the basis upon which is built up, and from which alone can be explained, the political and intellectual history of that epoch; and, consequently, the whole history of mankind (since the dissolution of primitive society, holding land in common ownership) has been a history of class struggles, contests between exploiting and exploited, ruling and oppressed classes; that the history of these class struggles forms a series of evolution in which, nowadays, a stage has been reached where the exploited and oppressed class--the proletariat--cannot attain its emancipation from the sway of the exploiting and ruling class--the bourgeoise--without, at the same time, and once and for all, emancipating society at large from all exploitation, oppression, class distinctions, and class struggles."[116]

In this classic statement of the theory, there are several fundamental propositions. First, that class divisions and class struggles arise out of the economic life of society. Second, that since the dissolution of primitive tribal society, which was communistic in character, mankind has been divided into economic groups or classes, and all its history has been a history of struggles between these classes, ruling and ruled, exploiting and exploited, being forever at war with each other. Third, that the different epochs in human history, stages in the evolution of society, have been characterized by the interests of the ruling class. Fourth, that a stage has now been reached in the evolution of society where the struggle assumes a form which makes it impossible for class distinctions and class struggles to continue if the exploited and oppressed class, the proletariat, succeeds in emancipating itself. In other words, the cycle of class struggles which began with the dissolution of rude, tribal communism, and the rise of private property, ends with the passing of private property in the means of social existence and the rise of Socialism. The proletariat in emancipating itself destroys all the conditions of class rule.

II

As we have already seen, slavery is historically the first system of class division which presents itself. Some ingenious writers have endeavored to trace the origin of slavery to the institution of the family, the children being the first slaves. It is fairly certain, however, that slavery originated in conquest. When a tribe was conquered and enslaved by some more powerful tribe, all the members of the vanquished tribe sunk to one common level of servility and degradation. Their exploitation as laborers was the principal object of their enslavement, and their labor admitted of little gradation. It is easy to see the fundamental class antagonisms which characterized slavery. Has there been no uprisings of the slaves, no active and conscious struggle against their masters, the antagonism of interests between them and their masters would be none the less apparent. But the overthrow of slavery was not the result of the rebellions and struggles of the slaves. While these undoubtedly helped, the principal factors in the overthrow of chattel slavery as the economic foundation of society were the disintegration of the system to the point of bankruptcy, and the rise of a new, and sometimes, as in the case of Rome, alien ruling class.

The class divisions of feudal society are not less obvious than those of chattel slavery. The main division, the widest gulf, divided the feudal lord and the serf. Often as brutally ill-treated as their slave-forefathers had been, the feudal serfs from time to time made abortive struggles. The class distinctions of feudalism were constant, but the struggles between the lords and the serfs were sporadic, and of comparatively little moment, just as the risings of their slave forefathers had been. But alongside of the feudal estate there existed another class, the free handicrafts-men and peasants, the former organized into powerful guilds. It was this class, and not the serf class, which was destined to challenge the rule of the feudal nobility, and wage war upon it. As the feudal class was a landed class, so the class represented by the guilds became a moneyed and commercial class, the pioneers of our modern capitalist class. As Mr. Brooks Adams[117] has shown very clearly, it was this moneyed, commercial class, which gave to the king the instrument for weakening and finally overthrowing feudalism. It was this class which built up the cities and towns from which was drawn the revenue for the maintenance of a standing army, thus liberating the king from his dependence upon the feudal lords. The capitalist class triumphed over the feudal nobility, and its interests became in their turn the dominant interests in society. Capitalism in its development effectually destroyed all those institutions of feudalism which obstructed its progress, leaving only those which were innocuous and safely to be ignored.

In capitalist society, the main class division is that which separates the employing, wage-paying class from the employed, wage-receiving class. Notwithstanding all the elaborate arguments made to prove the contrary, the frequently heard myth that the interests of Capital and Labor are identical, and the existence of pacificatory associations based upon that myth, there is no fact in the whole range of social phenomena more self-evident than the existence of an inherent, fundamental antagonism in the relationship of employer and employee. As individuals, in all other relations, they may have a commonality of interests, but as employer and employee they are fundamentally and necessarily opposed. They may belong to the same church, and so have religious interests in common; they may have common racial interests, as, for instance, if negroes, in protecting themselves against the attacks made in a book like *The Clansman*, or, if Jews, in opposing anti-Semitic movements; as citizens they may have the same civic interests, be equally opposed to graft in the city government, or equally interested in the adoption of wise sanitary precautions against epidemics. They may even have a common industrial interest in the general sense that they may be equally interested in the development of the industry in which they are engaged, and fear, equally, the results of a depression in trade. But their special interests as employer and employee are antithetical.

It cannot be denied that, in certain circumstances, these other interests may become so accentuated that the class antagonisms are momentarily lost sight of, or completely dwarfed in importance; nor is such a denial implied in the Socialist theory. It is not difficult to see that in the case of a general uprising against the members of their race, in which their lives are imperiled, Jewish employers and employees may forget their *class* interests and remember only that they are Jews. So with negroes and other oppressed races. The economic interests of the class may be engulfed in the solidarity of the race. It is not difficult, either, to see that in the presence of some great common danger or calamity, class interests may likewise be completely subordinated. An admirable example of this occurred at the time of the San Francisco earthquake and fire. The enormous demand for labor occasioned by that disaster practically enabled the artisans, most of whom were organized into unions, to demand and obtain almost fabulous wages. But there was no thought of taking advantage of the calamity. On the contrary, the unions immediately announced that they would make no attempt to do so. Not only that, but they voluntarily waived rules which in normal times they would have insisted upon with all their powers. The temporary overshadowing of the economic interests of classes by other special interests which have been thrust into special prominence, is not, however, evidence that these class interests do not prevail in normal times. Recognition of this fact effectually destroys much criticism of the theory.

The interest of the wage-worker, as wage-worker, is to receive the largest wage possible for the least number of hours spent in labor. The interest of the employer, as employer, on the other hand, is to secure from the worker as many hours of service, as much labor power, as possible for the lowest wage which the worker can be induced to accept. The workers employed in a factory may be divided by a hundred different forces. They may be divided by racial differences, for instance; but while preserving these differences in a large measure, they will tend to unite upon the basis of their economic interests. Some of the great labor unions, notably the United Mine Workers,[118] afford remarkable illustrations of this fact. If the difference of religious interests leads to division, the same unanimity of economic interests will sooner or later be developed. No impartial investigator who studies the influence of a great labor union which includes in its membership workers of various nationalities and adherents of various religious creeds, can fail to observe the fact that the community of economic interests which unites them is a powerful factor making for their amalgamation into a harmonious civic whole.

With the employers it is the same. They, too, may be divided by a hundred forces; the competition among them may be keen and fierce, but common economic interests will tend to unite them against the organizations of the workers they employ. Racial, religious, social, and other divisions and distinctions, may be maintained, but they will, in general, unite for the protection and furtherance of their common economic interests.

So much, indeed, belongs to the very primer stage of economic theory. Adam Smith is rather out of fashion nowadays, but there is still much in "The Wealth of Nations" which will repay our attention. No Socialist writer, not even Marx, has stated the fundamental principle of the antagonism between the employing and employed classes more clearly, as witness the following:--

"The workmen desire to get as much, the masters to give as little as possible. The former are disposed to combine in order to raise, the latter in order to lower the wages of labor.... Masters are always and everywhere in a sort of tacit, but constant and uniform, combination, not to raise the wages of labor above their actual rate. To violate this combination is everywhere a most unpopular action, and a sort of reproach to a master among his neighbors and equals.... Masters too sometimes enter into particular combinations to sink the wages of labor.... These are always conducted with the utmost silence and secrecy, till the moment of execution.... Such combinations, however, are frequently resisted by a contrary defensive combination of the workmen; who sometimes, too, without any provocation of this kind, combine of their own accord to raise the price of labor. Their usual pretenses are, sometimes the high price of provisions; sometimes the great profits which the masters make by their work. But whether these combinations be offensive or defensive, they are always abundantly heard of. In order to bring the point to a speedy decision, they have always recourse to the loudest clamor, and sometimes to the most shocking violence and outrage. They are desperate, and act with the extravagance and folly of desperate men, who must either starve, or frighten their masters into an immediate compliance with their demands. The masters upon these occasions are just as clamorous upon the other side, and *never cease to call aloud for the assistance of the civil magistrate, and the rigorous execution of those laws which have been enacted with so much severity against the combinations of servants, laborers, and journeymen.*"[119]

Thus Adam Smith. Were it essential to our present purpose, it would be easy to quote from all the great economists in support of the Socialist claim that the interests of the capitalist and those of the laborer are irreconcilably opposed. That individual workers and employers will be found who do not recognize their class interests is true, but that fact by no means invalidates the contention that, in general, men will recognize and unite upon a basis of common class interests. In both classes are to be found individuals who attach greater importance to the preservation of racial, religious, or social, than to economic, interests. But because the economic interest is fundamental, involving the very basis of life, the question of food, clothing, shelter, and comfort, these individuals are and must be exceptions to the general rule. Workers sink their racial and religious differences and unite to secure better wages, a reduction of their hours of labor, and better conditions in general. Employers, similarly, unite to oppose whatever may threaten their class interests, without regard to other relationships. The Gentile who is himself an anti-Semite has no qualms of conscience about employing Jewish workmen, at low wages, to compete with Gentile workers; he does not object to joining with Jewish employers in an Employers' Association, if thereby his economic interests may be safeguarded. And the Jewish employer, likewise, has no objection to joining with the Gentile employer for mutual protection, or to the employment of Gentile workers to fill the places of his employees, members of his own race, who have gone out on strike for higher wages.

III

The class struggle, therefore, presents itself in the present stage of social development, in capitalist countries, as a conflict between the wage-paying and the wage-paid classes. That is the dominating and all-absorbing conflict of the industrial age in which we live. True, there are other class interests more or less involved. This is especially true in the United States with its enormous agricultural industry, to which the description of the industrial conflict cannot be applied. There are the indefinite, inchoate, vague, and uncertain interests of that large, so-called middle class, composed of farmers, retailers, professional workers, and so on. The interests of this large class are not, and cannot be, as definitely defined. They vacillate, conforming now to the interest of the wage-workers, now to the interest of the employers. Thus the farmer may oppose an increase in the wages of farm laborers, because that touches him directly as an employer. His relation to the farm laborer is substantially that of the capitalist to the city worker, and his attitude upon that question is the attitude of the capitalist class as a whole. At the same time, he may heartily favor an increase of wages for miners, carpenters, bricklayers, shoemakers, printers, painters, factory workers, and non-agricultural laborers in general, for the reason that while a general rise of wages, resulting in a general rise of prices, will affect him slightly as a consumer, and compel him to pay more for what he buys, it will benefit him much more as a seller of the products of his farm. In short, consciously very often, but unconsciously oftener still, personal or class interests control our thoughts, opinions, beliefs, and actions.

It is impossible with the data at our disposal at present to make such an analysis of our population as will enable us to determine the particular class interests of the various groups. Of the twenty-four million men and boys engaged in industry there are some six million farmers and tenants; three million seven hundred and fifty thousand farm laborers; eleven million mechanics, laborers, clerks, and servants; one million five hundred thousand professional workers, agents, and the like; and about two million employers, large and small. Accurately to place each of these groups is out of the question until such time as we have a much more detailed study of our economic life than has yet been attempted. We may, however, roughly relate some of the groups.

First: It is evident that the interests of the eleven million wage-earners are, as a whole, opposed to those of the employing class. There may be exceptions, as in the case of those whose very occupation as confidential agents of the capitalists, overseers, and the like, places them outside of the sphere of working-class interests. They may not receive a salary much above the wage of the mechanic, yet their function is such as to place them psychologically with the capitalists rather than with the workers. It is also evident that, while their *interests* may be demonstrably antagonistic to those of the employers, not all of the wage-earners will be ***conscious*** of that fact. The ***consciousness*** of class interests develops slowly among rural and isolated workers, especially as between the small employer and his employee. And even when there is the consciousness of antagonistic interests among these workers it is very difficult for them actively to express it. Hence they cannot play an important part in the actual conflict of classes.

Second: We may safely place the three million seven hundred and fifty thousand farm laborers, as regards their economic ***interests***, with the general mass of wage-workers, with one important qualification. So far as they are in the actual relation of wage-paid laborers, hired by the month, week, or day, and bearing no other relation to their employers, they belong, in their economic interests, to the proletariat. But there are many farm laborers included in our enumeration who do not hold that relation to their employers. They are the sons of the farmers themselves, expecting to assume their fathers' positions, and their position as wage-paid laborers is largely nominal and fictitious. How many such there are it is impossible to ascertain with anything like certainty, and we can only say, therefore, that the position of the class, as such, must be determined without including these. But while this class has economic interests similar to those of the industrial proletariat, because of their isolation and scattered position, and because of the personal relations which they bear to their employers--farmer and laborer often working side by side, equally hard, and not infrequently having approximately the same standards of living--these cannot, to any very great extent, become an active factor in the class conflict in the same sense as the industrial wage-workers can, by engaging in strikes, boycotts, and other manifestations of the class war. Still, they may, and in fact do, play an important role in the ***political*** aspects of the struggle. Let a political movement of the proletariat arise and it will be found that these agricultural laborers will join it not less enthusiastically than their fellows from the factories in the cities. It would probably surprise most thoughtful Americans if they could see the organization maps in the offices of the Socialist Party of the United States, dotted with little red-capped pins denoting local organizations of the party. These are quite as common in the agricultural states as in the industrial states. So, too, in Germany. The movement is politically nearly as strong in the agrarian districts as elsewhere. This is a fact of vital significance, one which must not be lost sight of in studying the progress of Socialism in America.

Third: Of the exact position of the remaining groups it is very difficult to speak with anything like assurance. In an earlier chapter we have noticed the persistence of the small farm in America, and the fact that a class of small farmers forms a very important part of our population. As already observed, the economic condition of the small farmer is very often little, if any, superior to that of the laborers he employs. Elsewhere, I have shown that the actual income of the small farmer is not infrequently less than that of the hired laborer.[120] This is just as true of the small dealer, and the small manufacturer. But mere poverty of income, companionship in misery, the sharing of an equally poor existence, does not suffice to place the farmer in the proletarian class, as many Socialist writers have shown.[121] The small farmers constitute a distinct class. They are not, as the small dealers and manufacturers are, mere remnants of a disappearing class. The class is a permanent one, apparently, as much so as the class of industrial wage-workers. As a class it is just as essential to agricultural production as the industrial proletariat is essential to manufacture. It is thus a class analogous to the industrial proletariat, and Kautsky has well said that the small farmer is the "proletariat of the country." The exploitation of the small farmer is not direct, like that of the wage-worker by his employer, but indirect, through the great capitalist trusts and railroads. It also happens that these derive their chief income from the direct exploitation of the wage-workers, so that the small farmer and the wage-worker in the city factory have common exploiters. As they become conscious of this, the two classes will tend to unite their forces in the one sphere where such unity of action is possible, the sphere of political action.

This is also true, in some degree at least, of a considerable fraction of the one million five hundred thousand workers included in the professional and agent classes, and of the two million employers, the small dealers and manufacturers being included in this enumeration. That there is such a considerable fraction of each of these two classes whose interests lead them to make common cause with the proletariat is not at all a matter of theory or speculation, but of experience. These classes are represented very largely in the membership of the Socialist parties of this country and of Europe.

IV

Although it is sometimes so interpreted, the theory that classes are based upon commonality of interests does not imply that men are never actuated by other than selfish motives; that a sordid materialism is the only motive force at work in the world. Marx and Engels carefully avoided the use of the word *interests* in such manner as to suggest that material interests control the course of history. They invariably used the term *economic conditions*, and the careful reader will not fail to perceive that although economic conditions produce interests which form the basis of class divisions, it is not unusual for men to act contrary to their personal *interests* as a result of existing *conditions*. In general, class interests and personal interests coincide, but there are certainly occasions when they conflict. Many an employer, having no quarrel with his employees and confident that he will be the loser thereby, joins in a fight upon labor unions because he is conscious that the interests of his class are involved. In a similar way, workingmen enter upon sympathetic strikes, consciously, at an immediate loss to themselves, because they place class loyalty before personal gain. It is significant of class feeling and temper that when employers act in this manner, and lock out employees with whom they have no trouble, simply to help other employers to win their battles, they are lauded by the very newspapers which denounce the workers when they adopt a like policy.

It is also true that there are individuals in both classes who never become conscious of their class interests, and steadfastly refuse to join with the members of their class. The workingman who refuses to join a union, or who "scabs" when his fellow-workers go out on strike, may act from ignorance or from sheer self-interest and greed. His action may be due to his placing personal interest before the larger interest of his class, or from being too shortsighted to see that ultimately his own interests and those of his class must merge. Many an employer, likewise, may refuse to join in any concerted action of his class for either of these reasons, or he may even rise superior to his class and personal interests and support the workers because he believes in the justness of their cause, realizing perfectly well that their gain means loss to him or to his class. This ought to be a sufficient answer to those shallow critics who think that they dispose of the class struggle theory of modern Socialism by enumerating those of its leading exponents who do not belong to the proletariat.

The influence of class environment upon men's beliefs and ideals is a subject which our most voluminous ethicists have scarcely touched upon as yet. It is a commonplace saying that each age has its own standards of right and wrong, but little effort has been made, if we except the Socialists, to trace this fact to its source, to the economic conditions prevailing in the different ages.[122] Still less effort has been made to account for the different standards held by the different social classes at the same time, and by which each class judges the others. In our own day the idea of slavery is generally held in abhorrence. There was a time, however, when it was almost universally looked upon as a divine institution, alike by slaveholder and slave. It is simply impossible to account for this complete revolution of feeling upon any other hypothesis than that slave-labor then seemed absolutely essential to the life of the world. The slave lords of antiquity, and, more recently, the Southern slaveholders in our own country, all believed that slavery was eternally right. When the slaves took an opposite view and rebelled, they were believed to be in rebellion against God and nature. The Church represented the same view just as vigorously as it now opposes it. The slave owners who held slavery to be a divine institution, and the priests and ministers who supported them, were just as honest and sincere in their belief as we are in holding antagonistic beliefs to-day.

What was accounted a virtue in the slave was accounted a vice in the slaveholder. Cowardice and a cringing humility were not regarded as faults in a slave. On the contrary, they were the stock virtues of the pattern slave and added to the estimation in which he was held, just as similar traits are valued in personal servants--butlers, waiters, valets, footmen, and other flunkies--in our own day. But similar traits in the slaveholder, or the "gentleman" of to-day, would be regarded as terrible faults. As Mr. Algernon Lee very tersely puts it, "The slave was not a slave because of his slavish ideals and beliefs; the slave was slavish in his ideals and beliefs because he lived the life of a slave."[123]

In the industrial world of to-day we find a similar divergence of ethical standards. What the laborers regard as wrong, the employers regard as absolutely and immutably right. The actions of the workers in forming unions and compelling unwilling members of their own class to join them, even resorting to the bitter expedient of striking against them with a view to starving them into submission, seem terribly unjust to the employers and the class to which the employers belong. To the workers themselves, on the other hand, such actions have all the sanctions of conscience. Similarly, many actions of the employers, in which they themselves see no wrong, seem almost incomprehensibly wicked to the workers.

Leaving aside the wholesale fraud of our ordinary commercial advertisements, the shameful adulteration of goods, and a multitude of other such nefarious practices, it is at once interesting and instructive to compare the employers' denunciations of "the outrageous infringement of personal liberty," when the "oppressor" is a labor union, with some of their everyday practices. The same employers who loudly, and, let it be said, quite sincerely, condemn the members of a union who endeavor to bring about the discharge of a fellow-worker because he declines to join their organization, have no scruples of conscience about discharging a worker simply because he belongs to a union, and so effectually "blacklisting" him that it becomes almost or quite impossible for him to obtain employment at his trade elsewhere. They do not hesitate to do this secretly, conspiring against the very life of the worker. While loudly declaiming against the "conspiracy" of the workers to raise wages, they see no wrong in an "agreement" of manufacturers or mine owners to reduce wages. If the members of a labor union should break the law, especially if they should commit an act of violence during a strike, the organs of capitalist opinion teem with denunciation, but there is no breath of condemnation for the outrages committed by employers or their agents against union men and their families.

During the great anthracite coal strike of 1903, and again during the disturbances in Colorado in 1904, it was evident to every fair-minded observer that the mine owners were at least quite as lawless as the strikers.[124] But there was hardly a scintilla of adverse comment upon the mine owners' lawlessness in the organs of capitalist opinion, while they poured forth torrents of righteous indignation at the lawlessness of the miners. When labor leaders, like the late Sam Parks, for example, are accused of extortion and receiving bribes, the employers and their retainers, through pulpit, press, and every other avenue of public opinion, denounce the culprit, the bribe taker, in unmeasured terms--but the bribe giver is excused, or, at worst, only lightly criticised. These are but a few common illustrations of class conscience. Any careful observer will be able to add almost indefinitely to the number.

It would be easy to compile a catalogue of such examples as these from the history of the past few years sufficient to convince the most skeptical that class interests do produce a class conscience. Mr. Ghent aptly expresses a profound truth when he says: "There is a spiritual alchemy which transmutes the base metal of self-interest into the gold of conscience; the transmutation is real, and the resulting frame of mind is not hypocrisy, but conscience. It is a class conscience, and therefore partial and imperfect, having little to do with absolute ethics. But partial and imperfect as it is, it is generally sincere."[125] No better test of the truth of this can be made than by reading carefully for a few weeks the comments of half a dozen representative capitalist newspapers, and of an equal number of representative labor papers, upon current events. The antithetical nature of their judgments of men and events demonstrates the existence of a distinct class conscience. It cannot be interpreted in any other way.

V

A great many people, while admitting the important role class struggles have played in the history of the race, strenuously deny the existence of classes in the United States. They freely admit the class divisions and struggles of the Old World, but deny that a similar class antagonism exists in this country; they fondly believe the United States to be a glorious exception to the rule, and regard the claim that classes exist here as falsehood and treason. The Socialists are forever being accused of seeking to apply to American life judgments based upon European facts and conditions. It is easy to visualize the class divisions of monarchical countries, where there are hereditary ruling classes--even though these are only nominally the ruling classes in most cases--fixed by law. But it is not so easy to recognize the fact that, even in these countries, the power is held by the financial and industrial lords, and not by the kings and their titular nobility. The absence of a hereditary, titular ruling class serves to hide from many people the real class divisions existing in this country.

Nevertheless, there is a perceptible growth of uneasiness and unrest; a widening and deepening conviction that while we may retain the outward forms of democracy, and shout its shibboleths with patriotic fervor, its essentials are lacking. The feeling spreads, even in the most conservative circles, that we are developing, or have already developed, a distinct ruling class. The anomaly of a ruling class without legal sanction or titular prestige has seized upon the popular mind; titles have been created for our great "untitled nobility"--mock titles which have speedily assumed a serious import and meaning. Our financial "Kings," industrial "Lords," "Barons," and so on, have received their crowns and patents of nobility from the populace. President Roosevelt gives expression to the serious thought of our most conservative citizenry when he says: "In the past, the most direful among the influences which have brought about the downfall of republics has ever been the growth of the class spirit.... If such a spirit grows up in this republic, it will ultimately prove fatal to us, as in the past it has proven fatal to every community in which it has become dominant."[126]

With the exception of the chattel slaves, we have had no hereditary class in this country with a legally fixed status. But

"Man is more than constitutions,"

and there are other laws than those formulated in senates and recorded in statute books. The vast concentration of industry and wealth, resulting in immense fortunes on the one hand, and terrible poverty on the other, has separated the two classes by a chasm as deep and wide as ever yawned between czar and moujik, kaiser and vagrant, prince and pauper, feudal baron and serf. The immensity of the power and wealth thus concentrated into the hands of the few, to be inherited by their sons and daughters, tends to establish this class division hereditarily. Heretofore, passage from the lower class to the class above has been comparatively easy, and it has blinded people to the existing class antagonisms, though, as Mr. Ghent justly observes, it should no more be taken to disprove the existence of classes than the fact that so many thousands of Germans come to this country to settle is taken to disprove the existence of the German Empire.[127] The stereotyping of classes is undeniable. That a few men pass from one class to another is no disproof of this. The classes exist and the tendency is for them to remain permanently fixed, as a whole, in our social life.

But passage from the lower class to the upper tends to become, if not absolutely impossible and unthinkable, at least practically impossible, and as difficult and rare as the transition from pauperism to princedom in the Old World is. A romantic European princess may marry a penurious coachman, and so provide the world with a nine days' sensation, but such cases are no rarer in the royal courts of Europe than in our own plutoaristocratic court circles. Has there ever been a king in modern times with anything like the power of Mr. Rockefeller? Is any feature of royal recognition withheld from Mr. Morgan when he goes abroad in state, an uncrowned king, fraternizing with crowned but envious fellow-kings? The existence of classes in America to-day is as evident as the existence of America itself.

VI

Antagonisms of class interests have existed from the very beginning of civilization, though not always recognized. It is only the consciousness of their existence, and the struggle which results from that consciousness, that are new. As we suddenly become aware of the pain and ravages of disease, when we have not felt or heeded its premonitory symptoms, so, having neglected the fundamental class division of society, the bitterness of the strife resulting therefrom shocks and alarms us. So long as it is possible for the stronger and more ambitious members of an inferior class to rise out of that class and join the ranks of a superior class, so long will the struggle which ensues as the natural outgrowth of opposing interests be postponed.

Until quite recently, in the United States, this has been possible. Transition from the status of wage-worker to that of capitalist has been easy. But with the era of concentration and the immense capitals required for industrial enterprise, and the exhaustion of our supply of free land, these transitions become fewer and more difficult, and class lines tend to become permanently fixed. The stronger and more ambitious members of the lower class, finding it impossible to rise into the class above, thus become impressed with a consciousness of their class status. The average worker no longer dreams of himself becoming an employer after a few years of industry and thrift. The ambitious and aggressive few no longer look with the contempt of the strong for the weak upon their less aggressive fellow-workers, but become leaders, preachers of a significant and admittedly dangerous gospel of class consciousness.

President Roosevelt has assailed the preachers of class consciousness with all the energy of a confirmed moralizer. It is evident, however, that he has never taken the trouble to study either the preachers or their gospel. Never in his utterances has there been any hint given of a recognition of the fact that there could be no preaching of class consciousness had there been no classes. Never has he manifested the faintest recognition of the existence of conditions which develop classes, out of which the class consciousness of the propagandists springs naturally. He does not see that there is danger only when the preachers are not wise enough, nor sufficiently educated to see their position in its historical perspective; when in blind revolt they engender class hatred, personal hatred of the capitalist by the worker. But when there is the historical perspective, wisdom to see that economic conditions develop slowly, and that the capitalist is no more responsible for conditions than the worker, there is not only no personal hatred for the capitalist engendered, but, more important still, the workers get a new view of the relationship of the classes, and their efforts are directed to the bringing about of peaceful change.

The Socialists, accused as they are of seeking to stir up hatred and strife, by placing the class struggle in its proper light, as one of the great social dynamic forces, have done and are doing more to allay hatred and bitterness of feeling, and to save the world from the red curse of anarchistic vengeance, than all the Rooseveltian preaching in which thousands of venders of moral platitudes are engaged. The Socialist movement is vastly more powerful as a force against Anarchism, in its violent manifestations, than any other agency in the world. Wherever, as in Germany, the Socialist movement is strong, Anarchism is impotent and weak. The reason for this is the very obvious one here given. Class divisions are not created by Socialists, but developed in the womb of economic conditions. Class consciousness is not something which Socialism has developed. Before there was a Socialist movement, in the days of Luddite attacks upon machinery, and Captain Swing's rick-burners, there was class consciousness expressed in class revolt. Modern Socialism simply takes the class consciousness of the worker and educates it to see the futility of machine-destroying, or other foolish and abortive attacks upon capitalists and their property, and organizes it into a political movement for the peaceful transformation of society.

VII

Nowhere in the world, at any time in its history, has the antagonism of classes been more evident than in the United States at the present time. With an average of over a thousand strikes a year,[128] some of them involving, directly, tens of thousands of producers, a few capitalists, and millions of noncombatants, consumers; with strikes like this, boycotts, lockouts, injunctions, and all the other incidents of organized class strife reported daily by the newspapers, denials of the existence of classes, or of the struggle between them, are manifestly absurd. We have, on the one hand, organizations of workers, labor unions, with a membership of something over two million in the United States; one organization alone, the American Federation of Labor, having an affiliated membership of one million seven hundred thousand. On the other hand, we have organizations of employers, formed for the expressed purpose of fighting the labor unions, of which the National Association of Manufacturers is the most perfect type yet evolved.

While the leaders on both sides frequently deny that their organizations betoken the existence of a far-reaching fundamental class conflict, and, through ostensibly pacificatory organizations like the National Civic Federation, proclaim the "essential identity of interests between capital and labor"; while an intelligent and earnest labor leader like Mr. John Mitchell joins with an astute capitalist leader like the late Senator Marcus A. Hanna in declaring that "there is no necessary hostility between labor and capital," that there is no "necessary, fundamental antagonism between the laborer and the capitalist,"[129] a brief study of the constitutions of these class organizations, and their published reports, in conjunction with the history of the labor struggle in the United States, in which the names of Homestead, Hazelton, Coeur d'Alene and Cripple Creek appear in bloody letters, will show these denials to be the offspring of hypocrisy or delusion. If this much-talked-of unity of interests is anything but a stupid fiction, the great and ever increasing strife is only a matter of mutual misunderstanding. All that is necessary to secure permanent peace is to remove that misunderstanding. If we believe this, it is a sad commentary upon human limitations, upon man's failure to understand his own life, that not a single person on either side has arisen with sufficient intelligence and breadth of vision to state the relations of the two classes with clarity and force enough to accomplish that end, to make them understand each other.

Let us get down to fundamental principles.[130] Why do men organize into unions? Why was the first union started? Why do men pay out of their hard-earned wages to support unions now? The first union was not started because the men who started it did not understand their employers, or because they were misunderstood by their employers. The explanation involves a deeper insight into things than that. When the individual workingman, feeling that from the labor of himself and his fellows came the wealth and luxury of his employer, demanded higher wages, a reduction of the hours of labor, or better conditions in general, he was met with a reply from the employer--who understood the workingman's position very well, much better, in fact, than the workingman himself did--something like this, "If you don't like this job, and my terms, there are plenty of others outside ready to take your place." The workingman and the employer, then, understood each other perfectly. The employer understood the position of the worker, that he was dependent upon him, the employer, for opportunity to earn his bread. The worker understood that so long as the employer could discharge him and fill his place with another, he was powerless. The combat between the workers and the masters of their bread has from the first been an unequal one.

Nothing remained for the individual workingman but to join with his fellows in a collective and united effort. So organizations of workers appeared, and the employers could not treat the demands for higher wages or other improvements in conditions as lightly as before. The workers, when they organized, could take advantage of the fact that there were no organizations of the employers. Every strike added to the ordinary terrors of the competitive struggle for the employers. The manufacturer whose men threatened to strike often surrendered because he feared most of all that his trade, in the event of a suspension of work, would be snatched by his rival in business. So, by playing upon the inherent weakness of the competitive system as it affected the employers, the workers gained many substantial advantages. There is no doubt whatsoever that under these conditions the wage-workers got better wages, better working conditions, and a reduction in the hours of labor. It was in many ways the golden age of trade unionism. But there was an important limitation of the workers' power--the unions could not absorb the man outside; they could not provide all the workers with employment. That is an essential condition of capitalist industry, there is always the "reserve army of the unemployed," to use the expressive phrase of Friederich Engels. Rare indeed are the times when all the available workers in any industry are employed, and the time has probably never yet been when all the available workers in all industries were employed.

Notwithstanding this important limitation of power, it is incontrovertible that the workers were benefited by their organization. But only for a time. There came a time when the employers began to organize unions also. That they called their organizations by other and high-sounding names does not alter the fact that they were in reality unions formed to combat the unions of the workers. Every employers' association is, in reality, a union of the men who employ labor against the unions of the men they employ. When the organized workers went to individual, unorganized employers, who feared their rivals more than they feared the workers, or, rather, who feared the workers most of all because rivals waited to snatch their trade, a strike making their employees allies with their competitors, the employers were easily defeated. The workers could play one employer against another employer with constant success. But when the employers also organized, it was different. Then the individual employer, freed from his worst terrors, could say, "Do your worst. I, too, am in an organization." Then it became a battle betwixt organized capital and organized labor. When the workers went out on strike in one shop or factory, depending upon their brother unionists employed in other shops or factories, the employers of these latter locked them out, thus cutting off the financial support of the strikers. In other cases, when the workers in one place went out on strike, the employer got his work done through other employers, by the very fellow-members upon whom the strikers were depending for support. Thus the workers were compelled to face this dilemma, either to withdraw these men, thus cutting off their financial supplies, or to be beaten by their own members.

Under these changed conditions, the workers were beaten time after time. It was a case of the worker's cupboard against the master's warehouse, purse against bank account, poverty against wealth. The workers' chances are slight in such a combat! A strike means that the employers on one side, and the workers on the other, seek to force each other to surrender by waiting patiently to see who first feels the pinch of hardship and poverty. Employers and employees determine to play the waiting game. Each waits patiently in the hope that the other will weaken. At last one--most often the workers'--side weakens and gives up the struggle. When the workers are thus beaten in a strike, they are not convinced that their demands are unreasonable or unjust; they are simply beaten because their resources are too small to enable them to stand the struggle.

When the master class, the masters of jobs and bread, organized their forces, they set narrow and sharp boundaries to the power of labor organizations. Henceforth the chances of victory were overwhelmingly on the side of the employers. The workers learned by bitter and costly experience that they could not play the interests of individual employers against other employers' interests. Meantime, too, they have learned that they are not only exploited as producers, but also as buyers, as consumers. For long, dominated by economic theories, the Socialists refused to recognize this aspect of the labor struggle, though the workers felt it strongly enough. They set their fine-spun theories against the facts of life. Their contention was that wages being determined by the cost of living, it mattered nothing how much or how little the workers got in wages, the cost of living and wages adjusted themselves to each other. But in actual experience the workers found that when prices fall, wages are *quick* to follow, whereas when prices soar high, wages are *slow* to follow. Wages climb with leaden feet when prices soar with eagle wings. Because the workers are consumers, almost to the last penny of their incomes, having to spend practically every penny earned, that form of exploitation becomes a serious matter.

But against this exploitation the unions have ever been absolutely powerless. Workingmen have never made any very serious attempt to protect the purchasing capacity of their wages, notwithstanding its tremendous importance.[131] The result has been that not a few of the "victories" so dearly won by trade union action have turned out to be hollow mockeries. When better wages have been secured, prices have often gone up, most often, in fact, so that the net result has been little to the advantage of the workers. In many cases, where the advance in wages applied only to a restricted number of trades, the advance in prices becoming general, the total result has been against the working class as a whole, and little or nothing to the advantage of the few who received the advance in immediate wages. At this point, the need is felt of a social revolution, not a violent revolution, be it understood, but a comprehensive social change which will give to the workers the control of the implements of labor, and also of the product of their labor. In other words, the demand arises for independent, working-class action, aiming at the socialization of the means of production and the product.

VIII

A line of cleavage thus presents itself between those, on the one hand, who would continue the old methods of economic warfare, together with the advocates of physical force, and, on the other hand, the advocates of united political action by the working class, consciously directed toward the socialization of industry and its products. The measure of the crystallization of this latter force is represented by the strength of the political Socialist movement. Whoever has studied the labor movement during the past few years must have realized that there is a tremendous drift of sentiment in favor of that policy in the labor unions of the country. The clamor for political action in the labor unions presages an enormous advance of the political Socialist movement during the next few years.

The struggle between the capitalist and working classes must become a political issue, the supreme political issue. This must result, not only because the collective ownership of property can best be brought about by political methods, but also because the capitalists themselves have taken the industrial struggle into the political arena to suit themselves; and when the workers realize the issue and accept it, the capitalists will not be able to resist them. One is reminded of the saying of Marx that capitalism produces its own gravediggers. In taking the industrial issue into the political sphere, to suit their own immediate advantages, the capitalists were destined to reveal to the workers, sooner or later, their power and opportunity.

Realizing that all the forces of government are on their side, the legislative, judicial, and executive powers being controlled by their own class, the employers have made the fight against labor political as well as economic in its character. When the workers have gone on strike and the employers have not cared to play the "waiting game," choosing rather to avail themselves of the great reserve army of unemployed workers outside, the natural resentment of the strikers, finding themselves in danger of being beaten by members of their own class, has led to violence which has been remorselessly suppressed by all the police and military forces at the command of the government. In many instances, the employers have purposely provoked striking workers to violence, and then called upon the government to crush the revolt thus made. Workers have been shot down at the shambles in almost every state, no matter which political party has been in power. Nor have these forces of our class government been used merely to punish lawless union men and women on strike, to uphold the "sacred majesty of the law," as the hypocritical phrase goes. They have been also used to deny strikers the rights which belonged to them, and to protect capitalists and their agents in breaking the laws. No one can read with anything like an impartial spirit the records of the miners' strike in the Coeur d'Alene mine, Idaho, or the labor disturbances in the state of Colorado from 1880 to 1905 and dispute this assertion.

Most important of all has been the powerful opposition of the makers and interpreters of the law. A body of class legislation, in the interests of the employing class, has been created, while the workers have begged in vain for protective legislation. In no country of the world have the interests of the workers been so neglected as in the United States. There is practically no such thing as employers' liability for accidents to workers; no legislation worthy of mention relating to occupations which have been classified as "dangerous" in most industrial countries; women workers are sadly neglected. Whenever a law of distinct advantage to the workers in their struggle has been passed, a servile judiciary has been ready to render it null and void by declaring it to be unconstitutional. No more powerful blows have ever been directed against the workers than by the judiciary. Injunctions have been issued, robbing the workers of the most elemental rights of manhood and citizenship. They have forbidden things which no law forbids, and even things which the Constitution and statute law declare to be legal.

Mr. John Mitchell refers to this subject, in strong but not too strong terms. "No weapon," he says, "has been used with such disastrous effect against trade unions as the injunction in labor disputes. By means of it, trade unionists have been prohibited under severe penalties from doing what they had a legal right to do, and have been specifically directed to do what they had a legal right not to do. It is difficult to speak in measured tones or moderate language of the savagery and venom with which unions have been assailed by the injunction, and to the working classes, as to all fair-minded men, it seems little less than a crime to condone or tolerate it."[132] This is strong language, but who shall say that it is too strong when we remember the many injunctions which have been hurled at organized labor since the famous Debs case brought this weapon into general use?

In this celebrated case, which grew out of the Pullman strike, in 1894, Eugene V. Debs, president of the American Railway Union, was arrested and arraigned on indictments of obstructing the mails and interstate commerce. Although arraigned, he was not tried, the case being abandoned, despite his demands for a trial. President Cleveland's strike commission subsequently declared, "There is no evidence before the commission that the officers of the American Railway Union at any time participated in or advised intimidation, violence, or destruction of property." Realizing that it had no sort of evidence upon which a jury might be hoped to convict, a new way was found. Debs and his officers were enjoined in a famous "blanket" injunction directed against Debs and all other officials of the union, and "all persons whomsoever." For an alleged violation of that injunction, Judge Woods, without trial by jury, sentenced Debs to six months' imprisonment and his associates to three months'. The animus and class bias of the whole proceeding may be judged from the fact that President Cleveland selected to represent the United States Government, at Chicago, Mr. Edwin Walker, general counsel at that very time for the General Managers' Association, representing the twenty-four railroads centering or terminating in Chicago. And these railroads were operating in violation of the

Sherman Anti-Trust Law at the time.[133]

In 1899 an injunction was issued out of the United States Circuit Court of West Virginia against "John Smith and others," without naming the "others," in the interest of the Wheeling Railway Company. Two men, neither of them being John Smith, nor found to be the agent of "John Smith and others," were jailed for contempt of court![134] In 1900 members of the International Cigarmakers' Union, in New York City, were enjoined by Justice Freeman, in the Supreme Court, from even approaching their former employers for the purpose of attempting to arrange a peaceable settlement! The cigarmakers were further enjoined from publishing their grievances, or in any manner making their case known to the public, if the tendency of that should be to vex the plaintiffs or make them uneasy; from trying, even in a peaceful way, in any place in the city, even in the privacy of a man's own home, to persuade a new employee that he ought to sympathize with the union cause sufficiently to refuse to work for unjust employers; and, finally, the union was forbidden to pay money to its striking members to support them and their families. In the great steel strike of 1901, the members of the Amalgamated Association of Iron and Steel Workers were enjoined from peaceably discussing the merits of their claim with the men who were at work, even though the latter might raise no objection. In Pennsylvania, in the case of the York Manufacturing Company *vs.* Obedick, it was held that workmen had "no legal right" to persuade or induce other workmen to quit, or not to accept, employment.[135] In the strike of the members of the International Typographical Union against the Buffalo *Express*, the strikers were enjoined from discussing the strike, or talking about the paper in any way which might be construed as being against the paper. If one of the strikers advised a friend not to buy a "scab" paper, he was liable under the terms of that injunction to imprisonment for contempt of court. The members of the same union were, in the case of the Sun Printing and Publishing Company *vs*. Delaney and others, enjoined by Justice Bookstaver, in the Supreme Court of New York, from publishing their side of the controversy with the *Sun* as an argument why persons friendly to organized labor should not advertise in a paper hostile to it. In 1906 members of the same union were enjoined by Supreme Court Justice Gildersleeve from "making any requests, giving any advice, or resorting to any persuasion ... to overcome the free will of any person connected with the plaintiff [a notorious anti-union publishing company] or its customers as employees or otherwise."[136]

These are only a few examples of the abuse of the injunction in labor disputes, hundreds of which have been granted, many of them equally subversive of all sound principles of popular government. There is probably not another civilized country in which such judicial tyranny would be tolerated. It is not without significance that in West Virginia, where, as a result of an outcry against a number of particularly glaring abuses of the power to issue injunctions, the legislature passed a law limiting the right to issue injunctions, the Supreme Court decided that the law was unconstitutional, upon the ground that the legislature had no right to attempt to restrain the courts which were cooordinate with itself.

Even more dangerous to organized labor than the injunction is what is popularly known by union men as "Taff Vale law." Our judges have not been slow to follow the example set by the English judges in the famous case of the Taff Vale Railway Company against the officers of the Amalgamated Society of Railway Servants, a powerful labor organization. The decision in that case was most revolutionary. It compelled the workers to pay damages, to the extent of $115,000, to the railroad company for losses sustained by the company through a strike of its employees, members of the defendant union. That decision struck terror into the hearts of British trade unionists. At last they had to face a mode of attack even more dangerous than the injunction which their transatlantic brethren had so long been contending against. Taff Vale law could not long be confined to England. Very soon, our American courts followed the English example. A suit was instituted against the members of a lodge of the Machinists' Union in Rutland, Vermont, and the defendants were ordered to pay $2500. A writ was served upon each member and the property of every one of them attached. Since that time, numerous other decisions of a like nature have been rendered in various parts of the country. Thus the unions have been assailed in a vital place, their treasuries. It is manifestly foolish and quite useless for the members of a union to strike against an employer for any purpose whatever, if the employer is to be able to recover damages from the union. Taff Vale judge-made law renders the labor union *hors de combat* at a stroke.

IX

The immediate effect of the revolutionary judicial decision in England was to arouse the workers to the necessity for class-conscious political action. The cry went up that the unions must adopt a policy of independent political action. There is no doubt whatever that the tremendous advance of the Socialist movement in England during the past few years began as a result of the attack made upon the funds of the labor unions. From the moment of the Taff Vale decision the Socialist movement in England took rapid strides. A similar process is going on in this country, gathering momentum with every injunction against organized labor, every hostile enactment of legislatures, and every use of the judicial and executive powers to defeat the workers in their struggle against capitalism. The workers are being educated to political Socialism by the stern experiences resulting from capitalist rule. Underneath the thin veneer of party differences, the worker sees the class identity of the great political parties, and cries out, "A plague on both your houses!" The Socialist argument comes to him with a twofold force: not only does it show him how he is enslaved and exploited as a producer, but it convinces him that as a citizen he has it in his power to control the government and make it what he will. He can put an end to government by injunctions, to the use of police, state, and federal troops to break strikes, and to the sequestration of union funds by hostile judges. He can, if he so decides, own and control the government, and, through the government, own and control the essentials of life: be master of his own labor, his own bread, his own life.

If we take for granted that the universal increase of Socialist sentiment, and the growth of political Socialism, as measured by its rapidly increasing vote, presage this great triumph of the working class; that the heretofore despised and oppressed proletariat is, in a not far distant future, to rule instead of being ruled, the question arises, will the last state be better than the first? Will society be bettered by the change of masters?

The very form of the question must be denied. It is not a movement for a change of masters. To regard this struggle of the classes as one of revenge, of exploited masses ready to overturn the social structure that they may become exploiters instead of exploited, is to misread the whole movement. The political and economic conquest of society by the working class means the end of class divisions once and forever. A social democracy, a society in which all things essential to the common life and well-being are owned and controlled by the people in common, democratically organized, precludes the existence of class divisions in our present-day economic and political sense. Profit, through human exploitation, alone has made class divisions possible, and the Socialist regime will abolish profit. The working class, in emancipating itself, at the same time makes liberty possible for the whole race of man, and destroys the conditions of class rule.

NOTES:

[116] The **Communist Manifesto**, Kerr edition, page 8.

[117] In **Centralization and the Law: Scientific Legal Education, An Illustration**, edited by Melville M. Bigelow.

[118] See, for instance, **The Coal Mine Workers**, by Frank Julian Warne, Ph.D. (1905).

[119] Adam Smith, **The Wealth of Nations**, Vol. I, Book I, Chapter VIII.

[120] **The Common Sense of Socialism**, by John Spargo, page 131 (1908).

[121] See, for instance, **The American Farmer**, by A. M. Simons, page 130; **Agrarfrage**, by Karl Kautsky, pages 305-306.

[122] Mr. Ghent's excellent work, **Mass and Class**, and Karl Kautsky's **Ethics and the Materialistic Conception of History**, may be named as excellent examples of what Socialists have done in this direction.

[123] In **The Worker** (New York), March 25, 1905.

[124] Cf., for instance, **The Labor History of the Cripple Creek District**, by Benjamin McKie Rastall (1908), and Senate Document No. 122, being **A Report on Labor Disturbances in the State of Colorado, from 1880 to 1904, Inclusive**, by Carroll D. Wright (1905), for evidence of this from sources not specially friendly to the miners.

[125] **Mass and Class**, page 101.

[126] **Message to Congress**, January, 1906.

[127] *Mass and Class*, page 53.

[128] Vide *War of the Classes*, by Jack London, page 17.

[129] *Organized Labor*, by John Mitchell, page ix.

[130] The remainder of this chapter is largely reproduced from my little pamphlet, *Shall the Unions go into Politics?*

[131] This aspect of the exploitation of the laborers has been brought to the front very dramatically by the many recent "strikes" against high rents and high prices for meat and other commodities. Rent strikes and riots against high prices have become common events in our large cities.

[132] *Organized Labor*, by John Mitchell, page 324.

[133] See *Report of Commission of Investigation*, Senate Ex. Doc. No. 7, Fifty-third Congress, third session.

[134] Particulars are taken from a pamphlet by five members of the New York Bar and issued by the Social Reform Club, New York, in 1900.

[135] See the article by Judge Seabury, *The Abuses of Injunctions, in The Arena*, June, 1903.

[136] See the New York daily papers, January 31, 1906.

CHAPTER VII
KARL MARX AND THE ECONOMICS
OF SOCIALISM

I

The first approach to a comprehensive treatment by Marx of the materialistic conception of history appeared in 1847, several months before the publication of the ***Communist Manifesto***, in "La Misere de la Philosophie,"[137] the famous polemic with which Marx assailed J. P. Proudhon's ***La Philosophie de la Misere***. Marx had worked out his theory at least two years before, so Engels tells us, and in his writings of that period there are several evidences of the fact. In "La Misere de la Philosophie," the theory is fundamental to the work, and not merely the subject of incidental allusion. This little book, all too little known in England and America, is therefore important from this historical point of view. In it, Marx for the first time shows his complete confidence in the theory. It needed confidence little short of sublime to challenge Proudhon in the audacious manner of this scintillating critique. The torrential eloquence, the scornful satire, and fierce invective of the attack, have rather tended to obscure for readers of a later generation the real merit of the book, the importance of the fundamental idea that history must be interpreted in the light of economic development, that economic evolution determines social life. The book is important for two other reasons. First, it was the author's first serious essay in economic science--in the preface he boldly and frankly calls himself an economist--and, second, in it appears a full and generous recognition of that brilliant coterie of English Socialist writers of the Ricardian school from whom Marx has been unjustly, and almost spitefully, charged with "pillaging" his principal ideas.

What led Marx to launch out upon the troubled sea of economic science, when all his predilections were for the study of pure philosophy, was the fact that his philosophical studies had led him to a point whence further progress seemed impossible, except by way of economics. The Introduction to "A Contribution to the Critique of Political Economy" makes this perfectly clear. Having decided that "the method of production in material existence conditions social, political, and mental evolution in general," a study of economics, and especially an analysis of modern industrial society, became inevitable. During the year 1845, when the theory of the economic interpretation of history was absorbing his attention, Marx spent six weeks in England with his friend Engels, and became acquainted with the work of the Ricardian Socialists already referred to.[138] Engels had been living in England about three years at this time, and had made an exhaustive investigation of industrial conditions there, and become intimately acquainted with the leaders of the Chartist movement. His fine library contained most of the works of contemporary writers, and it was thus that Marx came to know them.

Foremost of this school of Socialists which had arisen, quite naturally, in the land where capitalism flourished at its best, were William Godwin, Charles Hall, William Thompson, John Gray, Thomas Hodgskin, and John Francis Bray. With the exception of Hall, of whose privately printed book, "The Effects of Civilisation on the People of the European States," 1805, he seems not to have known, Marx was familiar with the writings of all the foregoing, and his obligations to some of them, especially Thompson, Hodgskin, and Bray, were not slight. While the charge, made by Dr. Anton Menger,[139] among others, that Marx took his surplus value theory from Thompson is quite absurd, and rests, as Bernstein has pointed out, upon nothing but the fact that Thompson used the words "surplus value" frequently, but not at all in the same sense as that in which Marx uses them,[140] we need not attempt to dispute the fact that Marx gleaned much of value from Thompson and the two other writers. While criticising them, and pointing out their shortcomings, Marx himself frequently pays tributes of respect to each of them. His indebtedness to any of them, or to all of them, consists simply in the fact that he recognized the germinal truths in their writings, and saw far beyond what they saw.

Godwin's most important work, "An Inquiry Concerning Political Justice," appeared in 1793, and contains the germ of much that is called Marxian Socialism. In it may be found the broad lines of the thought which marks much of our present-day Socialist teaching, especially the criticism of capitalist society. Marx, however, does not appear to have been directly influenced by it to any extent. That he was influenced by it indirectly, through William Thompson, Godwin's most illustrious disciple, is, however, quite certain. Thompson wrote several works of a Socialist character, of which "An Inquiry into the Principles of the Distribution of Wealth most Conducive to Human Happiness, Applied to the newly proposed System of Voluntary Equality of Wealth," 1824, and "Labour Rewarded. The Claims of Labour and Capital Conciliated, or How to Secure to Labour the Whole Products of its Exertions," 1827, are the most important and best known. Thompson must be regarded as one of the greatest precursors of Marx in the development of modern Socialist theory. A Ricardian of the Ricardians, he states the law of wages in language that is almost as emphatic as Lassalle's famous *Ehernes Lohngesetz*, which Marx made the butt of his satire.[141] Accepting the view of Ricardo,--and indeed, of Adam Smith and other earlier English economists, including Petty,--that labor is the sole source of exchange value,[142] he shows by cogent argument the exploitation of the laborer, and uses the term "surplus value" to designate the difference between the cost of maintaining the laborer and the value of his labor product, assisted, of course, by machinery and other capital, which goes to the capitalist. By a most labored argument, Professor Anton Menger has attempted to create the impression that Marx took, without acknowledgment, his *theory of the manner in which surplus value is produced* from Thompson, simply because Thompson frequently used the *term itself*.[143] Marx never claimed to have originated the term. It is to be found in the writings of earlier economists than Thompson even, and Marx quotes an anonymous pamphlet entitled *The Source and Remedy of the National Difficulties. A Letter to Lord John Russell*, published in London in 1821, in which the phrase "the quantity of the surplus value appropriated by the capitalist" appears. [144] Nor did Marx claim to be the first to distinguish surplus value. That had been done very clearly by many others, including Adam Smith.[145] What is original in Marx is the explanation of the manner in which surplus value is produced.

John Gray's "A Lecture on Human Happiness," published in 1825, has been described by Professor Foxwell as being "certainly one of the most remarkable of Socialist writings,"[146] and the summary of the rare little work which he gives amply justifies the description. Gray published other works of note, two of which, "The Social System, a Treatise on the Principle of Exchange," 1831, and "Lectures on the Nature and Use of Money," 1848, Marx subjects to a rigorous criticism in "A Contribution to the Critique of Political Economy." Thomas Hodgskin's best-known works are "Labour Defended against the Claims of Capital," 1825, and "The Natural and Artificial Right of Property Contrasted," 1832. The former, which Marx calls "an admirable work," is only a small tract of thirty-four pages, but its influence in England and America was very great. Hodgskin was a man of great culture and erudition, with a genius for popular writing upon difficult topics. It is interesting to know that in a letter to his friend, Francis Place, he sketched a book which he proposed writing, "curiously like Marx's 'Capital,'" according to Place's biographer, Mr. Wallas,[147] and from which the conservative old reformer dissuaded him. John Francis Bray was a journeyman printer about whom very little is known. His "Labour's Wrongs and Labour's Remedy," published in Leeds in 1839, Marx calls "a remarkable work," and in his attack upon Proudhon he quotes from it extensively to show that Bray had anticipated the French writer's theories.[148]

The justification for this lengthy digression from the main theme of the present chapter lies in the fact that so many critics have sought to fasten the charge of dishonesty upon Marx, and claimed that the ideas with which his name is associated were taken by him, without acknowledgment, from these English Ricardians. As a matter of fact, no economist of note ever quoted his authorities, or acknowledged his indebtedness to others, more generously than did Marx, and it is exceedingly doubtful whether even the names of the precursors whose ideas he is accused of stealing would be known to his critics but for his frank recognition of them. No candid reader of Marx can fail to notice that he is most careful to show how nearly these writers approached the truth as he conceived it.

II

When the February revolution of 1848 broke out, Marx was in Brussels. The authorities there compelling him to leave Belgian soil, at the request of the Prussian government, he returned to Paris, but not for a long stay. The revolutionary struggle in Germany stirred his blood, and with Engels, Wilhelm Wolf, the intimate friend to whom he later dedicated the first volume of "Capital," and Ferdinand Freiligrath, the fiery poet of the movement, Marx started the *New Rhenish Gazette*. Unlike the first *Rhenish Gazette*, the new journal was absolutely free from control by business policy. Twice Marx was summoned to appear at the Cologne assizes, upon charges of inciting the people to rebellion, and each time he defended himself with superb audacity and skill, and was acquitted. But in June, 1849, the authorities suppressed the paper, because of the support it gave to the risings in Dresden and the Rhine Province. Marx was expelled from Prussia and once more sought a refuge in Paris, which he was allowed to enjoy only for a very brief time. Forbidden by the French government to stay in Paris, or any other part of France except Brittany, which, says Liebknecht, was considered "fireproof," Marx turned to London, the mecca of all political exiles, arriving there toward the end of June, 1849.

His removal to London was one of the crucial events in the life of Marx. It became possible for him, in the classic land of capitalism, to pursue his economic studies in a way that was not possible anywhere else in the world. As Liebknecht says: "Here in London, the metropolis (mother city) and the center of the world, and of the world of trade--the watch tower of the world whence the trade of the world and the political and economical bustle of the world may be observed, in a way impossible in any other part of the globe--here Marx found what he sought and needed, the bricks and mortar for his work. 'Capital' could be created in London only."[149]

Already much more familiar with English political economy than most English writers of his time, and with the fine library of the British Museum at his command, Marx felt that the time had at last arrived when he could devote himself to his long-cherished plan of writing a great treatise upon political economy as a secure basis for the theoretical structure of Socialism. With this object in view, he resumed his economic studies in 1850, soon after his arrival in London. The work proceeded slowly, however, principally owing to the long and bitter struggle with poverty which encompassed Marx and his gentle wife. For years they suffered all the miseries of acute poverty, and even afterward, when the worst was past, the principal source of income, at times almost the only source in fact, was the five dollars a week received from the **New York Tribune**, for which Marx acted as special correspondent, and to which he contributed some of his finest work.[150] There are few pictures more pathetic, albeit also heroic, than that which we have of the great thinker and his devoted wife struggling against poverty during the first few years of their stay in London. Often the little family suffered the pangs of hunger, and Marx and a group of fellow-exiles used to resort to the reading room of the British Museum, weak from lack of food very often, but grateful for the warmth and shelter of that hospitable spot. The family lived some time in two small rooms in a cheap lodging house on Dean Street, the front room serving as reception room and study, and the back room serving for everything else. In a diary note, Mrs. Marx has herself left us an impressive picture of the suffering of those early years in London. Early in 1852, death entered the home for the first time, taking away a little daughter. Only a few weeks later another little daughter died, and Mrs. Marx wrote concerning this event:--

"On Easter of the same year--1852--our poor little Francisca died of severe bronchitis. Three days the poor child was struggling with death. It suffered so much. Its little lifeless body rested in the small back room; we all moved together into the front room, and when night approached, we made our beds on the floor. There the three living children were lying at our side, and we cried about the little angel, who rested cold and lifeless near us. The death of the dear child fell into the time of the most bitter poverty ... (the money for the burial of the child was missing). In the anguish of my heart I went to a French refugee who lived near, and who had sometimes visited us. I told him our sore need. At once with the friendliest kindness he gave me two pounds. With that we paid for the little coffin in which the poor child now sleeps peacefully. I had no cradle for her when she was born, and even the last small resting place was long denied her. What did we suffer when it was carried away to its last place of rest!"[151]

The poverty, of which we have here such a graphic view, lasted for several years beyond the publication of the "Critique," on to the appearance of the first volume of "Capital." When this struggle is remembered and understood, it becomes easier to appreciate the life work of the great Socialist thinker. "It was a terrible time, but it was grand nevertheless," wrote Liebknecht years afterward to Eleanor Marx. As this is the last place in which the personality of Marx, or his personal affairs, will be discussed in this volume, and in view of constant misrepresentations on the part of unscrupulous opponents of Socialism, a further word concerning his family life may not be out of place. Those persons who regard Socialism as being antagonistic to the family relation, and fear it in consequence, will find no suggestion of support for that view in either the life of Marx or his teaching. The love of Marx and his wife for each other was beautiful and idyllic. A true account of their love and devotion would rank with the most beautiful love stories in literature. Their friends understood that, too, and there is a world of significance in the one brief sentence spoken by Engels, when told of the death of his friend's beautiful wife, who was likewise his own dear friend: "Mohr [Negro, a nickname given to Marx by his friends when young, on account of his mass of black hair and whiskers] is dead too," he said simply. He knew that from this blow Marx could not recover. It was indeed true. Though he lingered on for about three months after her death, the life of Marx really ended when the playmate of his boyhood, and the lover and companion of all the years of struggle, died with the name of her dear "Karl" upon her lips.

Marx was an ideal father as well as an ideal husband. Always passionately fond of children, he could not resist the temptation to join the games of children upon the streets, and in the neighborhoods where he lived the children soon learned to regard him as their friend. To his own children he was a real companion, always ready to amuse and to be amused by them.

III

The studious years spent in the reading room of the British Museum complete the anglicization of Marx. "Capital" is essentially an English work, the fact of its having been written in German, by a German writer, being merely incidental. No more distinctively English treatise on political economy was ever written, not even "The Wealth of Nations." Even the method and style of the book are, contrary to general opinion, much more distinctly English than German. I do not forget his Hegelian dialectic with its un-English subtleties, but against that must be placed the directness, vigor, and pointedness of style, and the cogent reasoning, with its wealth of concrete illustrations, which are as characteristically English. Marx belongs to the school of Petty, Smith, and Ricardo, and their work is the background of his. "Capital" was the child of English industrial conditions and English thought, born by chance upon German soil.

Toward the middle of the nineteenth century, English economic thought was entirely dominated by the ideas and methods of Ricardo, who has been described by Senior, not without justice, as "the most incorrect writer who ever attained philosophical eminence."[152] So far as such a sweeping criticism can be justified by looseness in the use of terms, it is justified by Ricardo's failing in this respect. That he should have attained the eminence he did, dominating English economic thought for so many years, in spite of the confusion which his loose and uncertain use of words occasioned, is not less a tribute to Ricardo's genius than evidence of the poverty of political economy in England at that time. In view of the constant and tiresome reiteration of the charge that Marx pillaged his labor-value theory from Thompson, Hodgskin, Bray, or some other more or less obscure writer of the Ricardian school, it is well to remember that there is nothing in the works of any of these writers connected with the theory of value which is not to be found in the earlier work of Ricardo himself. In like manner, the theory can be traced back from Ricardo to the master he honored, Adam Smith. Furthermore, almost a century before the appearance of "The Wealth of Nations," Sir William Petty had anticipated the so-called Ricardian labor-value theory of Smith and his followers.

Petty, rather than Smith, is entitled to be regarded as the founder of the classical school of political economy, and Cossa justly calls him "one of the most illustrious forerunners of the science of statistical research."[153] He may indeed fairly be said to have been the father of statistical science, and was the first to apply statistics, or "political arithmetick," as he called it, to the elucidation of economic theory. He boasts that "instead of using only comparative and superlative Words, and intellectual Arguments," his method is to speak "in Terms of Number, Weight, or Measure; to use only Arguments of Sense; and to consider only such Causes, as have visible Foundations in Nature; leaving those that depend upon the mutable Minds, Opinions, Appetites, and Passions of particular Men, to the Consideration of others."[154] The celebrated saying of this sagacious thinker that "labor is the father and active principle of wealth; lands are the mother," is more Marxian than Ricardian. Petty divided the population into two classes, the productive and non-productive, and insisted that the value of all things depends upon the labor it costs to produce them. This is, as we shall see, entirely Ricardian, but not Marxian. But these are the ideas Marx is supposed to have borrowed, without acknowledgment, from comparatively obscure followers of Ricardo, in spite of the fact that he gives abundant credit to the earlier writer. It has been asked with ample justification whether these critics of Marx have read either the works of Marx or his predecessors.

Adam Smith, who accepted the foregoing principles laid down by Petty, followed his example of basing his conclusions largely upon observed facts instead of abstractions. It is not the least of Smith's merits that, despite his many digressions, looseness of phraseology, and other admitted defects, his love for the concrete kept his feet upon the solid ground of fact. With his successors, notably Ricardo and John Stuart Mill, it was far otherwise. They made political economy an isolated study of abstract doctrines. Instead of a study of the meaning and relation of facts, it became a cult of abstractions, and the aim of its teachers seemed to be to render the science as little scientific, and as dull, as possible. They set up an abstraction, an "economic man," and created for it a world of economic abstractions. It is impossible to read either Ricardo or John Stuart Mill, but especially the latter, without feeling the artificiality of the superstructures they created, and the justice of Carlyle's description of such political economy as the "dismal science." With a realism greater even than Adam Smith's, and a more logical method than Ricardo or John Stuart Mill, Marx restored the science of political economy to its old fact foundations.

IV

The superior insight of Marx is shown in the very first sentence of his great work. The careful reader at once perceives that the first paragraph of the book strikes a keynote which distinguishes it from all other economic works comparable to it in importance. Marx was a great master of the art of luminous and exact definition, and nowhere is this more strikingly shown than in this opening sentence of "Capital": "The wealth of those societies *in which the capitalist mode of production prevails* presents itself as an immense accumulation of commodities, its unit being a single commodity."[155] In this simple, lucid sentence the theory of social evolution is clearly implied. The author repudiates, by implication, the idea that it is possible to lay down universal or eternal laws, and limits himself to the exploration of the phenomena appearing in a certain stage of historical development. We are not to have another abstract economic man with a world of abstractions all his own; lone, shipwrecked mariners upon barren islands, imaginary communities nicely adapted for demonstration purposes in college class rooms, and all the other stage properties of the political economists, are to be entirely discarded. Our author does not propose to give us a set of principles by which we shall be able to understand and explain the phenomena of human society at all times and in all places-- the Israel of the Mosaic Age, the nomadic life of Arab tribes, Europe in the Middle Ages, and England in the nineteenth century.

In effect, the passage under consideration says: "Political economy is the study of the principles and laws governing the production and distribution of wealth. Because of the fact that in the progress of society different systems of wealth production and exchange, and different concepts of wealth, prevail at different times, and at various places at the same time, we cannot formulate any laws which will apply to all times and all places. We must choose for examination and study a certain form of production, representing a particular stage of historical development, and be careful not to attempt to apply any of its laws to other forms of production, representing other stages of development. We might have chosen to investigate the laws which governed the production of wealth in the ancient Babylonian Empire, or in Mediaeval Europe, had we so desired, but we have chosen instead the period in which we live."

This that we call the capitalist epoch has grown out of the geographical discoveries and the mechanical inventions of the past three hundred years or so, especially of the seventeenth and eighteenth centuries. Its chief characteristic, from an economic point of view, is that of production for sale instead of direct use as in earlier stages of social development. Of course, barter and sale are much older than this epoch which we are discussing. In all ages men have exchanged their surplus products for other things more desirable to them, either directly by barter or through some medium of exchange. In the very nature of things, however, such exchange as this must have been incidental to the life of the people engaging in it, and not its principal aim. Under such conditions of society wealth consists in the possession of useful things. The naked savage, so long as he possessed plenty of weapons, and could get an abundance of fish or game, was, from the viewpoint of the society in which he lived, a wealthy man. In other words, the wealth of pre-capitalist society consisted in the possession of use-values, and not of exchange-values. Robinson Crusoe, for whom the possibility of exchange did not exist, was, from this pre-capitalist viewpoint, a very wealthy man.

In our present society, production is carried on primarily for exchange, for sale. The first and essential characteristic feature of wealth in this stage of social development is that it takes the form of accumulated exchange-values, or commodities. Men are accounted rich or poor according to the exchange-values they can command, and not according to the use-values they can command. To use a favorite example, the man who owns a ton of potatoes is far richer in simple use-values than the man whose only possession is a sack of diamonds, but, because in present society a sack of diamonds will exchange for an almost infinite quantity of potatoes, the owner of the diamonds is much wealthier than the owner of the potatoes. The criterion of wealth in capitalist society is exchangeable value as opposed to use-value, the criterion of wealth in primitive society. The unit of wealth is therefore a commodity, and we must begin our investigation with it. If we can analyze the nature of a commodity so that we can understand how and why it is produced, and how and why it is exchanged, we shall be able to understand the principle governing the production and exchange of wealth in this and every other society where similar conditions prevail, where, that is to say, the unit of wealth is a commodity, and wealth consists in an accumulation of commodities.

V

The visit to America, in 1907, of a distinguished English critic of Socialism, Mr. W. H. Mallock, had the effect of thrusting into prominence a common misconception of Marxian Socialism, and it is highly significant that, except in the Socialist press, none of the numerous comments which the series of university lectures delivered by that gentleman occasioned, called attention to the fact that they were based throughout upon a misstatement of the Marxian position. Briefly, Mr. Mallock insisted that Marx believed and taught that all wealth is produced by manual labor, and that, therefore, it ought to belong to the manual workers. In order that there may be no misstatement of our amiable critic's position, it will be best to quote his own words. He says, in Lecture I: "The practical outcome of the scientific economics of Marx is summed up in the formula which is the watchword of popular Socialism. 'All wealth is due to labor; therefore all wealth ought to go to the laborer'--a doctrine in itself not novel, but presented by Marx as the outcome of an elaborate system of economics"[156] (page 6). The careful reader will notice that Mr. Mallock does not profess to give the exact words of Marx, nor refer to any particular passage, but says that the formula quoted by him is the "practical outcome" of the economic system of Marx, "presented by Marx" as such. But to quote again: "Wealth, says Marx, not only ought to be, but actually can be distributed amongst a certain class of persons, namely, the laborers.... Because these laborers comprise in the acts of labor everything that is involved in the production of it" (page 7). Again: " ... Marx makes of his doctrine that labor alone produces all economic wealth" (page 7). Also: " ... that theory of production which the genius of Karl Marx invested with a semblance, at all events, of sober, scientific truth, and which ascribes all wealth to that ***ordinary manual labor which brings the sweat to the brow of the ordinary laboring man***" (page 12).[157] All the foregoing passages are taken from a single lecture, the first of the series. We will take only a few from the others: " ...

the doctrine of Marx that all productive effort is absolutely equal in productivity" (Lecture III, page 46); "Marx based the ethics of distribution on what purported to be an analysis of production" (Lecture IV, page 61); " ... Count Tolstoy, ... like Socialists of the school of Marx, declares that ordinary manual labor is the source of all wealth" (Lecture IV, page 76). "One is the attempt of Marx and his school, which represents ordinary manual labor as the sole producer of wealth" (Lecture IV, page 81); " ... the Marxian doctrine ... that manual labor is the sole producer of wealth" (Lecture V, page 115). It would be easy to add many other quotations very similar to these, but it is unnecessary. From the quotations given we can gather Mr. Mallock's conception of what Marx taught regarding the source of wealth.

It will be seen that Mr. Mallock alleges: (1) That Marx believed and taught that all wealth is produced by ordinary manual labor; (2) that he held, as a consequence, that all wealth ought to belong to the manual laborers, thus basing an ethic of distribution upon production; (3) that he taught that all productive effort is absolutely equal in productive value, in other words, that ten hours' work of one kind is economically as valuable as ten hours' of any other kind, so long as the labor is productive.

It is not easy to command the necessary self-restraint to reply with dignity to such wholesale misrepresentation as this. There is not the slightest scintilla of a foundation in fact for any one of the three statements. Not a single passage can be quoted from Marx which justifies any one of them. As we shall see, Marx specifically repudiated each one of them, a great deal more forcefully than Mr. Mallock does. That such misrepresentations of Marx should have been permitted to pass unchallenged in so many of our great colleges and universities is to our national shame. We will briefly consider the teaching of Marx under each of the three heads.

First, the source of wealth. It is true that such phrases as "Labor is the source of all wealth" are constantly met with in the popular literature of Socialism, but so far as that is the case it is not due to the teaching of Marx, but rather in spite of it. In the writings of the early Ricardian Socialists these phrases abound, but nowhere in all the writings of Marx will such a statement be found. For many years the opening sentence in the Programme of the German party contained the phrase "Labor is the source of all wealth and of all culture," ***but it was adopted in spite of the protest of Marx***. The Gotha Programme was adopted in 1875. A draft was submitted to

Marx and he wrote of it that it was "utterly condemnable and demoralizing to the party." Of the passage in question, he wrote: "Labor is **not** the source of all wealth. Nature is just as much the source of use-values (and of such, to be sure, is material wealth composed) as is labor, which itself is but the expression of a natural force, of human labor-power."[158] That the clause was adopted was a bitter disappointment to Marx, and was due to the insistence of the followers of Ferdinand Lassalle. To say that Marx held labor to be the sole source of wealth is to misrepresent his whole teaching.[159]

But while the Lassallians, and before them the Ricardians, used the **phrase**, it is evident that they assumed the inclusion of what Marx calls "Nature." They know very well that labor, mere exertion of physical strength, could produce nothing. If, for instance, a man were to spend all his strength trying to lift the pyramids, alone and unaided by mechanical power, it is quite evident to the meanest intellect that his exertions would not produce a single atom of wealth. It is equally obvious that if we take any use-value, whether it be an exchange-value or not being immaterial, we cannot eliminate from it the substance of which it is composed. Take, for example, the canoe of a savage, which is a simple use-value, and a meerschaum pipe, which is a commodity. In the canoe we have part of the trunk of a tree taken from the primeval forest, one of Nature's products. But without the labor of the savage it would never have become a canoe. It would have remained simply part of the trunk of a tree, and would not have acquired the use-value it has as a canoe. But it is likewise true that without the tree the canoe could not have existed. So with our meerschaum pipe. It is not simply a use-value: it is also an article of commerce, an exchange-value, a commodity. Its elements are, the silicate mineral which Nature provided and the form which human labor has given it. We can apply this test to every form of wealth, whether simple use-values or commodities, and we shall find that, in Mill's phrase, wealth is produced by the application of human labor to **appropriate natural objects**.

This brings us to the second point in Mr. Mallock's criticism, namely, that Marx held that only "ordinary manual labor" is capable of producing wealth, and that, therefore, all wealth ought to go to the manual laborers. One looks in vain for a single passage in all the writings of Marx which will justify this criticism. It may be conceded at once that if Marx taught anything of the kind, the defect in Marxian theory is fatal. But it must be proven that the defect exists--and the *onus probandi* rests upon Mr. Mallock. One need not be a trained economist or a learned philosopher to see how absurd such a theory must be. Suppose we take, for example, a man working in a factory, at a great machine, making screws. We go to that man and say: "Every screw here is made by manual labor alone. The machine does not count; the brains of the inventors of the machine have nothing to do with the making of screws." Our laborer might be illiterate and unable to read a single page of political economy with understanding, but he would know that our statement was foolish and untrue. Or, suppose we take the machine itself and say to the laborer: "That great machine with all its levers and wheels and springs working in such beautiful harmony was made entirely by manual workers, such as molders, blacksmiths, and machinists; no brain workers had anything to do with the making of it; the labor of the inventors, and of the men who drew the plans and supervised the making, had nothing to do with the production of the machine"--our laborer would rightly conclude that we were either fools or seeking to mock him as one.

Curiously enough, notwithstanding the frequent reiteration of this criticism of Marx by Mr. Mallock, he himself, in an unguarded moment, provides the answer by which Marx is vindicated! Thus, speaking of the great classical economists, Adam Smith, Ricardo, and John Stuart Mill, he points out that they included "all forms of living industrial effort, from those of a Watt or an Edison down to those of a man who tars a fence, grouped together under the common name of labor" (Lecture I, page 16). And again: "At present the orthodox economists and the socialistic economists alike give us *all human effort*[160] tied up, as it were, in a sack, and ticketed 'human labor'" (Lecture I, page 18). Now, if the Socialist includes in his definition of labor "all human effort," it stands to reason that he does not mean only "ordinary manual labor" when he uses the term. Thus Mallock answers Mallock and vindicates Marx!

Of course, Marx, like all the great economists, includes in his concept of labor every kind of productive effort, mental as well as physical, as Mr. Mallock, to the utter destruction of his disingenuous criticism, unconsciously--we must suppose--admitted. Take, for example, this definition: "By labor power or capacity for labor is to be understood the aggregate of those *mental and physical* capabilities existing in a human being, which he exercises when he produces a use-value of any description."[161] As against this luminous and precise definition, it is but fair to quote that of Mr. Mallock himself. He defines labor as "the faculties of an individual *applied to his own labor*"[162]--a meaningless jumble of words. The fifty-seven letters contained in that sentence would mean just as much if put in a bag, well shaken, and put on paper just as they happened to fall from the bag.

Marx never argued that the producers of wealth had a *right* to the wealth produced. The "right of labor to the whole of its produce" was, it is true, the keynote of the theories of the Ricardian Socialists. An echo of the doctrine appeared in the Gotha Programme of the German Socialists to which reference has already been made, and in the popular agitation of Socialism in this and other countries it is echoed more or less frequently. Just in proportion as the ethical argument for Socialism is advanced, and appeals made to the sense of justice, the rich idler is condemned and an ethic of distribution based upon production becomes an important feature of the propaganda. But Marx nowhere indulges in this kind of argument. Not in a single line of "Capital," or his minor economic treatises, can any hint of the doctrine be found. He invariably scoffed at the "ethical distribution" idea. In the judgment of the present writer, this is at once his great strength and weakness, but that is beside the point of this discussion. Suffice it to say, though it involves some reiteration, that Marx never took the position that Socialism *ought* to take the place of capitalism, because the producers of wealth *ought* to get the whole of the wealth they produce. His position was rather that Socialism *must* come, simply because capitalism *could not* last.

Finally, we come to the charge that Marx taught that "all productive effort is absolutely equal in productivity." Incredible as it may seem, it is nevertheless a fact that everything Marx has to say upon the subject is directly opposed to this notion, and that, as we shall see later on, his famous theory of value is not only not dependent upon a belief in the equal productivity of all productive effort, but would be completely shattered by it. Not only Marx, but also Mill, Ricardo, and Smith, his great predecessors, recognized the fact that all labor is not equally productive. Of course, it requires no special genius to demonstrate this. That a poor mechanic with antiquated tools will produce less in a given number of hours than an expert mechanic with good tools, for example, is too obvious for comment. The Marx assailed by Mr. Mallock, and numerous critics like him, is a myth. The real Marx they do not touch--hence the futility of their work. The Marx they attack is a man of straw, not the immortal thinker. Endowed

"With just enough of learning to misquote,"

their assaults are vain.

VI

Having thus disposed of some of the more prevalent criticisms of Marx as an economist, we are ready for a definite, consecutive statement of the economic theory of modern Socialism. First, however, a word as to the term "scientific" as commonly applied to Marxian Socialism. Even some of the friendliest of Socialist critics have contended that the use of the term is pretentious, bombastic, and altogether unjustified. From a certain narrow point of view, this appears to be an unimportant matter, and the vigor with which Socialists defend their use of the term seems exceedingly foolish, and accountable for only as a result of enthusiastic fetish worship--the fetish, of course, being Marx.

Such a view is very crude and superficial. It cannot be doubted that the Socialism represented by Marx and the modern political Socialist movement is radically different from the earlier Socialism with which the names of Fourier, Saint-Simon, Cabet, Owen, and a host of other builders of "cloud palaces for an ideal humanity," are associated. The need of some word to distinguish between the two is obvious, and the only question remaining is whether or not the word "scientific" is the most suitable and accurate one to make that distinction clear; whether the words "scientific" and "utopian" express with reasonable accuracy the nature of the difference. Here the followers of Marx feel that they have an impregnable position. The method of Marx is scientific. From the first sentence of his great work to the last, the method pursued is that of a painstaking scientist. It would be just as reasonable to complain of the use of the word "scientific" in connection with the work of Darwin and his followers, to distinguish it from the guesswork of Anaximander, as to cavil at the distinction made between the Socialism of Marx and Engels and their followers, and that of visionaries like Owen and Saint-Simon.

Doubtless both Marx and Engels lapsed occasionally into Utopianism. We see instances of this in the illusions Marx entertained regarding the Crimean War bringing about the European Social Revolution; in the theory of the increasing misery of the proletariat; in Engels' confident prediction, in 1845, that a Socialist revolution was imminent and inevitable; and in the prediction of both that an economic cataclysm must create the conditions for a sudden and complete revolution in society. These, I say, are Utopian ideas, evidences that the founders of scientific Socialism were tinctured with the older ideas of the Utopists, and even more with their spirit. But when we speak of "Marxism," what mental picture does the word suggest, what intellectual concept is the word a name for? Is it these forecasts and guesses, and the exact mode of realizing the Socialist ideal which Marx laid down, or is it the great principle of social evolution determined by economic development? Is it his naive and simple description of the process of capitalist concentration, in which no hint appears of the circuitous windings that carried the actual process into unforeseen channels, or the broad fact that the concentration has taken place and that monopoly has come out of competition? Is it his statement of the extent to which labor is exploited, or the *fact* of the exploitation? If we are to judge Marx by the essential things, rather than by the incidental and non-essential things, then we must admit his claim to be reckoned with the great scientific sociologists and economists.

After all, what constitutes scientific method? Is it not the recognition of the law of causation, putting exact knowledge of facts above tradition or sentiment; accumulating facts patiently until sufficient have been gathered to make possible the formulation of generalizations and laws enabling us to connect the present with the past, and in some measure to foretell the outcome of the present, as Marx foretold the culmination of competition in monopoly? Is it not to see past, present, and future as one whole, a growth, a constant process, so that instead of vainly fashioning plans for millennial Utopias, we seek in the facts of to-day the stream of tendencies, and so learn the direction of the immediate flow of progress? If this is a true concept of scientific method, and the scientific spirit, then Karl Marx was a scientist, and modern Socialism is aptly named Scientific Socialism.

NOTES:

[137] An English edition of this work, translated by H. Quelch, was published in 1900 under the title *The Poverty of Philosophy*.

[138] Cf. F. Engels, Preface to *La Misere de la Philosophie*, English translation, *The Poverty of Philosophy*, page iv.

[139] *The Right to the Whole Produce of Labour*, by Anton Menger, 1899.

[140] Edward Bernstein, *Ferdinand Lassalle as a Social Reformer*, page ix.

[141] *Criticism of the Gotha Programme*, from the posthumous papers of Karl Marx.

[142] It should perhaps be pointed out here, to avoid misunderstanding, that Ricardo hedged this doctrine about with important qualifications--not always observed by his followers--till it no longer remained the simple proposition stated above. See Dr. A. C. Whitaker's *History and Criticism of the Labour Theory of Value in English Political Economy*, page 57, for a suggestive treatment of this point.

[143] *The Right to the Whole Produce of Labour.*

[144] Cf. *Capital*, Vol. I, page 644, and Vol. II, page 19, Kerr edition.

[145] Cf., for instance, *The Wealth of Nations*, Vol. I, Chapter VI.

[146] Introduction to Menger's *The Right to the Whole Produce of Labour*.

[147] *The Life of Francis Place*, by Graham Wallas, M.A., London, 1898, page 268.

[148] For this brief sketch of the works of these Ricardian Socialist writers I have drawn freely upon Menger's *The Right to the Whole Produce of Labour*, and Professor Foxwell's Introduction thereto.

[149] *Karl Marx: Biographical Memoirs*, by Wilhelm Liebknecht, translated by E. Untermann, 1901, page 32.

[150] Much of this work has been collated and edited by Marx's daughter, the late Mrs. Eleanor Marx-Aveling, and her husband, Dr. Edward Aveling, and published in two volumes, *The Eastern Question* and *Revolution and Counter-Revolution*.

[151] The note is quoted by Liebknecht, *Memoirs of Marx*, page 177, and in the Introduction to *Revolution and Counter-Revolution*, by the editor, Eleanor

Marx-Aveling.

[152] *Political Economy*, page 115.

[153] Luigi Cossa, *Guide to the Study of Political Economy*, English translation, 1880.

[154] *The Economic Writings of Sir William Petty*, edited by Charles Henry Hull, Vol. I, page 244.

[155] The italics are mine.--J. S.

[156] All quotations from Mr. Mallock are taken from the volume containing the text of his lectures, entitled *Socialism*, published by The National Civic Federation, New York, 1907.

[157] The italics are mine.--J. S.

[158] *Letter on the Gotha Programme*, by Karl Marx, published in the collection of the posthumous writings of Marx and Engels, edited by Mehring, 1902. See a translation of the letter by Dr. Harriet E. Lothrop, *International Socialist Review*, May, 1908.

[159] I note that my friend, Mr. J. R. Macdonald, M.P., "Whip" of the Labour Party in the British House of Commons, so misrepresents Marx in his admirable little book, *Socialism*, page 54.

[160] Italics mine.--J. S.

[161] The italics are mine. The passage occurs on page 186, Vol. I, of *Capital*, Kerr edition. In the last of the series of lectures printed in his book, Mr. Mallock attempts a reply to the criticism of an American Socialist, Mr. Morris Hillquit who quoted this passage from Marx to show that Mr. Mallock was in error in saying that Marx regarded manual labor as the sole source of wealth. He evades the real point, namely, that Marx clearly included mental as well as physical labor in his use of the term, and with an ingenuity equaled only by the disingenuousness of the argument, seeks refuge in the fact that it does not cover the special "directive ability" which is a special function, "a productive force distinct from labor." The trick will not do. The fact is that Marx clearly and precisely covers that point in another place. The reader is referred to Chapter XIII of Part IV, Vol. I, of *Capital*, pages 363-368, Kerr edition, for a brilliant and honest treatment of the whole subject of the place of the "directing few" in modern industry. We shall treat the matter briefly later on.

[162] Italics mine.--J. S. The passage occurs in Lecture III, page 36.

CHAPTER VIII
OUTLINES OF SOCIALIST ECONOMIC THEORY

I

The *geist* of social and political evolution is economic, according to the Socialist philosophy. This view of the importance of man's economic relations involves some very radical changes in the methods and terminology of political economy. The philosophical view of social and political evolution as a world-process, through revolutions formed in the matrices of economic conditions, at once limits and expands the scope of political economy. It destroys on the one hand the idea of the eternality of economic laws and limits them to particular epochs. On the other hand, it enhances the importance of the science of political economy as a study of the motive force of social evolution. With Marx and his followers, political economy is more than an analysis of the production and distribution of wealth; it is a study of the principal determinant factor in the social and political progress of society, consciously recognized as such.

The sociological viewpoint appears throughout the whole of Marxian economic thought. It appears, for instance, in the definition of a commodity as the unit of wealth *in those societies in which the capitalist mode of production prevails*. Likewise wealth and capital connote special social relations or categories. Wealth, which in certain simpler forms of social organization consists in the ownership of use-values, under the capitalist system consists in the ownership of exchange-values. Capital is not a thing, but a social relation between persons established through the medium of things. Robinson Crusoe's spade, the Indian's bow and arrow, and all similar illustrations given by the "orthodox" economists, do not constitute capital any more than an infant's spoon is capital. They do not serve as the medium of the social relation between wage-worker and capitalist which characterizes the capitalist system of production. The essential feature of capitalist society is the production of wealth in the commodity form; that is to say, in the form of objects that, instead of being consumed by the producer, are intended to be exchanged or sold at a profit. Capital, therefore, is wealth set aside for the production of other wealth with a view to its exchange at a profit. A house may consist of certain definite quantities of bricks, timber, lime, iron, and other substances, but similar quantities of these substances piled up without plan will not constitute a house. Bricks, timber, lime, and iron become a house only in certain circumstances, when they bear a given ordered relation to each other. "A negro is a negro; it is only under certain conditions that he becomes a slave. A certain machine, for example, is a machine for spinning cotton; it is only under certain defined conditions that it becomes capital. Apart from these conditions, it is no more capital than gold *per se* is money; capital is a social relation of production."[163]

This sociological principle pervades the whole of Socialist economics. It appears in every economic definition, practically, and the terminology of the orthodox political economists is thereby often given a new meaning, radically different from that originally given to it and commonly understood. The student of Socialism who fails to appreciate this fact will most frequently land in a morass of confusion and difficulty, but the careful student who fully understands it will find it of great assistance. Take, as an illustration, the phrase "the abolition of capital" which frequently occurs in Socialist literature. The reader who thinks of capital as consisting of *things*, such as machinery, materials of production, money, and so on, finds the phrase bewildering. He wonders how it is conceivable that production should go on if these things were done away with. But the student who fully understands the sociological principle outlined above comprehends at once that it is not proposed to do away with the *things*, but with *certain social relations expressed through them*. He understands that the "abolition of capital" no more involves the destruction of the physical things than the abolition of slavery involved the destruction of the slave himself. What is aimed at is the social relation which is established through the medium of the things commonly called capital.

II

In common with all the great economists, Socialists hold that wealth is produced by human labor applied to appropriate natural objects. This, as we have seen, does not mean that labor is the sole source of wealth. Still less does it mean that the mere expenditure of labor upon natural objects must inevitably result in the production of wealth. If a man spends his time digging holes in the ground and filling them up again, or dipping water from the ocean in a bucket and pouring it back again, the labor so expended upon natural objects would not produce wealth of any kind. Nor is the productivity of mental labor denied. In the term "labor" is implied the totality of human energies expended in production, regardless of whether those energies be physical or mental. In modern society wealth consists of social use-values, commodities.

We must, therefore, begin our analysis of capitalist society with an analysis of a commodity. "A commodity," says Marx, "is, in the first place, an object outside us, a thing that by its properties satisfies human wants of some sort or another. The nature of such wants, whether, for instance, they spring from the stomach or from fancy, makes no difference. Neither are we here concerned to know how the object satisfies these wants, whether directly as means of subsistence, or indirectly as means of production."[164] But a commodity must be something more than an object satisfying human wants. Such objects are simple use-values, but commodities are something else in addition to simple use-values. The manna upon which the pilgrim exiles of the Bible story were fed, for instance, was not a commodity, though it fulfilled the conditions of this first part of our definition by satisfying human wants. We must carry our definition further, therefore. In addition to use-value, then, a commodity must possess exchange-value. In other words, it must have a social use-value, a use-value to others, and not merely to the producer.

Thus, things may have the quality of satisfying human wants without being commodities. To state the matter in the language of the economists, use-values may, and often do, exist without economic value, value, that is to say, in exchange. Air, for example, is absolutely indispensable to life, yet it is not--except in special, abnormal conditions--subject to sale or exchange. With a use-value that is beyond computation, it has no exchange-value. Similarly, water is ordinarily plentiful and has no economic value; it is not a commodity. A seeming contradiction exists in the case of the water supply of cities where water for domestic use is commercially supplied, but a moment's reflection will show that it is not the water, but the social service of bringing it to a desired location for the consumer's convenience that represents economic value. Over and above that there is, however, the element of monopoly-price which enters into the matter. With that we have not, at this point, anything to do. Under ordinary circumstances, water, like light, is plentiful; its utility to man is not due to man's labor, and it has, therefore, no economic value. But in exceptional circumstances, as in an arid desert or in a besieged fortress, a millionaire might be willing to give all his wealth for a little water, thus making the value of what is ordinarily valueless almost infinite. What may be called natural use-values have no economic value. And even use-values that are the result of human labor may be equally without economic value. If I make something to satisfy some want of my own, it will have no economic value unless it will satisfy the want of some one else. So, unless a use-value is social, unless the object produced is of use to some other person than the producer, it will have no value in the economic sense: it will not be ***exchangeable***.

A commodity must therefore possess two fundamental qualities. It must have a use-value, must satisfy some human want or desire; it must also have an exchange-value arising from the fact that the use-value contained in it is social in its nature and exchangeable for other exchange-values. With the unit of wealth thus defined, the subsequent study of economics is immensely simplified.[165]

The trade of capitalist societies is the exchange of commodities against each other, through the medium of money. Commodities utterly unlike each other in all apparent physical properties, such as color, weight, size, shape, substance, and so on, and utterly unlike each other in respect to the purposes for which intended and the nature of the wants they satisfy, are exchanged for one another, sometimes equally, sometimes in unequal ratio. The question immediately arises: what is it that determines the relative value of commodities so exchanged? A dress suit and a kitchen stove, for example, are very different commodities, possessing no outward semblance to each other, and satisfying very different human wants, yet they may, and actually do, exchange upon an equality in the market. To understand the reason for this similarity of value of dissimilar commodities, and the principle which governs the exchange of commodities in general, is to understand an important part of the mechanism of modern capitalist society.

This is the problem of value which all the great economists have tried to solve. Sir William Petty, Adam Smith, David Ricardo, John Stuart Mill, and Karl Marx developed what is known as the labor-value theory as the solution of the problem. This theory, as developed by Marx, not in its cruder forms, is one of the cardinal principles in Socialist economic theory. The Ricardian statement of the theory is that the relative value of commodities to one another is determined by the relative amounts of human labor embodied in them; that the quantity of labor embodied in them is the determinant of the value of all commodities. When all their differences have been carefully noted, all commodities have at least one quality in common. The dress suit and the kitchen range, toothpicks and snowshoes, pink parasols and sewing-machines, are unlike each other in every other particular save one--they are all products of human labor, crystallizations of human labor-power. Here, then, say the Socialists, as did the great classical economists, we have a hint of the secret of the mechanism of exchange in capitalist society. The amount of labor-power embodied in their production is in some way connected with the measure of the exchangeable value of the commodities.

Stated in the simple, crude form, that the quantity of human labor crystallized in them is the basis and measure of the value of commodities when exchanged against one another, the labor theory of value is beautifully simple. At least, the formula is simplicity itself. At the same time, it is open to certain very obvious criticisms. It would be absurd to contend that the day's labor of a coolie laborer is equal in productivity to the day's labor of a highly skilled mechanic, or that the day's labor of an incompetent workman is of equal value to that of the most proficient. To refute such a theory is as beautifully simple as the theory itself. In all seriousness, arguments such as these are constantly used against the Marxian theory of value, notwithstanding that they do not possess the slightest relation to it. Marxism is very frequently "refuted" by those who do not trouble themselves to understand it.

The idea that the quantity of labor embodied in them is the determinant of the value of commodities was held by practically all the great economists. Sir William

Petty, for example, in a celebrated passage, says of the exchange-value of corn: "If a man can bring to London an ounce of silver out of the earth in Peru in the same time that he can produce a bushel of corn, then one is the natural price of the other; now, if by reason of new and more easy mines a man can get two ounces of silver as easily as formerly he did one, then the corn will be as cheap at ten shillings a bushel as it was before at five shillings a bushel, *caeteris paribus*."[166]

Adam Smith, following Petty's lead, says: "The real price of everything, what everything really costs to the man who wants to acquire it, is the toil and trouble of acquiring it. What everything is really worth to the man who has acquired it, and who wants to dispose of it or exchange it for something else, is the toil and labor which it can save to himself, and which it can impose on other people.... Labor was the first price, the original purchase money, that was paid for all things.... If among a nation of hunters, for example, it usually costs twice the labor to kill a beaver which it does to kill a deer, one beaver would naturally be worth or exchange for two deer. It is natural that what is usually the produce of two days' or two hours' labor, should be worth double of what is usually the produce of one day's or one hour's labor."[167]

Benjamin Franklin, whose merit as an economist Marx recognized, takes the same view and regards trade as being "nothing but the exchange of labor for labor, the value of all things being most justly measured by labor."[168] From the writings of almost every one of the great classical economists of England it would be easy to compile a formidable and convincing volume of similar quotations, showing that they all took the same view that the quantity of human labor embodied in commodities determines their value. One further quotation, from Ricardo, must, however, suffice. He says:--

"To convince ourselves that this (quantity of labor) is the real foundation of exchangeable value, let us suppose any improvement to be made in the means of abridging labor in any one of the various processes through which the raw cotton must pass before the manufactured stockings come to the market to be exchanged for other things; and observe the effects which will follow. If fewer men were required to cultivate the raw cotton, or if fewer sailors were employed in navigating, or shipwrights in constructing, the ship in which it was conveyed to us; if fewer hands were employed in raising the buildings and machinery, or if these, when raised, were rendered more efficient; the stockings would inevitably fall in value, and command less of other things. They would fall because a less quantity of labor was necessary to their production, and would therefore exchange for a smaller quantity of those things in which no such abridgment of labor had been made."[169]

It is evident from the foregoing quotations that these great writers regarded the quantity of human labor crystallized in them as the basis of all commodity values, and their real measure. The great merit of Ricardo lies in his development of the idea of social labor as against the simple concept of the labor of particular individuals, or sets of individuals. In the passage cited, he includes in the term "quantity of human labor" not merely the total labor of those immediately concerned in the making of stockings, from the cultivation of the raw cotton to the actual making of stockings in the factory, but all the labor indirectly expended, even in the making and navigating of ships, and the building of the factories. One does, indeed, find hints of the social labor concept in Adam Smith, but it is Ricardo who first clearly develops it. Marx further developed this principle, and all criticisms of the labor-value theory in Marxian economic theory which are based upon the assumption that quantity of labor means the simple, direct labor embodied in commodities fall of their own weight.

Thus, if we take any commodity, we shall find that it is possible to ascertain with tolerable certainty the amount of direct labor embodied in it, but that it is equally as impossible to ascertain the amount of the indirect expenditure of labor power which entered into its making. In the case of a table, for example, it may be possible to trace with some approximation to accuracy the labor involved in felling the tree and preparing the lumber out of which the table was made; the labor directly spent in bringing the lumber to the factory, and the direct labor expended in making out of the lumber a finished table; allowance may also be made for the labor embodied in the nails, glue, stain, and other articles used in making the table. So we have a fairly accurate statement of the direct labor embodied in the table. But what of the labor used to make the tools of the men who felled the trees and prepared the lumber? What of the coal miner and the iron miner and the tool maker? And what of the numerous and incalculable expenditures of labor to make the railroads, the railway engines, and to provide these with steam-power? What, also, of the machinery in the factory, and of the factory buildings themselves, and, back of them, again, the tool makers and the providers of raw materials? It is obvious that no human intellect could ever unravel the tangled skein of human labor, and that in actual exchange there can be no calculation of the respective labor content of commodities. If the law of value holds good, it must operate mechanically, automatically. And this it does, through the incidence of bargaining and the law of supply and demand.

We have noted elsewhere the variations in human capacity and productiveness. Superficial critics still frequently charge Marx with having overlooked this very obvious fact, whereas it has not only been fully treated by him, but was actually covered by Smith and Ricardo before Marx! With these writers and their followers it is the law of averages which solves the difficulties arising from variations in individual capacity and productivity. It is the *average* amount of labor expended in killing the beaver which counts, not the actual individual labor in a specified case. Nor did these writers overlook the important differentiation between simple, unskilled labor and labor that is highly skilled. If A in ten hours' labor produces exactly double the amount of exchange-value which B produces in the same time devoted to labor of another kind, it is obvious that the labor of B is not equal in value to that of A. Quantity of labor cannot, therefore, be measured, in individual cases, by time units. Despite a hundred passages which, detached from their context, seem to imply the contrary, Adam Smith recognized this very clearly, and attempted to solve the riddle by a differentiation of skilled and unskilled labor in which he likens skilled labor to a machine; and insists that the labor and time spent in acquiring the skill which distinguishes skilled labor must be reckoned.[170]

Another frequent criticism of the Marxian theory has not only been answered by Marx himself--is, in fact, ruled out by the terms of the theory itself--but was amply replied to by Ricardo.[171] The criticism in question consists in the selection of what may be called "unique values," or scarcity values, articles which cannot be reproduced by labor, and whose value is wholly independent of the quantity of labor originally necessary to produce them. Such articles are unique specimens of coins and postage stamps, autograph letters, rare manuscripts, Stradivarius violins, Raphael pictures, Caxton books, articles associated with great personages--such as Napoleon's snuffbox--great auks' eggs, and so on *ad infinitum*. No possible amount of human labor could reproduce these articles, reproduce, that is to say, the exact utilities in them. Napoleon's snuffbox might be exactly duplicated so far as its physical properties are concerned, but the association with Napoleon's fingers, the sentimental quality which gives it its special utility, is not reproducible. But the trade of capitalist society does not consist in the manufacture and sale of these things, which, after all, form a very insignificant part of the exchange-values of the world.

III

Marx saw the soul of truth in the labor-value theory, as propounded by his predecessors, especially Ricardo, and devoted himself to its development and systematization. He has been accused of plagiarizing his theory from the Ricardians, but it is surely not plagiarism when a thinker sees the germ of truth in a theory, and, separating it from the mass of confusion and error which envelops it, restates it in scientific fashion with all its necessary qualifications. This is precisely what Marx did. He developed the idea of social labor which Ricardo had propounded, disregarding entirely individual labor. He recognized the absurdity of the contention that the value of commodities is determined by the amount of labor, either individual or social, ***actually embodied in them***. If two workers are producing precisely similar commodities, say coats, and one of them expends twice as much labor as the other and uses tools and methods representing twice the social labor, it is clearly foolish to suppose that the exchange-value of his coat will be twice as great as that of the other worker, regardless of the fact that their utility is equal. Labor, Marx pointed out, has two sides, the qualitative and the quantitative. The qualitative side, the difference in quality between specially skilled and simply unskilled labor, is easily recognized, though the relative value of the one compared with the other may be somewhat obscured. The secret of that obscurity lies hidden in the quantitative side of labor. Here we must enter upon an abstract inquiry, that part of the Marxian theory which is most difficult to comprehend. Yet, it is not so very difficult, after all, to understand that the years devoted to learning his trade, by a mechanical engineer, for instance, during all of which years he must be provided with the necessities of life, must be reckoned somewhere and somehow; and that when they are so reckoned, his day's labor may be found to contain, concentrated, so to speak, an amount of labor time equivalent to two or even many days' simple unskilled labor time. It may be, and in fact is, quite impossible to set forth mathematically the relation of the two, for the reason that the process of developing skilled labor is too complex to be unraveled. Of the fact, however, there can be no doubt.

The real law of value, then, according to Marx, is as follows: Under capitalism, *in free competition*, the value of all commodities, other than those unique things which cannot be reproduced by human labor, is determined by the amount of *abstract* labor embodied in them; or, better, by the amount of social human labor power necessary, on the average, for their production. We may conveniently illustrate this theory by a concrete example. Let us, therefore, return to our coat-makers. Now, always assuming their equal utility, no one will be willing to pay twice as much for the coat produced by the slow worker with poor tools as for the other. If the more economical methods of production employed by the man who makes his coats in half the time taken by the other man are the methods usually employed in the manufacture of coats, and the time he takes represents the average time taken to produce a coat, then the average value of coats will be determined thereby, and coats produced by the slower, less economical process will command only the same price in the market, the fact that they may embody twice the amount of actual labor counting for nothing. If we reverse the order of this proposition, and suppose the slower, less economical methods to be those generally prevailing in the manufacture of coats, and the quicker, more economical methods to be exceptional, then, all other things being equal, the exchange-value, of coats will be determined by the amount of labor commonly consumed, and the fortunate producer who adopts the exceptional, economical methods will, for a time, reap a golden harvest. Only for a time, however. As the new methods prevail, competition being the impelling force, they become less and less exceptional, and, finally, the regular, normal methods of production and the standard of value.

It is this very important qualification, fundamental to the Marxian theory, which is most often lost sight of by the critics. They persist in applying to individual commodities the test of comparing the amounts of labor-power actually consumed in their production, and so confound the Marxian theory with its crude progenitors. In refuting this crude theory, they are quite oblivious of the fact that Marx himself accomplished that by no means difficult feat. To state the Marxian theory accurately, we must qualify the bald statement that the exchange-value of commodities is determined by the amount of labor embodied in them, and state it in the following manner: ***The exchange-value of commodities is determined by the amount of average labor at the time socially necessary for their production.*** This is determined, not absolutely in individual cases, but approximately in general, by the bargaining and higgling of the market, to adopt Adam Smith's well-known phrase.

Now, this theory applies to those things, exclusive of the category of "unique values," which cannot be made by labor and are commonly supposed to owe their value to their rarity. For example, we may take diamonds. A man walking along the great wastes of the African ***karoo*** comes across a little stream. As he stoops to drink, he sees in the water a number of glittering diamonds. To pick them out is the work of a few minutes only, but the diamonds are worth many thousands of dollars. The law of value above outlined applies just as much to them as to any other commodity. The value of diamonds is determined by the amount of labor expenditure necessary ***on an average*** to procure them. If the normal method of obtaining diamonds were simply to go to the nearest stream and pick them out, their value would fall, possibly to zero:--

> "When we have nothing else to wear
> But cloth of gold and satins rare,
> For cloth of gold we cease to care--
> Up goes the price of shoddy."

IV

Most writers do not distinguish between price and value with sufficient clearness, using the terms as if they were synonymous and interchangeable. Where utilities are exchanged directly one for another, as in the barter of primitive society, there is no need of a price-form to express value. In highly developed societies, however, where the very magnitude of production and exchange makes direct barter impossible, and where the objects to be exchanged are not commonly the product of individual labor, a medium of exchange becomes necessary; a something which is generally recognized as a safe and stable commodity which can be used to express in terms of its own weight, size, shape, or color, the value of other commodities to be exchanged. This is the function of money. In various times and places wheat, shells, skins of animals, beads, powder, tobacco, and a multitude of other things, have served as money, but for various reasons, more or less obvious, the precious metals, gold and silver, have been most favored.

In all commercial countries to-day, one or other of these metals, or both of them, serves as the recognized medium of exchange. They are commodities also, and when we say that the value of a commodity is a certain amount of gold, we equally express the value of that amount of gold in terms of the commodity in question. As commodities, the precious metals are subject to the same laws as other commodities. If gold should be discovered in such abundance that it became as plentiful and easy to obtain as coal, its value would be no greater than that of coal. It might, conceivably, still be used as the medium of exchange, but it would--unless protected by legislation or otherwise from the operation of economic law, and so given a monopoly-price--have an exchange-value equal to that of coal, a ton of the one being equal to a ton of the other--provided, of course, that its utility remained. Since the scarcity of gold is an important element in its utility valuation, creating and fostering the desire for its possession, that utility-value might largely disappear if gold became as plentiful as coal, in which case it would not have the same value as coal, and might cease to be a commodity at all.

Price, then, is the expression of value in terms of some other commodity, which, generally used for that purpose of expressing the value of other commodities, we call money. It is only an approximation of value, and subject to a much greater fluctuation than value itself. It may, for a time, fall far below or rise above value, but in a free market--the only condition in which the operation of the law may be judged--sooner or later the equilibrium will be regained. Where monopoly exists, the free market condition being non-existent, price may be constantly elevated above value. Monopoly-price is an artificial elevation of price above value, and must be considered separately as the abrogation of the law of value.

Failure to discriminate between value and its price-expression, or symbol, has led to endless difficulty. It lies at the bottom of the naive theory that value depends upon the relation of supply and demand. Lord Lauderdale's famous theory has found much support among later economists, though it is now rather unpopular when stated in its old, simple form. Disguised in the so-called Austrian theory of final utility, it has attained considerable vogue.[172] The theory is plausible and convincing to the ordinary mind. Every day we see illustrations of its working: prices are depressed when there is an oversupply, and elevated when the demand of would-be consumers exceeds the supply of the commodities they desire to buy. It is not so easy to see that these effects are temporary, and that there is an automatic adjustment going on. Increased demand raises prices for a while, but it also calls forth an increase in supply which tends to restore the old price level, or may even force prices below it. In the latter case, the supply falls off and prices find their real level. The relation of supply to demand causes an oscillation of prices, but it is not the determinant of value. When prices rise above a certain level, demand slackens or ceases, and prices are inevitably lowered. Prices may and do fall with a decreased demand, but it is clear that unless the producers can get a price approximately equal to the value of their commodities, they will cease to produce them, and the supply will diminish or cease altogether. Ultimately, therefore, the fluctuations of price through the lack of equilibrium between supply and demand adjust themselves, and prices must tend constantly to approximate values.

Monopoly-price is, as already observed, an artificial price in the sense that the laws of free market exchange do not apply to it. The "unique utilities," things not reproducible by human labor, command what might be termed natural monopoly-prices. There are many other commodities, however, the price of which is not regulated by the quantity of social human labor necessary to produce them, but simply by the desire of the purchasers and the means they have of gratifying it and the power of the sellers to control the market and exclude effective competition. Since Karl Marx wrote, the exceptions to his law of value have become more numerous, as a result of the changes in industrial and commercial conditions. The development of great monopolies and near-monopolies has greatly increased the number of commodities which, for considerable periods, are placed outside the sphere of the labor-value theory, their price depending upon their marginal utility, irrespective of the labor actually embodied in them or necessary to their reproduction. It may, in the opinion of the present writer, be said in criticism of the followers of Marx that they have not carried on his work, but largely contented themselves with repeating generalizations which, true when made, no longer fit all the facts. But that is not a criticism of Marx, or of his work. What he professed to make was an analysis of the methods of production and exchange in competitive capitalist society. His followers have largely failed to allow for the enormous changes which have taken place, and go on repeating, unchanged, his phrases.

Professor Seligman has pointed out that Ricardo's contention that value is determined by the cost of production, and the contention of Jevons that value is determined by marginal utility, are not mutually exclusive, but, on the contrary, complementary to each other.[173] The present writer has long contended that the marginal utility theory and the Marxian labor-value theory are likewise not antagonistic but complementary.[174] This is not the place to enter into the elaborate discussion which this contention involves. Only a brief indication of the argument for the claim is here and now possible. First, as we have seen, Marx is very careful to insist that utility is essential to value, and that the utility must be a social utility. But social utility does not come of itself, from the skies or elsewhere. It is, so far as the vast majority of commodities is concerned, the product of labor. It is true that the value of a thing is never independent of its social utility; it is likewise true that this is determined by the social labor necessary to the reproduction of that utility. To regard the two theories as antagonistic, it seems to be necessary to say either (1) that the quantity of social labor necessary to produce certain commodities determines their value, utterly regardless of the amount of their social utility, or (2) that we estimate the social utility of commodities, estimate what we are willing to pay for them, utterly regardless of the labor necessary, on an average, for their reproduction. The latter contention would be absurd, and the former would involve the abandonment of the initial premises of the Marxian theory, contained in his definition of a commodity. In so far as the basis of social utility is the social labor necessary for its production, the labor-value theory of Marx may be said, I think, to include the marginal utility law, as one of the forms in which it operates.

V

Labor, the source and determinant of value, has, ***per se***, no value. Only when it is embodied in certain forms has it any value. If a man labors hard digging holes and refilling them, his labor has no value. What the capitalist buys is not labor, but labor-power. Wages in general is a form of payment for a given amount of labor-power, measured by duration and skill. The laborer sells brain and muscle power, which is thus placed at the temporary disposal of the capitalist to be used up like any other commodity that he buys. The philosopher Hobbes, in his "Leviathan," clearly anticipated Marx in thus distinguishing between labor and laboring power in the saying, "The value or worth of a man is ... so much as would be given for the Use of his Power." The power to labor assumes the commodity form, being at once a use-value and an exchange-value. At first sight it appears that piecework is an exception to the general rule that the capitalist buys labor-power and not labor itself. It seems that when piece-wages are paid it is not the machine, the living labor-power, but the product of the machine, labor actually performed, that is bought. Superficially, this is so, of course, but it does not affect the principle laid down, because, as a matter of fact, the piecework system is only one of the means used to secure a maximum of labor-power. The average output of pieceworkers in a trade always tends to become the standard output for the time-workers, and, on the other hand, the average wage of pieceworkers tends to keep very near the standard of time-wages.

Now, as a commodity, labor-power is subject to the same laws as all other commodities. Its price, wages, fluctuates just as the price of all other commodities does, and bears the same relation to its value. It may be temporarily affected by the preponderance of supply over demand, or of demand over supply; it may be made the subject of monopoly in certain cases. There is, therefore, no such thing as an "iron law" of wages, any more than there is an "iron law" of prices for other commodities. Lassalle took the Ricardian law of wages and, by means of his characteristic exaggeration, distorted it out of all semblance to truth. Says Ricardo: "The natural price of labor, therefore, depends on the price of the food, necessaries, and conveniences required for the support of the laborer and his family. With a rise in the price of food and necessaries, the natural price of labor will rise; with the fall in their price, the natural price of labor will fall."[175] This Lassalle made the basis of his famous "iron law," according to which 96 per cent of the wage-workers were precluded from improving their economic position. Lassalle's chief fault lay in that he made no allowance whatever for either state interference, or the organized influence of the workers themselves. He also attaches too little importance to what Marx calls the traditional standards of living.[176] It is nevertheless true that the price of la-bor-power, wages, tends to approximate its value, just as the price of all other com-modities tends, under normal conditions, to approximate their value.

And just as the value of other commodities is determined by the amount of so-cial labor necessary on an average for their reproduction, so the value of labor-power is likewise determined. Wages tend to a point at which they will cover the average cost of the necessary means of subsistence for the workers and their families, in any given time and place, under the conditions and according to the standards of living generally prevailing. Trade union action, for example, may force wages above that point, or undue stress in the competitive labor market may force wages below it. While, however, a trade union may bring about what is virtually a monopoly-price for the labor-power of its members, there is always a counter tendency in the other direction, sometimes even to the lowering of the standard of subsistence itself to the minimum of things required for physical existence.

To class human labor-power with pig iron as a commodity, subject to the same laws, may at first seem fantastic to the reader, but a careful survey of the facts will fully justify the classification. The capacity of the worker to labor depends upon his securing certain things; his labor-power has to be reproduced from day to day, for which a certain supply of food, clothing, and other necessities of life is essential. Even with these supplied constantly, the worker sooner or later wears out and dies. If the race is not to be extinguished, a certain supply of the necessities of life must be provided for the children during the years of their development to the point where their labor-power becomes marketable. The average cost of production in the case of labor-power includes, therefore, the necessities for a wife and family as well as for the individual worker. Far from being the iron law Lassalle imagined, this law of wages is one of considerable elasticity. The standard of living itself, far from being a fixed thing, determined only by the necessities of physical existence, varies according to occupational groups; to localities sometimes, as a result of historical development; to nationality and race, as a result of tradition; to the general standard of intelligence, and the degree in which the workers are organized for the promotion of their economic interests. The advance in the culture of the people as a whole, expressing itself in legislation for compulsory education, the abolition of child labor, improvement of housing and general sanitary conditions, and so on, tends to raise the standard of living. Finally, the fluctuations in the price of labor-power due to the operation of the law of supply and demand are much more important than Lassalle imagined.

This living commodity, labor-power, differs in one remarkable way from all other commodities, in that when it is used up in the process of the production of other commodities in which it is embodied, it creates new value in the process of being used up, and embodies that new value in the commodity it assists to produce. In the case of raw materials and machinery this is not so. In the manufacture of tables, for example, the wood used up is transformed into tables, embodied in them, but the wood has added nothing to its own value. The same is true of machinery. But with human labor-power it is otherwise. The capitalist buys from the laborer his labor-power at its full value as a commodity. But the laborer, in embodying that labor-power in some concrete form, creates more value than his wages represents. For the commodity he sells, his *power* to labor, he has been paid its full value, namely, the social labor-cost of its production; but that power may be capable of producing the equivalent of twice its own cost of production. This is the central idea of the famous and much-misunderstood Marxian theory of surplus-value, by which the method of capitalism, the exploitation of the wage-workers, and the resulting class antagonisms of the system are explained. This theory becomes the groundwork of all the social theories and movements protesting against and seeking to end the exploitation of the laboring masses. To understand it is, therefore, of paramount importance.

VI

As we have seen in an earlier chapter, Marx was not the first to recognize that the secret of capitalism, the object of capitalist industry, is the extraction of surplus-value from the labor-power of the worker. Nor was he the first to use the term. By no means a happy term, since it adds to the difficulty of comprehending the meaning and nature of *value*, Marx took it from the current economic discussion of his time as a term already fairly well understood. What we owe to the genius of Marx is an explanation of the manner in which surplus-value is extracted by the capitalist from the labor-power of the worker, and the part it plays in capitalist society.

The essence of the theory can be very briefly stated, but its demonstration involves, naturally, a more extensive study. Under normal conditions, the worker will produce a value equivalent to his means of subsistence, or to the wages actually paid to him, in a very small number of hours. If he owned and controlled the means of production,--land, machinery, raw materials, and so on,--he would, therefore, need to work only so many hours as the production of the necessities of life for himself and his family required. But the laborer in capitalist society does not own the means of production, that condition being quite incompatible with machine production upon a large scale. A separation of the worker from the ownership of the means of production has taken place as one of the inevitable results of industrial evolution. So the laborer must sell the only commodity he has to sell, namely, his labor-power. He sells the utility of that commodity to the capitalist for its exchange-value, or market price. Like any other commodity, the utility of labor-power, its use-value, belongs to the purchaser, the capitalist. It is his to use as he sees fit. He has it used to produce other commodities which he in turn hopes to sell--has the labor-power used up in the manufacture of other commodities, just as he has the raw materials used up. He buys, for example, the labor-power of the workers for a day of ten hours. In five hours, say, the worker creates value equivalent to his wages, but he does not cease at that point. He goes on working for another five hours, thus producing in a day double the amount of his wages, the exchange-value of the labor-power he sold the capitalist. Thus the capitalist, having paid wages equivalent to the product of five hours, receives the product of ten hours. This balance represents the surplus-value (Mehrwerth).

This takes place all through industry. If the capitalist employs a thousand workers under these conditions, each day he receives the product of five thousand hours over and above the product actually paid for. This constitutes his income. If the capitalist owned the land, machinery, and raw materials, absolutely, without incumbrances of any kind, the whole of that surplus-value would, naturally, belong to him. But as a general rule this is not the case. He rents the land and must pay rent to the landlord, or he works upon borrowed capital and must pay interest upon loans, so that the surplus-value extracted from the laborer must be divided into rent, interest, and profit. But how the surplus-value is divided among landlords, moneylenders, creditors, speculators, and actual employers is a matter of absolutely no moment to the workers as a class. That is why such movements as that represented by the followers of Henry George fail to vitally interest the working class. [177] The division of the surplus-value wrung from the toil of the workers gives rise to much quarrel and strife within the ranks of the exploiting class, but the working class recognizes, and vaguely and instinctively feels where it does not clearly recognize, that it has no interest in these quarrels. All that interests it vitally is how to lessen the extent of the exploitation to which it is subjected, and how ultimately to end that exploitation altogether. That is the objective of the movement for the socialization of the means of life.

Such, briefly stated, is the theory. We may illustrate it by the following example: Let us say the average cost of a day's subsistence is the product of five hours' social labor, which is represented by a wage of $1 per day. In a factory there are 1000 workers. Their labor-power they have sold at its exchange value, $1 per day per man, a total of $1000. They use up $1000 worth of labor-power, then. They also use up $1000 worth of raw material and wear out the plant to the extent of $100 in the course of their work. Now, instead of working five hours each, that being the amount of time necessary to reproduce the value of their wages, as above described, they all work ten hours. Thus, in place of the $1000 they received as wages for the labor-power they sold, they create labor ***products***, valued at just twice that sum, $2000. According to our suppositions, therefore, the gross value of the day's product will be $3100, the whole of it belonging to the capitalist, for the simple and sufficient reason that he bought and paid for, at their full value as commodities, all the elements entering into its production, the machinery, materials, and labor-power. The capitalist pays,--

For labor-power	$1000	
For materials	1000	
For repairs and replacement of machinery	100	

He receives, for the gross product	3100	$2100
The surplus-value is, therefore	1000	

and this sum is the fund from which rent, interests, and profits must be paid.

It will be observed that there is no moral condemnation of the capitalist involved in this illustration. He simply buys the commodity, labor-power, at its full market price, as in the case of all other commodities. No ethical argument enters into it at all. It is very evident, however, that the interest of the capitalist will be to get as much surplus-value as possible, by buying labor-power at the lowest price possible, prolonging the working day, and intensifying the productivity of the labor-power he buys, while the interest of the workman will be equally against these things. Here we have the cause of class antagonism--not in the speeches of agitators, but in the facts of industrial life.

This is the Marxian theory of surplus-value in a nutshell. Rent, interest, and profit, the three great divisions of capitalist income into which this surplus-value is divided, are thus traced to the exploitation of labor, resting fundamentally upon the ownership by the exploiting class of the means of production. Other economists, both before and since Marx, have tried to explain the source of capitalist income in very different ways. An early theory was that profit originates in exchange, through "buying cheap and selling dear." That this is so in the case of individual traders is obvious. If A sells to B commodities above their value, or buys commodities from him below their value, it is plain that he gains by it. But it is equally plain that B loses. If one group of capitalists gains what another group loses, the gains and losses balance each other; there is no gain to the capitalist class as a whole. Yet that is precisely what occurs--the capitalist class as a whole does gain, and gain enormously, despite the losses of individual members of that class. It is that gain to the great body of capitalists, that general increase in their wealth, which must be accounted for, and which exchange cannot explain. Only when we think of the capitalist class buying labor-power from outside its own ranks, generally at its natural value, and using it, is the problem solved. The commodity which the capitalist buys creates a value greater than its own in being used up.

The theory that profit is the wages of risk is answerable in substantially the same way. It does not in any way explain the increase in the aggregate wealth of the capitalist class to say that the individual capitalist must have a chance to receive interest upon his money in order to induce him to turn it into capital, to hazard losing it wholly or in part. While the theory of risk helps to explain some features of capitalism, the changes in the flow of capital into certain forms of investment, and, to some small extent, the commercial crises incidental thereto, it does not explain the vital problem, the source of capitalist income. The chances of gain, as a premium for the risks involved, explain satisfactorily enough the action of the gambler when he enters into a game of roulette or faro. It cannot be said, however, that the aggregate wealth of the gamblers is increased by playing roulette or faro. Then, too, the risks of the laborers are vastly more vital than those of the capitalist. Yet the premium for their risks of health and life itself does not appear, unless, indeed, it be in their wages, in which case the most superficial glance at our industrial statistics will show that wages are by no means highest in those occupations where the risks are greatest and most numerous. Further, the wages of the risks for capitalists and laborers alike are drawn from the same source, the product of the laborers' toil.

To consider, even briefly, all the varied theories of surplus-value other than these would be a prolonged, dull, and profitless task. The theory of abstinence, that profit is the just reward of the capitalist for saving part of his wealth and using it as a means of production, is answerable by *a priori* arguments and by a vast volume of facts. Abstinence obviously produces nothing; it can only save the wealth already produced by labor, and no automatic increase of that saved-up wealth is possible. If it is to increase without the labor of its owner, it can only be through the exploitation of the labor of others, so that the abstinence theory in no manner controverts the Marxian position. On the other hand, we see that those whose wealth increases most rapidly are not given to frugality or abstinence by any means. It may, certainly, be possible for an individual to save enough by practicing frugality and abstinence to enable him to invest in some profitable enterprise, but the source of his profit is not his abstinence. That must be sought elsewhere. Abstinence may provide him with the means for taking the profit, but the profit itself must come from the value created by human labor-power over and above its cost of production.

Still less satisfactory is the idea that surplus-value is nothing more than the "wages of superintendence," or the "rent of ability." This theory has been advocated with much specious argument. Essentially it involves the contention that there is no distinction between wages and profits, or between capitalists and laborers; that the capitalist is a worker, and his profits simply wages for his useful and highly important work of directing industry. It is a bold theory with a very small basis of fact. Whoever honestly considers it, must, one would think, see that it is both absurd and untrue. Not only is the larger part of industry to-day managed by salaried employees who have no part, or only a very insignificant part, in the ownership of the concerns they manage, but the profits are distributed among shareholders who, as shareholders, have never contributed service of any kind to the industries in which they are shareholders. Whatever services are performed, even by the figure-head "dummy" directors of companies, are paid for before profits are considered at all. This is the invincible answer to such criticisms as that of Mr. Mallock, that Marx and his followers have not recognized "the functions of the directive ability of the few." When all the salaries of the directing "few" have been paid, as well as the wages of the many, and the cost of all materials and maintenance of machinery, there remains a surplus to be distributed among those who belong neither to the "laboring many" nor the "directing few." That profit Mr. Mallock cannot explain away. Marx himself, in "Capital," called attention to the "directing ability of the few," quite as clearly as Mr. Mallock has done. He first shows how the "collective power of masses" is really a new creation; that it involves a special kind of leadership, or directing authority, just as an orchestra does; then he proceeds to point out the development of a special class of supervisors and directors of industry, "a special kind of wage laborer.... The ***work of supervision becomes their established and exclusive function***."[178] Socialists, contrary to Mr. Mallock, have not overlooked the function exercised by the directing few, but they have pointed out that when these have been paid, their salaries being sometimes almost fabulous, there is still a surplus-value to be distributed among those who have not shared in the production, either as mental or manual workers. As Mr. Algernon Lee says:--

"The profits produced in many American mills, factories, mines, and railway systems go in part to Englishmen or Belgians or Germans who never set foot in America, and who obviously can have no share in even the mental labor of direction. A certificate of stock may belong to a child, to a maniac, to an imbecile, to a prisoner behind the bars, and it draws profit for its owner just the same. Stocks and bonds may lie for months or years in a safe-deposit vault, while an estate is being disputed, before their ownership is determined; but whoever is declared to be the owner gets the dividends and interest "earned" during all that time."[179]

It is an easy task to set up imaginary figures labeled "Marxism," and then to demolish them by learned argument--but the occupation is as fruitless as it is easy. It remains the one central fact of capitalism, however, that a surplus-value is created by the working class and taken by the exploiting class, from which develops the class struggle of our time.

NOTES:

[163] *The People's Marx*, by Gabriel Deville, page 288.

[164] *Capital*, Vol. I, Kerr edition, page 41.

[165] Professor J. S. Nicholson, a rather pretentious critic of Marx, has called sunshine a commodity because of its utility, *Elements of Political Economy*, page 24. Upon the same ground, the song of the skylark and the sound of ocean waves might be called commodities. Such use of language serves for nothing but the obscuring of thought.

[166] William Petty, *A Treatise on Taxes and Constitutions* (1662), pages 31-32.

[167] *The Wealth of Nations*, Vol. I, Chapters V-VI.

[168] Benjamin Franklin, *Remarks and Facts Relative to the American Paper Money* (1764), page 267.

Marx thus speaks of Franklin as an economist: "The first sensible analysis of exchange-value as labor-time, made so clear as to seem almost commonplace, is to be found in the work of a man of the New World, where the bourgeois relations of production, imported together with their representatives, sprouted rapidly in a soil which made up its lack of historical traditions with a surplus of *humus*. That man was Benjamin Franklin, who formulated the fundamental law of modern political economy in his first work, which he wrote when a mere youth (A Modest Inquiry into the Nature and Necessity of a Paper Currency), and published in 1721." *A Contribution to the Critique of Political Economy*, by Karl Marx, English translation by N. I. Stone, 1894, page 62.

[169] David Ricardo, *Principles of Political Economy and Taxation*, Chapter I, Sec. III.

[170] *Wealth of Nations*, Book I, Chapter X.

[171] *Principles of Political Economy and Taxation*, Chapter I, Sec. 1, Sec. 4.

[172] See "The Final Futility of Final Utility," in H. M. Hyndman's *Economics of Socialism*, for a remarkable criticism of the "final utility" theory, showing its identity with the doctrine of supply and demand as the basis of value.

I refer to the theory of final or marginal utility as the "so-called Austrian theory" for the purpose, mainly, or calling attention to the fact that, as Professor Seligman has ably and clearly demonstrated, it was conceived and excellently stated by W. F. Lloyd, Professor of Political Economy at Oxford, in 1833. (See the paper, *On Some Neglected British Economists*, in the *Economic Journal*, V, xiii, pages 357-363.) This was two decades before Gossen and a generation earlier than Menger and Jevons. In view of this fact, the criticism of Marx for his lack of originality by members of the "Austrian" school is rather amusing.

[173] *Principles of Economics*, by Edwin R. A. Seligman (1905), page 198.

[174] Cf., for instance, my little volume, in the *Standard Socialist Series* (Kerr), entitled *Capitalist and Laborer*; Part II, *Modern Socialism*, page 112.

[175] *Principles of Political Economy and Taxation*, Chapter V, Sec. 35.

[176] *Value, Price, and Profit*, by Karl Marx, Chapter XIV.

[177] It is worthy of note that the taxation of land values, commonly associated with the name of Henry George, was advocated as a palliative in the *Communist Manifesto* of Marx and Engels.

[178] *Capital*, by Karl Marx, Vol. I, Chapter XIII, of Part IV.

[179] *The Worker* (New York), February 5, 1905.

CHAPTER IX
OUTLINES OF THE SOCIALIST STATE

I

Many persons who have thought of Socialism as a scheme, the plan of a new social edifice, have been disappointed not to find in all the voluminous writings of Marx any detailed description of such a plan, any forecast of the future. But when they have grasped the fundamental principles of the Marxian system of thought, they realize that it would be absurd to attempt to give detailed specifications of the Socialist state. As the Socialist movement has outgrown the influence of the early Utopians, its adherents have abandoned the habit of speculating upon the practical application of Socialist principles in future society. The formulation of schemes, more or less detailed, has given place to firm insistence that Socialism must be regarded as a principle, namely, the efficient organization of wealth production and distribution to the end that the exploitation of the wealth producers by a privileged class may be rendered impossible. Whatever contributes to that end is a contribution to the fulfillment of the Socialist ideal.

Still, it is natural and inevitable that earnest Socialists and students of Socialism should seek something more tangible by way of a description of the future state than the bald statement that it will be free from the struggle between exploiting and exploited classes. The question is, can we go further in our attempt to scan the future without entering the realms of Utopian speculation? If Socialism is, objectively considered, a state of society which is being developed in the womb of the present, are there any signs by which its peculiar form and spirit, as distinguished from the form and spirit of the present, may be visualized? Within certain limits, an affirmative answer seems possible to each of these questions. There are certain fundamental principles which may be said to be essential to the existence of Socialist society. Without them, the Socialist state cannot exist. Regardless of the fact that Karl Marx never attempted to describe his ideal, to give such a description of his concept of the next epoch in evolution as would enable us to compare it with the present and to measure the difference, it is probable that every Socialist makes, privately at least, his own forecast of the manner in which the new society must shape itself.

There is nothing Utopian or fantastic in trying to ascertain the tendencies of economic development; nothing unscientific in trying to read out of the pages of social evolution such lessons as may be contained therein. So long as we bear in mind that our forecasts must not take the form of plans for the arbitrary shaping of the future, specifications of the Cooeperative Commonwealth, but that they must, on the contrary, be based upon the facts of life--not abstract principles born in the heart's desire--and attempt to discern the tendencies of social and economic evolution, we are upon safe ground. Such forecasts may indeed be helpful, not only in so far as they provide us with a more or less concrete picture of the ideal to be aimed at, but also, and even more important, in that they at once enable us to gauge from time to time the progress made by society toward the realization of the ideal, and to formulate our policies most effectively. Especially as there are certain fundamental principles essential to the existence of a Socialist state, we may take these and correlate them, and these principles, together with our estimate of economic tendencies, drawn from the facts of the present, may provide us with a suggestive and approximate outline of the Socialist society of the future. So far we may proceed with full scientific sanction; beyond are the realms of fancy and dream, the Elysian Fields of Utopia.[180] We must not set about our task with the mental attitude so well displayed by the yearning of Omar--

> "Ah Love! could you and I with Him conspire
> To grasp this sorry Scheme of Things entire,
> Would not we shatter it to bits--and then
> Remold it nearer to the Heart's Desire!"

From that spirit only vain dreams and fantastic vagaries can ever come. What we must bear in mind is that the social fabric of to-morrow, like that of yesterday, whose ruins we contemplate to-day, will not spring up, complete, in response to our will, but will grow out of social experience and needs.

II

One of the greatest and most lamentable errors in connection with the propaganda of modern Socialism has been the assumption of its friends, in many instances, and its foes, in most instances, that Socialism and Individualism are entirely antithetical concepts. Infinite confusion has been caused by setting the two against each other. Society consists of an aggregation of individuals, but it is something more than that in just the same sense as a house is something more than an aggregation of bricks. It is an organism, though as yet an imperfectly developed one. While the units of which it is composed have distinct and independent lives within certain limits, they are, outside of those limits, interdependent and inter-related. Man is governed by two great forces. On the one hand, he is essentially an egoist, ever striving to attain individual freedom; on the other hand, he is a social animal, ever seeking association and avoiding isolation. This duality expresses itself in the life of society. There is a struggle between its members motived by the desire for individual expression and gain; and, alongside of it, a sense of solidarity, a movement to mutual, reciprocal relations, motived by the gregarian instinct. All social life is necessarily an oscillation between these two motives. The social problem in its last analysis is nothing more than the problem of combining and harmonizing social and individual interests and actions springing therefrom.

In dealing with this social problem, the problem of how to secure harmony of social and individual interests and actions, it is necessary first of all to recognize that both motives are equally important and necessary agents of human progress. The idea largely prevails that Socialists ignore the individual motive and consider only the social motive, just as the ultra-individualists have erred in an opposite discrimination. The Socialist ideal has been conceived to be a great bureaucracy. Mr. Anstey gave humorous and vivid expression to this idea in **Punch** some years ago, when he represented the citizens of the Socialist state as being all clothed alike, known only by numbers, strangers to all the joys of family life, plodding through their allotted tasks under a race of hated bureaucrats, and having the solace of chewing gum in their leisure time as a specially paternal provision. Some such mental picture must have inspired Herbert Spencer's "Coming Slavery," and it must be confessed that the early forms of Socialism which consisted mainly of detailed plans of cooeperative commonwealths afforded some excuse for the idea. Most intelligent Socialists, if called upon to choose between them, would probably prefer to live in Thibet under a personal despotism, rather than under the hierarchies of most of the imaginary commonwealths which Utopian Socialists have depicted.

Even in the later propaganda of the modern political Socialist movement, there has been more than enough justification for those who regard Socialism as impossible except under a great bureaucracy. In numberless Socialist programmes and addresses Socialism has been defined as meaning "The social ownership and control of all the means of production, distribution, and exchange." Critics of Socialism are not to be seriously blamed if they take such "definitions" at their face value and interpret them quite literally. It is not difficult to see that in order to place "all means of production, distribution, and exchange" under social ownership and control, the creation of such a bureaucracy as the world has never seen would be necessary. A needle is a means of production quite as much as an electric power machine in a factory is, the difference being in their degrees of efficiency. A jackknife is, likewise, in certain circumstances, a means of production, just as surely as a powerful planing machine is, the difference being in degrees of efficiency. So a market basket is a means of distribution quite as surely as an ocean steamship is; a wheelbarrow quite as much as a locomotive. They differ in degrees of efficiency, that is all. The idea that the housewife in the future, when she wants to sew a button upon a garment, will be obliged to go to some department and "take out" a needle, having it properly checked in the communal accounts, and being responsible for its return, is, of course, worthy only of opera bouffe. So is the notion of the state owning wheelbarrows and market baskets and making their private ownership illegal. "The socialization of *all* the means of production, distribution, and exchange," literally interpreted, is folly. But none of those using the phrase must be regarded as seriously contemplating its literal interpretation. For many years the phrase was included in the statement of its "Object" by the English Social Democratic Federation, and even now it appears in a slightly modified form, the word "all" being omitted,[181] perhaps because of its tautological character. For several years the writer was a member of the Federation, actively engaged in the propaganda, and how we spent much of our time explaining to popular audiences in halls and upon street corners that the socialization of jackknives, needles, sewing machines, market baskets, beer mugs, frying pans, and toothpicks was not our aim, is a merry memory.

When this is understood, the nightmare of the bureaucracy of Socialism vanishes. It is no longer necessary to fret ourselves asking how a government is to own and manage everything without making slaves of its citizens. The question propounded by that venerable and distinguished Canadian scholar, Professor Goldwin Smith,[182] whether a government can be devised which shall hold all the instruments of production, distribute to the citizens their tasks, pick out inventors, philosophers, artists, and laborers, and set them to work, without destroying personal liberty, loses its force when it is remembered that Socialism involves no such necessity.

The Socialist ideal may be said to be a form of social organization in which every individual will enjoy the greatest possible amount of freedom for self-development and expression; and in which social authority will be reduced to the minimum necessary for the preservation and insurance of that right to all individuals. There is an incontestable right of the individual to full and free self-development and expression so long as no other individual's right to a like freedom is infringed upon. No individual right can be an **absolute** right in a society, but must be subject to such restrictions as may be necessary to safeguard the like right of every other individual, and of society as a whole. **Absolute** personal liberty is not possible; to grant it to any one individual would be equivalent to denying it to others. If, in a certain community, a need is commonly felt for a system of drainage to protect the citizens against the perils of a possible outbreak of typhoid or some other epidemic disease, and all the citizens agree upon a scheme except two or three, who, in the name of personal liberty, declare that their property must not be touched, what is to be done? If the citizens, out of solicitude for the personal liberty of the objecting individuals, abandon or modify their plans, is it not clear that the liberty of the many has been sacrificed to the liberty of the few, which is the essence of tyranny?

Absolute individual liberty is incompatible with social liberty. The liberty of each must, in Mill's phrase, be bounded by the like liberty of all. Absolute personal liberty is a chimera, a delusion.

Even the Anarchist must come to a realization of the fact that liberty is not an absolute, but a relative and limited, right. Kropotkin, for example, realizes that, even under Anarchism, any individual who did not live up to his obligations, or who persisted in conducting himself in a manner obnoxious or injurious to the community, would have to be expelled.[183] This is very like Spencer's practical abandonment of the doctrine of *laissez faire* individualism. Says he: "Many facts have shown us that while the individual man has acquired liberty as a citizen and greater religious liberty, he has also acquired greater liberty in respect of his occupations; and here we see that he has simultaneously acquired greater liberty of combination for industrial purposes. Indeed, in conformity with the universal law of rhythm, ***there has been a change from excess of restriction to deficiency of restriction***. As is implied by legislation now pending, the facilities for forming companies and raising compound capitals have been too great."[184] Here is a very definite confession of the insufficiency of natural law, the failure of the *laissez faire* theory, and a virtual appeal for restrictive and coercive legislation.

This is inevitable. The dual forces which serve as the motives of individual and collective action, spring, unquestionably, from the fact that individuals are at once alike and unlike, equal and unequal. Alike in our needs of certain fundamental necessities, such as food, clothing, shelter, cooeeperation for producing these necessities, for protection from foes, human and other, we are unlike in tastes, appetites, temperaments, character, will, and so on, till our diversity becomes as great and as general as our likeness. Now, the problem is to insure equal opportunities of full development to all these diversely constituted and endowed individuals, and, at the same time, to maintain the principle of equal obligations to society on the part of every individual. This is the problem of social justice: to insure to each the same social opportunities, to secure from each a recognition of the same obligations toward all. The basic principle of the Socialist state must be justice; no privileges or favors can be extended to individuals or groups of individuals.

III

Politically, the organization of the Socialist state must be democratic. Socialism without democracy is as impossible as a shadow without light. The word "Socialism" applied to schemes of paternalism, and to government ownership when the vital principle of democracy is lacking, is a misnomer. As with Peter Bell--

"A primrose by a river's brim,   A yellow primrose was to him"

and nothing more than that, so there are many persons to whom Socialism signifies nothing more than government ownership. Yet it ought to be perfectly clear that Russia, with her state-owned railways, and liquor and other monopolies, is no nearer Socialism than the United States. The same applies to Germany with her state railways. Externally similar in one respect to Socialism, they radically differ. In so far as they prepare the necessary forms for Socialism, all examples of public ownership may be said to be "socialistic," or making for Socialism. What they lack is a spiritual quality rather than a mechanical one. They are not democratic. Socialism is political democracy allied to industrial democracy.

Justice requires that the legislative power of society rest upon universal adult suffrage, the political equality of all men and women, except lunatics and criminals. It is manifestly unjust to exact obedience to the laws from those who have had no share in making them and can have no share in altering them. Of course, there are exceptions to this principle. We except (1) minors, children not yet arrived at the age of responsibility agreed upon by the citizens; (2) lunatics and certain classes of criminals; (3) aliens, non-citizens temporarily resident in the state.

Democracy in the sense of popular self-government, the "government of the people, by the people, and for the people," of which political rhetoricians boast, is only approximately attainable in any society. While all can equally participate in the legislative power, all cannot participate directly in the administrative power, and it becomes necessary, therefore, to adopt the principle of delegated authority, representative government. But care must be taken to preserve a maximum of power in the hands of the people. In this respect the United States Constitution is defective. It is not, and was not intended by its framers to be, a democratic instrument,[185] and we are vainly trying to-day to make democratic government through an undemocratic medium. The political democracy of the Socialist state must be real, keeping the power of government in the hands of the people.

How is this to be done? Direct legislation by the people might be realized through the adoption of the principles of popular initiative and referendum. Or, if representative legislative bodies should be deemed best, these measures, together with proportional representation and the right of recall, might be adopted. There is no apparent reason why *all* legislation, except temporary legislation as in war time, famine, plague, and such abnormal conditions, could not be directly initiated and enacted, leaving only the just and proper enforcement of the law to delegated authority. In practically all the political programmes of Socialist parties throughout the world, these principles are included at the present time; not merely as means to secure a greater degree of political democracy within the existing social state, but also, and primarily, to prepare the required political framework of democracy for the industrial commonwealth of the future.

The great problem for such a society, politically speaking, consists in choosing wisely the trustees of delegated power and authority, and seeing that they justly and wisely use it for the common good, without abuse, either for the profit of themselves or their friends, and without prejudice to any portion of society. Will there be abuses? Will not political manipulators and bosses betray their trusts? To these questions, and all other questions of a like nature, the Socialist can only give one answer, namely, that there is no such a thing as an "automatic democracy," that eternal vigilance will be the price of liberty under Socialism as it has ever been. There can be no other safeguard against the usurpation of power than the popular will and conscience ever alert upon the watch-towers. With political machinery so responsive to the popular will when it is asserted and an alert and vigilant electorate, political democracy attains its maximum development. Socialism requires that development.

IV

With these general principles prevised, we may consider, briefly, the respective rights of the individual and of society. The rights of the individual may be summarized as follows: There must be freedom of movement, including the right to withdraw from the domain of the government, to migrate at will to other territories. Freedom of movement is a fundamental condition of personal liberty, but it is easy to see that it cannot be made an absolute right. Quarantine laws, for social protection, for example, may seriously inconvenience the individual, but be imperatively necessary for all that. There must be immunity from arrest, except for infringing others' rights, with compensation of some kind for improper arrest; respect of the privacy of domicile and correspondence; full liberty of dress, subject to decency; freedom of utterance, whether by speech or publication, subject only to the protection of others from insult, injury, or interference with their equal liberties, the individual being held responsible to society for the proper use of that right. Freedom of the individual in all that pertains to art, science, philosophy, and religion, and their teaching, or propaganda, is essential. The state can have nothing to do with these matters, they belong to the personal life alone.[186] Art, science, philosophy, and religion cannot be protected by any authority of the state, nor is such authority needed.

Subject to the ultimate control of society, certainly, but normally free from collective authority and control, these may be regarded as imperative rights of the individual. Doubtless many Socialists, in common with many Individualists, would considerably extend the list. Some, for instance, would include the right to possess and bear arms for the defense of person and property. On the other hand, it might be objected with good show of reason by other Socialists that such a right must always be liable to abuses imperiling the peace of society, and that the same ends would be served more surely if individual armament were made impossible. Again, some Socialists, like some Individualists, would include in the category of private acts outside the sphere of law and social authority the union of the sexes. They would do away with legal intervention in marriage and make it and the parental relation exclusively a private concern. On the other hand, probably an overwhelming majority of Socialists would object. They would insist that the state must, in the interest of the children, and for its own self-preservation, assume certain responsibilities for, and exercise a certain control over, all marriages. They would have the state insist upon such conditions as mature age, freedom from dangerous diseases and physical defects. While believing that under Socialism marriage would no longer be subject to economic motives,--matrimonial markets for titles and fortunes no longer existing,--and that the maximum of personal freedom together with the minimum of social authority would be possible in the union of the sexes, they would still insist upon the necessity of that minimum of legal control.

The abolition of the legal marriage tie, and the substitution therefor of voluntary sex union, which so many people believe to be part of the Socialist programme, is not only not a part of that programme, but is probably condemned by more than ninety-five per cent of the Socialists of the world, and favored by no appreciable proportion of Socialists more than non-Socialists. There is no such thing as a Socialist view of marriage, any more than there is a Republican or Democratic view of marriage; or any more than there is a Socialist view of vaccination, vivisection, vegetarianism, or homeopathy. The same may be said of the drink evil and tobacco smoking. Some Socialists would prohibit both smoking and drinking; others would permit smoking, but prohibit the manufacture of intoxicating liquors; most Socialists recognize the evils, especially of drunkenness, but believe that it would be foolish at this time to state in what manner the evils must be dealt with by the Socialist state.

Our hasty summary by no means exhausts the category of personal liberties, nor does it rigidly define such liberties. To presume to do that would be a piece of charlatanry, social quackery of the worst type. It is not for the Socialist of to-day to determine what the citizens of a generation hence shall do. The citizens of the future, like the citizens of to-day, will be living human beings, not mere automatons; they will not accept places and forms imposed upon them, but make their own. The object of this phase of our discussion is simply to show that individual freedom would by no means be crushed out of existence by the Socialist state. The intolerable bureaucracy of collectivism is wholly an imaginary evil. There is nothing in the nature of Socialism as it is understood to-day by its adherents which would prevent a wide extension of personal liberties in the social regime.

In the same general manner, we may summarize the principal functions of the state[187] as follows: the state has the right and power to organize and control the economic system, comprehending in that term the production and distribution of all social wealth, wherever private enterprise is dangerous to the social well-being, or is inefficient; the defense of the community from invasion, from fire, flood, famine, or disease; the relations with other states, such as trade agreements, boundary treaties, and the like; the maintenance of order, including the juridical and police systems in all their branches; and public education in all its departments. It will be found that these five functions include all the services which the state may properly undertake, and that not one of them can safely be intrusted to private enterprise. On the other hand, it is not at all necessary to assume that the state must have an ***absolute monopoly*** of any one of these groups of functions in the social organism. It would not be necessary, for example, for the state to prohibit its citizens from entering into voluntary relations with the citizens of other countries for the promotion of international friendship, for trade reciprocity, and so on. Likewise, the juridical functions being in the hands of the state would not prevent voluntary arbitration; or the state guardianship of the public health prevent voluntary associations of citizens from taking measures to advance the health of their communities. On the contrary, all such efforts would be advantageous to the state. Our study becomes, therefore, a study of social physiology.

The principle already postulated, that the state must undertake the production and distribution of wealth wherever private enterprise is dangerous, or inefficient, clarifies somewhat the problem of the industrial organization of the Socialist regime, which is a vastly more difficult problem than that of its political organization. Socialism by no means involves the suppression of all private industrial enterprises. Only when these fail in efficiency or result in injustice and inequality of opportunities does socialization present itself. There are many petty, subordinate industries, especially the making of articles of luxury, which might be well allowed to remain in private hands, subject only to such general regulation as might be found necessary for the protection of health and the public order. For example, suppose that the state undertakes the production of shoes upon a large scale as a result of the popular conviction that private enterprise in shoemaking is either inefficient or injurious to society in that the manufacturers exploit the shoemakers on the one hand, and, through the establishment of monopoly-prices, the consumers upon the other hand. The state thus becomes the employer of shoeworkers and the vender of shoes to the citizens. But A, being a fastidious citizen, does not like the factory product of the state any more than he formerly did the factory product of private enterprise. Under the old conditions, he used to employ B, a shoemaker who does not like factory work, a craftsman who likes to make the whole shoe. Naturally, B was not willing to work for wages materially lower than those he could earn in the factory. A willingly paid enough for his hand-made shoes to insure B as much wages as he would get in the factory. What reason could the state possibly have for forbidding the continuance of such an arrangement between two of its citizens?

Or take the case of a farmer maintaining himself and family upon a modest acreage, by his own labor. He exploits no one, and the question of inefficiency does not present itself as a public question, for the reason that there is plenty of farming land available, and any inefficiency of the small farmer does not injure the community in any manner. What object could the state have in taking away that farm and compelling the farmer to work upon a communal, publicly owned and managed farm? Of course, the notion is perfectly absurd.[188] On the other hand, there are things, natural monopolies, which cannot be safely left to private enterprise. The same is true of large productive and distributive enterprises upon which great masses of the people depend. Land ownership[189] and all that depends thereon, such as mining, transportation, and the like, must be collective.

It will help us to get rid of the difficulty presented by petty industry and agriculture if we bear in mind that collective ownership is not, as is commonly supposed, the supreme, fundamental condition of Socialism. It is proposed only as a means to an end, not as the end itself. The wealth producers are exploited by a class whose source of income is the surplus-value extracted from the workers. Instinctively, the workers struggle against that exploitation, to reduce the amount of surplus-value taken by the capitalists to a minimum. To do away with that exploitation social ownership and control is proposed. If the end could be attained more speedily by other methods, those methods would be adopted. It follows, therefore, that to make collective property of things not used as a means of exploiting labor does not necessarily form part of the Socialist programme. True, some such things might be socialized in response to an urgent demand for efficiency, but, of necessity, the struggle will be principally concerned with the socializing of the means of production which are used as means of exploitation by a class deriving its income from the surplus-value produced by another class. It is easy enough to see that, according to this principle of differentiation, it would be necessary to socialize the railroad, but not at all necessary to socialize the wheelbarrow; while it would be necessary to socialize a clothing factory, it would not be necessary to take away a woman's domestic sewing machine. Independent, self-employment, as in the case of a craftsman working in his own shop with his own tools, or groups of workers working cooeperatively, is quite consistent with Socialism.

In the Socialist state, then, certain forms of private industry will be tolerated, and perhaps even definitely encouraged by the state, but the great fundamental economic activities will be collectively managed. The Socialist state will not be static and, consequently, what at first may be regarded as being properly the subject of private enterprise may develop to an extent or in directions which necessitate its transformation to the category of essentially social properties. Hence, it is not possible to give a list of things which would be socialized and another list of things which would remain private property, but perfectly possible to state the principle which must be the chief determinant of the extent of socialization. With this principle in mind it is fairly possible to sketch the outlines at least of the economic development of the collectivist commonwealth; the conditions essential to that stage of social evolution at which it will be possible and natural to speak of capitalism as a past and outgrown stage, and of the present as the era of Socialism.

Socialists, naturally, differ very materially upon this point. Probably, however, an overwhelming majority of the leaders of Socialist thought in Europe and this country would agree with the writer that it is fairly probable that the economic structure of the new society will include at least the following measures of socialization: (1) Ownership of all natural resources, such as land, mines, forests, waterways, oil wells, and so on; (2) operation of all the means of transportation and communication other than those of purely personal service; (3) operation of all industrial production involving large compound capitals and associated labor, except where carried on by voluntary, democratic cooeperation, with the necessary regulation by the state; (4) organization of all labor essential to the public service, such as the building of schools, hospitals, docks, roads, bridges, sewers, and the like; the construction of all the machinery and plant requisite to the social production and distribution, and of things necessary for the maintenance of those engaged in such public services as the national defense and all who are wards of the state; (5) a monopoly of the monetary and credit functions, including coinage, banking, mortgaging, and the extension of credit to private enterprise.

With these economic activities undertaken by the state, a pure democracy differing vitally from all the class-dominated states of history, private enterprise would by no means be excluded, but limited to an extent making the exploitation of labor and public needs and interests for private gain impossible. Socialism thus becomes the defender of individual liberty, not its enemy.

V

As owner of the earth and all the major instruments of production and exchange, society would occupy a position which would enable it to insure that the physical and mental benefits derived from its wealth, its natural resources, its collective experience, genius, and labor, were universalized as befits a democracy. It would be able to guarantee to all its citizens the right to labor, through preventing private or class monopolization of the land and instruments of production and social opportunities in general. It would be in a position to make every development from competition to monopoly the occasion for further socialization. Thus there would be no danger to the state in permitting, or even fostering, private industry within the limits described. As the organizer of the vast body of labor essential to the operation of the main productive and distributive functions of society, and to the other public services, the state would automatically, so to speak, set the standards of income and leisure which private industry would be compelled, by competitive force, to observe. The regulation of production, too, would be possible, and as a result the crises arising from glutted markets would disappear. Finally, in the control of all the functions of credit, the state would effectually prevent the exploitation of the mass of the people through financial agencies, one of the greatest evils of our present system.

The application of the principles of democracy to the organization and administration of these great economic services of production, exchange, and credit is a problem full of alluring invitations to speculation. "This that they call the Organization of Labor," said Carlyle, "is the Universal Vital Problem of the World." This description applies not to what we commonly mean by the "organization of labor," namely, the organization of the laborers in unions for class conflict, but to the organization of the brain and muscle of the world to secure the greatest efficiency. This is the great central problem of the socialization of industry and the state, before which all other problems pale into insignificance. It is comparatively easy to picture an ideal political democracy; and the main structural economic organization of the Socialist regime, with its private and public functions more or less clearly defined, is not very difficult of conception. These are foreshadowed with varying degrees of distinctness in present society, and the light of experience illumines the pathway before us. It is when we come to the methods of organization and management, the *spirit* of the economic organization of the future state, that the light fails and we must grope our way into the great unknown with imagination and our sense of justice for guides.

Most Socialist writers who have attempted to deal with this subject have simply regarded the state as the greatest employer of labor, carrying on its business upon lines not materially different from those adopted by the great corporations of to-day. Boards of experts, chosen by civil service methods, directing all the economic activities of the state--such is their general conception of the industrial democracy of the Socialist regime. They believe, in other words, that the methods now employed by the capitalist state, and by individual and corporate employers within the capitalist state, would simply be extended under the Socialist regime. If this be so, a psychological anomaly in the Socialist propaganda appears in the practical abandonment of the claim that, as a result of the class conflict in society, the public ownership evolved within the capitalist state is essentially different from, and inferior to, the public ownership of the Socialist ideal. It is perfectly clear that if the industrial organization under Socialism is to be such that the workers employed in any industry have no more voice in its management than the postal employees in this country, for example, have at the present time, it cannot be otherwise than absurd to speak of it as an industrial democracy.

Here, in truth, lies the crux of the greatest problem of all. We must face the fact that, in anything worthy the name of an industrial democracy, the terms and conditions of employment cannot be wholly decided without regard to the will of the workers themselves on the one hand, nor, on the other hand, by the workers alone without reference to the general body of the citizenry. If the former method fails to satisfy the requirements of democracy by ignoring the will of the workers in the organization of their work, the alternate method involves a hierarchical government, equally incompatible with democracy. Some way must be found by which the industrial government of society, the organization of production and distribution, may be securely and fairly based upon the dual basis of common civic rights and the rights of the workers in their special relations as such.

And here we are not wholly left to our imaginations, not wholly without experience to guide us. In actual practice to-day, in those industries in which the organization of the workers into unions has been most successful, the workers, through their organizations, do exercise a certain amount of control over the conditions of their employment. Their right to share in the determination of the conditions of labor is conceded. They make trade agreements, for instance, in which such matters as wages, hours of labor, apprenticeship, output, engagement and discharge of workers, and numerous other matters, are provided for and made subject to the joint control of the workers and their employers. Of course, this share in the control of the industry in which they are employed is a right enjoyed only as a fruit of conquest, won by war and maintained by ceaseless vigilance and armed strength. It is not inconceivable that in the Socialist state there might be a frank extension of this principle. The workers in the main groups of industries might form autonomous organizations for the administration of their special interests, subject only to certain fundamental laws of the state. Thus the trade unions of to-day would evolve into administrative politico-economic organizations, after the manner of the mediaeval guilds, and become constructive agencies in society instead of mere agencies of class warfare as at present.

The economic organization of the Socialist state would consist, then, of three distinct divisions, as follows: (1) Private production and exchange, subject only to such general supervision and control by the state as the interests of society demand, such as protection against monopolization, sanitary laws, and the like; (2) voluntary cooeperation, subject to similar supervision and control; (3) production and distribution by the state, the administration to be by the autonomous organizations of the workers in industrial groups, subject to the fundamental laws and government of society as a whole.[190]

VI

Two other functions of the economic organization of society remain to be considered, the distribution of labor and its remuneration. In the organization of industry society will have to achieve a twofold result, a maximum of general, social efficiency, on the one hand, and of personal liberty and comfort to the workers on the other. The state would not only guarantee the right to labor, but, as a corollary, it would impose the duty of labor upon every competent person. The Pauline injunction, "If any man will not work, neither shall he eat," would be applied in the Socialist state to all except the incompetent to labor. The immature child, the aged, the sick and infirm members of society, would alone be exempted from labor. The result of this would be that instead of a large unemployed army, vainly seeking the right to work, on the one hand, accompanied by the excessive overwork of the great mass of the workers fortunate enough to be employed, a vast increase in the number of producers from this one cause alone would make possible much greater leisure for the whole body of workers. Benjamin Franklin estimated that in his day four hours' labor from every adult male able to work would be more than sufficient to provide wealth enough for human wants; and it is certain that, without resorting to any standards of Spartan simplicity, Franklin's estimate could be easily realised to-day with anything approaching a scientific organization of labor.

Not only would the productive forces be enormously increased by the absorption of those workers who under the present system are unemployed, and those who do not labor or seek labor; in addition to these, there would be a tremendous transference of potential productive energy from occupations rendered obsolete and unnecessary by the socialization of society. Thus there are to-day tens of thousands of bankers, lawyers, traders, middlemen, speculators, advertisers, and others, whose functions, necessary to the capitalist system, would in most cases disappear. Because of this, they would be compelled to enter the producing class. The possibilities of the scientific organization of industry are therefore almost unlimited. Every gain made by the state in the direction of economy of production would test the private enterprise existing and urge it onward in the same direction. Likewise, every gain made by the private producers would test the social production and urge it onward. Whether socialized production extended its sphere, or remained confined to its minimum limitations, would depend upon the comparative success or failure resulting. The state would not be a force outside of the people, arbitrarily extending its functions regardless of their will. The decision would rest with the people; they would *be* the state, and would, naturally, resort to social effort only where it demonstrated its ability to serve the community more efficiently than private enterprise, with greater comfort and liberty to the individual and to the community.

While in the Socialist regime labor would be compulsory, it is inconceivable that a free people would tolerate a bureaucratic rule assigning to each individual his or her proper task, no matter how ingenious the assignment might be. Even if the bureaucracy were omniscient, such a condition of life would be intolerable. Just as it is necessary to insist that all must be secured in their right to labor, and required to labor, it is necessary also that the choice of one's occupation should be as far as possible personal and free, subject only to the laws of supply and demand. The greatest amount of personal freedom compatible with the requisite efficiency would be secured to the workers in their chosen occupations through their craft organizations.

But, it will be objected, all occupations are not equally desirable. There are certain forms of work which, disagreeable in themselves, are just as essential to the well-being of society as the most artistic and pleasing. Who will do the dirty work, and the dangerous work, under Socialism? Will these occupations also be left to choice, and, if so, will there not be an insurmountable difficulty arising from the natural reluctance of men to choose such work?

In answering the question and affirming the principle of free choice--for so it must be answered--the Socialist is called upon to show that the absence of compulsion would not involve the neglect of these disagreeable, but highly important, social services; that it would be compatible with social safety to leave them to personal choice. In the first place, much of this kind of work that is now performed by human labor could be more efficiently done by mechanical means. Much of the work done by sweated women and children in our cities is in fact done in competition with machines. Machinery has been invented, and is now available, to do thousands of the disagreeable and hurtful things now done by human beings. Professor Franklin H. Giddings is perfectly right when he says: "Modern civilization does not require, it does not need, the drudgery of needle-women or the crushing toil of men in a score of life-destroying occupations. If these wretched beings should drop out of existence and no others take their places, the economic activities of the world would not greatly suffer. A thousand devices latent in inventive brains would quickly make good any momentary loss."[191]

When, in England, a law was passed forbidding the practice of forcing little boys through chimneys, to clean them, chimneys did not cease to be swept. Other, less disagreeable and less dangerous, means were quickly invented. When the woolen manufacturers were prevented from employing little boys and girls, they invented the piecing machine.[192] Thousands of instances might be compiled in support of the contention of Professor Giddings, equally as pertinent as these. Another important point is that the amount of such disagreeable and dangerous work to be done would be very much less than now. That would be an inevitable result of the scientific organization of industry. It is likely that, if the subject could be properly investigated, it could be shown that the amount of such labor involved in wasteful and unnecessary advertising alone is enormous.

Addressing an audience composed mainly of scientific men upon the subject of Socialism, the writer was once questioned upon this phase of the subject. "Gentlemen," was the reply, "it is impossible for me to say exactly how the intelligence of the people in a more or less remote future will solve the problem. The Socialist state will be a democracy, not a dictatorship. But if I were dictator of society to-day and wanted to solve the problem, I should assign to such men as yourselves all the most disagreeable and dangerous tasks I could find. This I should do because I should know that at once your inventive brains would begin to devise mechanical and other means of doing the work. You would make sewer cleaning as pleasant as any other occupation in the world." There was, of course, nothing original in the reply, but the men of science recognized its force, and it fairly states one important part of the Socialist answer to the objection we are discussing. Still, with all possible reduction of the quantity of such work to be done, and with all the mechanical genius brought to bear upon it, we may freely concede that, for a long time to come, there must be some work quite dangerous, altogether disagreeable and repellent, and a great difference in the degree of attractiveness of some occupations as compared with some others. But an occupation repellent in itself might be made attractive, if the hours of labor were relatively few as compared with other occupations. If six hours be regarded as the normal working day, it is quite easy to believe that, for sake of the larger leisure, with its opportunities for the pursuit of special interests, many a man would gladly accept a disagreeable position for three hours a day.

The same holds true of superior remuneration. Under the Socialist regime, just as to-day, many a man would gladly exchange his work for less pleasant work, if the remuneration offered were higher. To the old Utopian ideas of absolute equality and uniformity of income these methods would be fatal, but they are not at all incompatible with modern, scientific Socialism. Nothing could well be sillier, or more futile, than the Rooseveltian attacks upon the Socialism of to-day as if it meant equality of possession, or equality of anything except opportunity.[193] Finally, in connection with this question, we must not forget that there is a natural inequality of talent, of power. In any state of society most men will prefer to do the things they are best fitted for, the things they can do best. The man who feels himself to be best fitted to be a hewer of wood or a drawer of water will choose that rather than some loftier task. There is no reason at all to suppose that leaving the choice of occupation to the individual would involve the slightest risk to society.

While equality of remuneration, meaning by that uniformity of reward for labor, is not an essential condition of the Socialist regime, it may be freely admitted that ***approximate equality of income*** is the ideal to be ultimately aimed at. Otherwise, if there should be the present inequality of remuneration, represented by the enormous salary of a manager like Mr. Schwab, to quote a conspicuous example, and the meager wage of the average laborer, class formations must take place and the old problems incidental to economic inequality reappear. There is no need to regard uniformity of reward for all as the only solution of this problem, however. Given such an industrial democracy as is herein suggested as the essential condition of Socialism, there is little reason to doubt that gradually, by the free play of economic law, approximate equality would be attained. This brings us to the method of the remuneration of labor.

VII

Socialists are too often judged by their shibboleths, rather than by the principles which those shibboleths imperfectly express, or seek to express. Declaiming, rightly, against the wages system as a form of slave labor,[194] the "abolition of wage slavery," forever inscribed on their banners, the average man is forced to the conclusion that the Socialists are working for a system in which the workers will divide their actual products and then barter the surplus for the surplus products of other workers. Either that, or the most rigid system of governmental production and a method of distributing rations and uniforms similar to that which obtains in the military organization of present-day governments. It is easily seen, however, that such plans do not conform to the democratic ideals of the Socialists, on the one hand, nor would either of them, on the other hand, be compatible with the wide personal liberty herein put forward as characteristic of the Socialist state.

The earlier Utopian Socialists did propose to do away with wages; in fact, they proposed to do away with money altogether, and invented various forms of "Labor Notes" as a means of giving equality of remuneration for given quantities of labor, and providing a medium for the exchange of wealth. But when the Socialists of to-day speak of the "abolition of wages," or of the wages system, they use the words in the same sense as they speak of the abolition of capital: ***they would abolish only the social relations implied in the terms***. Just as they do not mean by the abolition of capital the destruction of the machinery and implements of production, but the social relation in which they are used to create profit for the few, so, when they speak of the abolition of the wages system, they mean only the use of wages to exploit the producers for the gain of the owners of the means of production and exchange. Though the name "wages" might not be changed, a money payment for labor in a democratic arrangement of industry, representing an approximation to the full value of the labor, minus only its share of the cost of maintaining the public services, and the weaker, dependent members of society, would be vastly different from a money payment for labor by one individual to other individuals, representing an approximation to their cost of living, bearing no definite relation to the value of their labor products, and paid in lieu of those products with a view to the gathering of a rich surplus value by the payer.

Karl Kautsky, perhaps the greatest living exponent of the theories of modern Socialism, has made this point perfectly clear. He accepts without reserve the belief that wages, unequal and paid in money, will be the method of remuneration for labor in the Socialist regime.[195] When too many laborers rush into certain branches of industry, the natural way to lessen their number and to increase the number of laborers in other branches where there is need for them, will be to reduce wages in the one and to increase them in the other. Socialism, instead of being defined as an attempt to make men equal, might perhaps be more justly and accurately defined as a social system based upon the natural inequalities of mankind. Not human equality, but equality of opportunity, and the prevention of the creation of artificial inequalities by privilege, is the essence of Socialism.

What, it may be asked, will society do to prevent the hoarding of wealth on the one hand, and the exploitation of the spendthrift by the abstinent upon the other? Here, as throughout this discussion, we must be careful to refrain from laying down dogmatic rules, giving categorical replies to questions which the future will settle in its own way. At best, we can only reason as to what possible answers are compatible with the fundamental principles of Socialism. Thus we may safely answer that in the Socialist regime society will not attempt to dictate to the individual how he shall spend his income. If Jones prefers ***objets d'art***, and Smith prefers fast horses or a steam yacht, each will be free to follow his inclinations so far as his resources will permit. If, on the contrary, one should prefer to hoard his wealth, he would be free to do so. The inheritance of such accumulated property, other than personal objects, of course, might be denied, the state being made the only possible inheritor of such accumulated property. Even in the absence of such a regulation, the inheritance of hoarded wealth would not be a serious matter and would speedily adjust itself. There would be no opportunity for its ***investment***, so that at most individuals inheriting such property would be enabled to live idly, or with extra luxury, until it was spent. The fact of inheriting property would not give the individual power over the life and labor of others. By either method, full play for individual liberty would be coupled with full economic security for society. There would be no danger of the development of a ruling class as a result of natural inequalities.

With such conditions as these, it is not difficult nor in any sense romantic to suppose that the tendency to hoard wealth would largely disappear. In the same way we must regard the possibilities of the exploitation of man by man developing in the Socialist state, through the wastefulness and improvidence of the one and the frugality, abstinence, and cunning of the other, as slight. With the credit functions entirely in the hands of the state, the improvident man would be able to obtain credit upon the same securities as from a private creditor, without extortion. Society would further secure itself against the weakness and failure of the improvident by insuring all its members against sickness, accident, and old age.

VIII

The administration of justice is necessarily a social function in a democratic society. All juridical functions should be socialized in the strict sense of being maintained at the social expense for the free service of its citizens. Court fees, advocates' charges, and other expenses incidental to the administration of justice in present society are all anti-democratic and subversive of justice.

Finally, education is likewise a social necessity which society itself must assume responsibility for. We have discovered that for self-protection society must insist upon a certain minimum of education for every child able to receive it; that it is too vital a matter to be left to the option of parents or the desires of the immature child. We have made a certain minimum of education compulsory and free; the Socialist state would make a minimum--probably much larger than our present minimum--compulsory, but it would also make *all* education free. From the first stages, in the kindergartens, to the last, in the universities, education must be wholly free or equality of opportunity cannot be realized. So long as a single barrier exists to prevent any child from receiving all the education it is capable of profiting by, democracy is unattained.

Whether the Socialist state could tolerate the existence of elementary schools other than its own, such as privately conducted kindergartens, religious schools, and so on, is by no means agreed upon by Socialists. It is like the question of marriage, a matter which is wholly beyond the scope of present knowledge. The future will decide for itself. There are those who believe that the state would not content itself with refusing to permit religious doctrines or ideas to be taught in the schools, but would go further, and, as the protector of the child, guard its independence of thought in later life as far as possible by forbidding religious teaching of any kind in schools for children below a certain age. It would not, of course, attempt to prevent parental instruction in religious beliefs in the home. Beyond the age prescribed, religious education, in all other than public institutions of learning, would be freely admitted. This restriction of religious education to the years of judgment and discretion implies no hostility to religion on the part of the state, but complete neutrality. Not the least important of the rights of the child is the right to be protected from influences which bias the mind and destroy the possibilities of independent thought in later life, or make it attainable only as a result of bitter, needless, tragic experience. This is one view. On the other hand, there are probably quite as many Socialists who believe that the state would not attempt to prevent the religious education of children of any age, in schools voluntarily maintained for that purpose, independent of the public schools. They believe that the state would content itself with insisting that these religious schools must be so built and equipped as not to imperil the lives or the health of the children attending them, and so conducted as not to interfere with the public schools,--all of which means simply that, like vaccination, and the form of marriage contract, the question will be settled by the future in its own way. There is nothing in the fundamental principles of Socialism, nor any body of facts in our present experience, from which we can judge the manner of that settlement.

In this brief outline of the Socialist state as the writer, in common with many of his associates, conceives it, there are many gaps. The temptation to fill in the outline somewhat more in detail is strong, but that is beyond the borderland which divides scientific and Utopian methods. The purpose of the outline is mainly to show that the ideal of the Socialism of to-day is something far removed from the network of laws and the oppressive bureaucracy commonly imagined; something wholly different in spirit and substance from the mechanical arrangement of human relations imagined by Utopian romancers. If the Socialist propaganda of to-day largely consists of the advocacy of laws for the protection of labor and dealing with all kinds of evils, it must be remembered that these are to *ameliorate conditions in the existing social order*. Many of the laws for which Socialists have most strenuously fought have their *raison d'etre* in the conditions of capitalist society, and would be quite unnecessary under Socialism. If a reference to one's personal work may be pardoned, I will cite the matter of the feeding of school children, in the public schools, at the public expense. I have, for many years, advocated this measure, which is to be found in most Socialist programmes, and which the Socialists of other countries have to a considerable extent carried into practical effect. Yet, I am free to say that the plan is not my ideal of the manner in which children should be fed. It is, at best, a palliative, a necessary evil, rendered necessary by the conditions of capitalist society. One hopes that in the Socialist regime, home life would be so far developed as to make possible the proper feeding and care of all children in their homes. This is but an illustration. The Socialist ideal of the state of the future, when private property is no longer an instrument of oppression used by the few against the many, is not a life completely enmeshed in a network of government, but a life controlled by government as little as possible; not a life ruled and driven by a powerful engine of laws, but a life as spontaneous and free as possible--a maximum of personal freedom with a minimum of restraint.

> "These things shall be! A loftier race
> Than e'er the world hath known shall rise
> With flower of freedom in their souls
> And light of science in their eyes."[196]

NOTES:

[180] Cf. *Das Erfurter Program*, by Karl Kautsky.

[181] Cf. Ensor's *Modern Socialism*, page 351.

[182] *Labour and Capital: a Letter to a Labour Friend*, by Goldwin Smith, D.C.L. (Macmillan, 1907).

The reader of Professor Smith's little book is referred, for the Socialist answer to his criticisms, to a small volume by the author of this book: *Capitalist and Laborer: an Open Letter to Professor Goldwin Smith*, D.C.L. (Kerr, *Standard Socialist Series*), 1907.

[183] *La Conquete du pain*, Pierre Kropotkin, 5th edition, Paris, 1895, page 202.

[184] *The Principles of Sociology*, by Herbert Spencer, Vol. III, page 534.

[185] Cf. *The Spirit of American Government*, by J. Allen Smith, LL.B. Ph.D., for a discussion of this subject.

[186] This statement must not be interpreted too narrowly, of course. While the nature of these things makes possible an infinitely wider range of personal liberty than is possible in some other things, individual liberty must *ultimately* be governed by the liberty of others. A fanatical religious sect practicing human sacrifice, for instance, could not be tolerated by any civilized society. Obscenity in art is another example.

[187] I use the word "state" throughout this discussion in its largest, most comprehensive sense, as meaning the whole political organization of society.

[188] This view is fully shared by Kautsky, *Agrarfrage*, pages 443-444, and by Paul Lafargue, *Revue Politique et Parliamentaire*, October, 1898, page 70.

[189] Of course, this does not mean that there must not be private *use* of land.

[190] The student who cares to pursue the subject will find that this analysis is, in the main, agreed to by the most eminent exponents of Marxian Socialism to-day. Cf., for instance, Kautsky's *Das Erfurter Program*; the same writer's *The Social Revolution*, especially pages 117, 159; Vandervelde, quoted by Ensor, *Modern Socialism*, page 205; also, Vandervelde's *Collectivism*, page 46. Jaures, the brilliant French Socialist, may not perhaps be strictly included in the category of "eminent Marxists," but he accepts the position of Kautsky, see *Studies in Socialism*, by Jean Jaures, pages 36-40. See, also, Engels, *Die Bauernfrage in Frankreich und Deutschland*, published in *Die Neue Zeit*, 1894-1895, No. 10; Kautsky, *Die Agrarfrage*; and Simons, *The American Farmer*. That most of these deal with petty agriculture rather than petty industry is true, but the principle holds in regard to both.

[191] "Ethics of Social Progress," by Professor Franklin H. Giddings in *Philanthropy and Social Progress* (1893), page 226.

[192] "The Economics of Factory Legislation," in *The Case For the Factory Acts*, by Mrs. Sidney Webb, page 50.

[193] See, for instance, Mr. Roosevelt's speech at Matinecock, L.I., near Oyster Bay, July 11, 1908, as reported in the daily papers by the Associated Press. Also, the Republican National Platform, 1908, which states that Socialism stands for "equality of possession," while the Republican Party stands for "equality of opportunity"--a complete misrepresentation, both of Socialism and the Republican Party!

[194] For condemning the wages system as a form of slavery, Socialists are often vigorously condemned, but there are few sociologists of repute who question the truth of the Socialist claim. Herbert Spencer, for example, is as vigorous in asserting that wage-labor is a form of slavery as any Socialist. See *The Principles of Sociology*, Vol. III, Chapter 18.

[195] See Kautsky's *Das Erfurter Program*, and also *The Social Revolution*, especially pages 128-135; Anton Menger, *L'Etat Socialiste*, page 35; and Vandervelde's *Collectivism*, pages 149-150.

[196] J. Addington Symonds.

CHAPTER X
THE MEANS OF REALIZATION[197]

I

You ask me how the goal I have described is to be attained: "The picture," you say, "is attractive, but we would like to know how we are to reach the Promised Land which it pictures. Show us the way!" The question is a fair one, and I shall try to answer it with candor, as it deserves. But I cannot promise to tell how the change will be brought about, to describe the exact process by which social property will supplant capitalist private property. The only conditions under which any honest thinker could give such an answer would necessitate a combination of circumstances which has never existed, and which no one seriously expects to develop. To answer in definite terms, saying, "This is the manner in which the change will be made," one would have to know the exact time of the change; precisely what things would be socialized; the thought of the people, their temper, their courage. In a word, omniscience would be necessary to enable one to make such a reply.

All that is possible in this connection for the candid Socialist is to point out those tendencies which he believes to be making for the Socialist ideal, those tendencies in society, whether political or economic, which are making for industrial democracy; to consider frankly the difficulties which must be overcome before the transition from capitalism can be effected, and to suggest such means of overcoming these as present themselves to the mind, always remembering that other means may be developed which we cannot now see, and that great storms of elemental human passion may sweep the current into channels unsuspected.

Those who are familiar with the writings of Marx know that, in strange contrast with the fundamental principles of that theory of social evolution which he so well developed, he lapsed at times into the Utopian habit of predicting the sudden transformation of society. Capitalism was to end in a great final "catastrophe" and the new order be born in the travail of a "social revolution." I remember that when I joined the Socialist movement, many years ago, the Social Revolution was a very real event, inevitable and nigh at hand, to most of us. The more enthusiastic of us dreamed of it; we sang songs in the spirit of the ***Chansons Revolutionaires***, one of which, as I recall, told plainly enough what we would do--

"When the Revolution comes."

Some comrades actually wanted to have military drill at our business meetings, merely that we might be ready for the Revolution, which might occur any Monday morning or Friday afternoon. If this seems strange and comic as I relate it to-day, please remember that we were very few and very young, and, therefore, very sure that we were to redeem the world. We lived in a state of revolutionary ecstasy. Some of us, I think, must have gone regularly to sleep in the mental state of Tennyson's May Queen, with words equivalent to her childish admonition--

"If you're waking call me early,"

so fearful were we that the Revolution might start without us!

There can be no harm in these confessions to-day, for we have grown far enough beyond that period to laugh at it in retrospect. True, there is still a good deal of talk about the Social Revolution, and there may be a few Socialists here and there who use the term in the sense I have described; who believe that capitalism will come to a great crisis, that there will be a rising of millions in wrath, a night of fury and agony, and then the sunrise of Brotherhood above the blood-stained valley and the corpse-strewn plain. But most of us, when we use the old term, by sheer force of habit, or as an inherited tradition, think of the Social Revolution in no such spirit. We think only of the change that must come over society, transferring the control of its life from the few to the many, the change that is now going on all around us. When the time comes that men and women speak of the state in which they live as Socialism, and look back upon the life we live to-day with wonder and pity, they will speak of the period of revolution as including this very year, and, possibly, all the years included in the lives of the youngest persons present. At all events, no considerable body of Socialists anywhere in the world to-day, and no Socialist whose words have any influence in the movement, believe that there will be a sudden, violent change from capitalism to Socialism.

If it seemed necessary, abundant testimony to the truthfulness of this claim could be produced. But I shall content myself with two witnesses--chosen from the multitude of available witnesses for reasons which will unfold themselves. The first witness is Marx himself. I choose his testimony, mainly, because there is no other name so great as his, and, secondly, to show that his profoundest thought rejected the idea of sudden social transformations which at times he seemed to favor. It is 1850. Marx is in London, actively engaged in a German Communist movement with its Central Committee in that great metropolis. The majority are impatient, feverishly urging revolt; they are under the illusion that they can make the Social Revolution at once. Marx tells them, on the contrary, that it will take fifty years "not only to change existing conditions but to change yourselves and make your-selves worthy of political power." They, the majority, say on the other hand, "We ought to get power at once, or else give up the fight." Marx tries vainly to make them see this, and resigns when he fails, scornfully telling them that they "substi-tute revolutionary phrases for ***revolutionary evolution***."[198] Mark well that term, "revolutionary evolution," for it bears out the description I have attempted of the sense in which we speak of revolution in the Socialist propaganda of to-day. And mark well, also, that Marx gave them fifty years simply to make themselves worthy of political power.

As the second witness, I choose Liebknecht, whose name must always be as-sociated with those of Marx, Engels, and Lassalle, in Socialist history. Not alone be-cause of the fact that Liebknecht, more than almost any other man, has influenced the tactics of the international Socialist movement, but for the additional reason that detached phrases of his are sometimes quoted in support of the opposite view. Words spoken in oratorical and forensic passion, or in the bravado of irresponsible youthfulness, and texts torn from their contexts, are used to show that Liebknecht anticipated the violent transformation of society. But heed this, one of many similar statements of his maturest and profoundest thought: "But we are not going to attain Socialism at one bound. The transition is going on all the time, and the important thing for us ... is not to paint a picture of the future--which in any case would be useless labor--but to forecast a practical programme for the intermediate period, to formulate and justify measures that shall be applicable at once, and that will serve as aids to the new Socialist birth."[199]

So much, then, for quotations from the mightiest of all our hosts. What I would make clear is not merely that the greatest of Socialist theorists and tacticians agree that the change will be brought about gradually, and not by one stroke of revolutionary action, but that, more important still, the Socialist Party of this country, and all the Socialist parties of the world, are based upon that idea. That is why they have their political programmes, aiming to make the conditions of life better now, in the transition period, and also to aid in the happy, peaceful birth of the new order.

II

Having disposed of the notion that Socialists expect to realize their ideals by a single stroke, and thus swept away some of the greatest obstacles which rise before the imagination of the student of Socialism, we obtain a clearer vision of the problem. And that is no small advance toward its solution.

Concerning the political organization of the Socialist state, so far as the extension of political democracy is concerned, not much need be said. You can very readily comprehend that this may be done by legal, constitutional means. Step by step, just as we attain power enough to do so, we shall extend the power of the people until we have a complete political democracy. Where, as in some of the Southern States, there is virtually a property qualification for the franchise, where that remnant of feudalism, the poll tax, remains, Socialists, whenever they come into power in those states, or whenever they are strong enough to force the issue, will insist upon making the franchise free. And where, as in this state, there is a sex qualification for the franchise, women being denied the suffrage, they will work unceasingly to do away with that relic of barbarism. By means of such measures as the Initiative and Referendum, and election of judges by the people, the sovereignty of the people will be established. It may be that without some constitutional amendments it will be found impossible to make political democracy complete. In that case, moving along the line of least resistance, they will do all that they can within the limits of the Constitution as it is, changing it whenever by reason of their power they deem that practicable.

As to the organization of the industrial life of the Socialist state, bringing industry from private to public control, here, too, Socialists will work along the line of least resistance. First of all, it must be remembered that there are tendencies to that end within society at present. Every development of industry and commerce, from competition to monopoly, so far as it centers the control in few hands and organizes the industry or business, makes it possible to take it over without dislocation, and, at the same time, makes it the interest of a larger number to help in bringing about that transfer. In like manner every voluntary cooeperative organization of producers makes for the Socialist ideal. This is a far less important matter in the United States than in England and other European countries. Finally, we have the enormous extension of public functions developed already in capitalist society, and being constantly extended. Our postal system, public schools, state universities, libraries, museums, art galleries, parks, bureaus of research and information, hospitals, sanatoria, municipal ferries, water supply, fire departments, health boards, lighting systems, these, and a thousand other activities of our municipalities and states, and the nation, are so many forms created by capitalism to meet its own needs which belong, however, to Socialism and require only to be infused with the Socialist spirit. This will be done as they come under the influence of Socialists elected to various legislative and administrative bodies in ever increasing number as the movement grows.

All this is not difficult to comprehend. What is more likely to perplex the average man is the method by which Socialists propose to effect the transfer of individual or corporate property to the collectivity. Will it be confiscated, taken without recompense; and if so, will it not be necessary to take the bank savings of the poor widow as well as the millions of the millionaire? On the other hand, if compensation is given, will there not be still a privileged class, a wealthy class, that is, and a poorer class? These are the questions I see written upon your faces as I look down upon them and read the language of their strained interest. Every face seems a challenge to answer these questions. I shall try to answer them with perfect candor, as far as that is possible within the limits of our time. May I not ask you, then, to follow carefully a brief series of propositions, or postulates, which I shall, with your permission, lay before you?

First: The act of transfer, whether it take the form of confiscation or otherwise, must be the will of a legal majority of the people. If the unit is the city, a legal majority of the citizens there; if the unit is the state, then a legal majority of the citizens of the state; if the unit is the nation, then a legal majority in the nation. I use the term "legal majority" to indicate my profound conviction that the process itself must be a legal, constitutional process. Of course, in the event of some great upheaval occurring, such as, for example, the rising of a suffering and desperate people in consequence of some terrific panic or period of depression, brought on by capitalist misrule, or by war, this might be swept away. Throughout the world's history such upheavals have occurred, when the people's wrath, or their desperation, has assumed the form of a cyclone, and in such times laws have been of no more resistance than straws in the pathway of the cyclone sweeping across the plain. Omitting such dire happenings from our calculations--for so we must wish to do--we may lay down this principle of the imperative necessity for a legal majority, acting in legal manner.

Second: The process must be gradual. There will be no *coup de force*. No effort will be made to socialize those industries which have not been made ready by a degree of monopolization. This we can say with confidence, if for no other reason than that we cannot conceive a legal majority being stirred sufficiently to take action in the absence of some degree of oppression or danger, such as monopoly alone contains. Further, as a matter of hard, practical sense, it is not conceivable that any government will ever be able to deal with all the industries at one time. The railroads may be first to be taken, or it may be the mines in one state and the oil wells in another. The important point is to see that the process of socialization *must* be piecemeal and gradual. This does not mean that it must be a *slow* process, suggesting the slowness of geologic formations, but that it must be gradual, progressive, advancing from step to step, and giving opportunities for adjusting things. Otherwise there would be chaos and anarchy.

Third: The manner of the acquisition must be determined by the people at the time, and not fixed by us in advance, according to some abstract principle. If the people decide to take any particular individual or corporate property without compensation, that will be done. And they will have great historic precedents for their action. The Socialists of Europe could point to the manner in which many of the feudal estates and rights were confiscated, while American Socialists could point to the manner in which, without indemnity or compensation, chattel slavery was abolished.

So much is said merely by way of explanation, first, that the manner of acquiring private and corporate property and making it social property is not to be decided in advance, and secondly, that there are historic precedents for confiscation. On the other hand, there is no good reason why compensation should not be paid for such properties. You start! You have been more shocked than if I had said we should seize the properties and cut the throats of the proprietors! Be assured: I am not forgetting my promise to be frank with you, nor am I expressing my personal opinion merely when I say that there is nothing in the theory of modern Socialism which precludes the possibility of compensation. There is no Socialist of repute and authority in the world, so far as my knowledge goes, who makes a contrary claim. I should regard it as unworthy to lay down as the Socialist position views which were my own, and which were not shared by the great body of Socialist thinkers throughout the world. It is not less nor more than the truth that all the leading Socialists of the world agree that compensation could be paid without doing violence to a single Socialist principle, and most of them favor it.[200]

Once more I shall appeal to the authority of Marx. Engels wrote in 1894: "We do not at all consider the indemnification of the proprietors as an impossibility, whatever may be the circumstances. How many times has not Karl Marx expressed to me the opinion that if we could buy up the whole crowd it would really be the cheapest way of relieving ourselves of them."[201] Not only Marx, then, in the most intimate of his discussions with Engels, his bosom friend, but Engels himself, in almost his last days, refused to admit the impossibility of paying indemnity for properties socialized, "whatever may be the circumstances."

Now, as to the difficulties--especially as to the widow's savings. The socialization of non-productive wealth is not contemplated by any Socialist, no matter whether it consist of the widow's savings in a stocking or the treasures in the safe deposit vaults of the rich. Mere wealth, whether in money or precious gems and jewels, need not trouble us. Non-productive wealth is outside of our calculation. In the next place, as I have attempted to make clear, the petty business, the individual store, the small workshop, and the farm operated by its owner, would not, necessarily, nor probably, be disturbed. We have to consider only the great agencies of exploitation, industries operated by many producers of surplus-value for the benefit of the few. Let us, for example, take a conspicuous industrial organization, the so-called Steel Trust. Suppose the Socialists to be in power: there is a popular demand for the socialization of the steel industry. The government decides to take over the plant of the Steel Trust and all its affairs, and the support of the vast majority of the people is assured. First a valuation takes place, and then bonds, government bonds, are issued. Unlike what happens too often at the present time, the price fixed is not greatly in excess of the value the people acquire--one of the means by which the capitalists fasten their clutches on the popular throat. The Socialist *spirit* enters into the business. Bonds are issued to all the shareholders in strict proportion to their holdings, and so the poor widow, concerning whose interests critics of Socialism are so solicitous, gets bonds for her share. She is therefore even more secure than before, since it is no longer possible for unscrupulous individuals to plunder her by nefarious stock transactions.

So far, good and well. But, you may rightly say, this will not eliminate the unearned incomes. The heavy stockholders will simply become rich bondholders. Temporarily, that is true. But when that has been accomplished in a few of the more important industries, they will find it difficult to invest their surplus incomes profitably. There will also be a surplus to the state over and above the amounts annually paid in redemption of the bonds. Finally, it will be possible to adopt measures for eliminating the unearned incomes entirely by means of taxation, such as the progressive income tax, property and inheritance taxes. Taxation is, of course, a form of confiscation, but it is a form which has become familiar, which is perfectly legal, and which enables the confiscatory process to be stretched out over a long enough period to make it comparatively easy, to reduce the hardship to a minimum. By means of a progressive income tax, a bond tax, and an inheritance tax, it would be possible to eliminate the unearned incomes of a class of bondholders from society within a reasonable period, without inflicting injury or hardship upon any human being.

I do not, let me again warn you, set this plan before you as one which Socialism depends upon, which must be adopted. I do not say that the Socialist parties of the world are pledged to this method, for they are not. The subject is not mentioned in any of our programmes, so far as I recall them at this moment. We are silent upon the subject, not because we fear to discuss it, but because we realize that the matter will be decided when the question is reached, and that each case will be decided upon its merits. Still, it is but fair to express my belief that it is to the interest of the workers, no less than of the rest of society, that the change to a Socialist state be made as easy and peaceable as possible. Socialists, being human beings and not monsters, naturally desire that the transition to Socialism shall be made with as little friction and pain as possible. Left to their own choice, I am confident that those upon whom the task of effecting the change falls will not choose the way of violence, if the way of peace is left open to them.

Within the limits of this opportunity, I have tried to be as frank as I am to myself in those constant self-questionings which are inseparable from the work of the serious propagandist and honest teacher. Further I cannot go. If I have not been able to tell definitely how the change ***will*** be wrought, I have at least been able, I hope, to show that it ***may*** be brought about peaceably and without bloodshed. If this has given any one a new view of Socialism--opened, as it were, a doorway through which you can get a glimpse of the City Beautiful, and the way leading to its gates--then my reward is infinitely precious.

NOTES:

[197] From the stenographic report of an address given to some students of Socialism in New York, October, 1907.

[198] Cf. Jaures, ***Studies in Socialism***, page 44.

[199] Quoted by Jaures, ***Studies in Socialism***, page 93.

[200] The reader is referred to Kautsky's books, ***Das Erfurter Program*** and ***The Social Revolution***, and to Vandervelde's admirable work, ***Collectivism***, for confirmation of this statement.

The Codes Of Hammurabi And Moses
W. W. Davies

QTY

The discovery of the Hammurabi Code is one of the greatest achievements of archaeology, and is of paramount interest, not only to the student of the Bible, but also to all those interested in ancient history...

Religion   **ISBN:** *1-59462-338-4*   **Pages:132**

MSRP $12.95

The Theory of Moral Sentiments
Adam Smith

QTY

This work from 1749. contains original theories of conscience amd moral judgment and it is the foundation for systemof morals.

Philosophy **ISBN:** *1-59462-777-0*   **Pages:536**

MSRP $19.95

Jessica's First Prayer
Hesba Stretton

QTY

In a screened and secluded corner of one of the many railway-bridges which span the streets of London there could be seen a few years ago, from five o'clock every morning until half past eight, a tidily set-out coffee-stall, consisting of a trestle and board, upon which stood two large tin cans, with a small fire of charcoal burning under each so as to keep the coffee boiling during the early hours of the morning when the work-people were thronging into the city on their way to their daily toil...

Pages:84

Childrens   **ISBN:** *1-59462-373-2*   *MSRP $9.95*

My Life and Work
Henry Ford

QTY

Henry Ford revolutionized the world with his implementation of mass production for the Model T automobile. Gain valuable business insight into his life and work with his own auto-biography... "We have only started on our development of our country we have not as yet, with all our talk of wonderful progress, done more than scratch the surface. The progress has been wonderful enough but..."

Pages:300

Biographies/   **ISBN:** *1-59462-198-5*   *MSRP $21.95*

The Art of Cross-Examination
Francis Wellman

QTY

I presume it is the experience of every author, after his first book is published upon an important subject, to be almost overwhelmed with a wealth of ideas and illustrations which could readily have been included in his book, and which to his own mind, at least, seem to make a second edition inevitable. Such certainly was the case with me; and when the first edition had reached its sixth impression in five months, I rejoiced to learn that it seemed to my publishers that the book had met with a sufficiently favorable reception to justify a second and considerably enlarged edition. ..

Pages:412

Reference   ISBN: *1-59462-647-2*   *MSRP $19.95*

On the Duty of Civil Disobedience
Henry David Thoreau

QTY

Thoreau wrote his famous essay, On the Duty of Civil Disobedience, as a protest against an unjust but popular war and the immoral but popular institution of slave-owning. He did more than write—he declined to pay his taxes, and was hauled off to gaol in consequence. Who can say how much this refusal of his hastened the end of the war and of slavery ?

Law   ISBN: *1-59462-747-9*

Pages:48

MSRP $7.45

Dream Psychology Psychoanalysis for Beginners
Sigmund Freud

QTY

Sigmund Freud, born Sigismund Schlomo Freud (May 6, 1856 - September 23, 1939), was a Jewish-Austrian neurologist and psychiatrist who co-founded the psychoanalytic school of psychology. Freud is best known for his theories of the unconscious mind, especially involving the mechanism of repression; his redefinition of sexual desire as mobile and directed towards a wide variety of objects; and his therapeutic techniques, especially his understanding of transference in the therapeutic relationship and the presumed value of dreams as sources of insight into unconscious desires.

Psychology   ISBN: *1-59462-905-6*

Pages:196

MSRP $15.45

The Miracle of Right Thought
Orison Swett Marden

QTY

Believe with all of your heart that you will do what you were made to do. When the mind has once formed the habit of holding cheerful, happy, prosperous pictures, it will not be easy to form the opposite habit. It does not matter how improbable or how far away this realization may see, or how dark the prospects may be, if we visualize them as best we can, as vividly as possible, hold tenaciously to them and vigorously struggle to attain them, they will gradually become actualized, realized in the life. But a desire, a longing without endeavor, a yearning abandoned or held indifferently will vanish without realization.

Pages:360

Self Help   ISBN: *1-59462-644-8*   *MSRP $25.45*

QTY

The Rosicrucian Cosmo-Conception Mystic Christianity *by Max Heindel*   ISBN: *1-59462-188-8*   **$38.95**
The Rosicrucian Cosmo-conception is not dogmatic, neither does it appeal to any other authority than the reason of the student. It is: not controversial, but is: sent forth in the, hope that it may help to clear...   New Age/Religion Pages 646

Abandonment To Divine Providence *by Jean-Pierre de Caussade*   ISBN: *1-59462-228-0*   **$25.95**
"The Rev. Jean Pierre de Caussade was one of the most remarkable spiritual writers of the Society of Jesus in France in the 18th Century. His death took place at Toulouse in 1751. His works have gone through many editions and have been republished...   Inspirational/Religion Pages 400

Mental Chemistry *by Charles Haanel*   ISBN: *1-59462-192-6*   **$23.95**
Mental Chemistry allows the change of material conditions by combining and appropriately utilizing the power of the mind. Much like applied chemistry creates something new and unique out of careful combinations of chemicals the mastery of mental chemistry...   New Age Pages 354

The Letters of Robert Browning and Elizabeth Barret Barrett 1845-1846 vol II   ISBN: *1-59462-193-4*   **$35.95**
by Robert Browning and Elizabeth Barrett   Biographies Pages 596

Gleanings In Genesis (volume I) *by Arthur W. Pink*   ISBN: *1-59462-130-6*   **$27.45**
Appropriately has Genesis been termed "the seed plot of the Bible" for in it we have, in germ form, almost all of the great doctrines which are afterwards fully developed in the books of Scripture which follow...   Religion/Inspirational Pages 420

The Master Key *by L. W. de Laurence*   ISBN: *1-59462-001-6*   **$30.95**
In no branch of human knowledge has there been a more lively increase of the spirit of research during the past few years than in the study of Psychology, Concentration and Mental Discipline. The requests for authentic lessons in Thought Control, Mental Discipline and...   New Age/Business Pages 422

The Lesser Key Of Solomon Goetia *by L. W. de Laurence*   ISBN: *1-59462-092-X*   **$9.95**
This translation of the first book of the "Lernegton" which is now for the first time made accessible to students of Talismanic Magic was done, after careful collation and edition, from numerous Ancient Manuscripts in Hebrew, Latin, and French...   New Age/Occult Pages 92

Rubaiyat Of Omar Khayyam *by Edward Fitzgerald*   ISBN: *1-59462-332-5*   **$13.95**
Edward Fitzgerald, whom the world has already learned, in spite of his own efforts to remain within the shadow of anonymity, to look upon as one of the rarest poets of the century, was born at Bredfield, in Suffolk, on the 31st of March, 1809. He was the third son of John Purcell...   Music Pages 172

Ancient Law *by Henry Maine*   ISBN: *1-59462-128-4*   **$29.95**
The chief object of the following pages is to indicate some of the earliest ideas of mankind, as they are reflected in Ancient Law, and to point out the relation of those ideas to modern thought.   Religion/History Pages 452

Far-Away Stories *by William J. Locke*   ISBN: *1-59462-129-2*   **$19.45**
"Good wine needs no bush, but a collection of mixed vintages does. And this book is just such a collection. Some of the stories I do not want to remain buried for ever in the museum files of dead magazine-numbers an author's not unpardonable vanity..."   Fiction Pages 272

Life of David Crockett *by David Crockett*   ISBN: *1-59462-250-7*   **$27.45**
"Colonel David Crockett was one of the most remarkable men of the times in which he lived. Born in humble life, but gifted with a strong will, an indomitable courage, and unremitting perseverance...   Biographies/New Age Pages 424

Lip-Reading *by Edward Nitchie*   ISBN: *1-59462-206-X*   **$25.95**
Edward B. Nitchie, founder of the New York School for the Hard of Hearing, now the Nitchie School of Lip-Reading, Inc, wrote "LIP-READING Principles and Practice". The development and perfecting of this meritorious work on lip-reading was an undertaking...   How-to Pages 400

A Handbook of Suggestive Therapeutics, Applied Hypnotism, Psychic Science   ISBN: *1-59462-214-0*   **$24.95**
by Henry Munro   Health/New Age/Health/Self-help Pages 376

A Doll's House: and Two Other Plays *by Henrik Ibsen*   ISBN: *1-59462-112-8*   **$19.95**
Henrik Ibsen created this classic when in revolutionary 1848 Rome. Introducing some striking concepts in playwriting for the realist genre, this play has been studied the world over.   Fiction/Classics/Plays 308

The Light of Asia *by sir Edwin Arnold*   ISBN: *1-59462-204-3*   **$13.95**
In this poetic masterpiece, Edwin Arnold describes the life and teachings of Buddha. The man who was to become known as Buddha to the world was born as Prince Gautama of India but he rejected the worldly riches and abandoned the reigns of power when...   Religion/History/Biographies Pages 170

The Complete Works of Guy de Maupassant *by Guy de Maupassant*   ISBN: *1-59462-157-8*   **$16.95**
"For days and days, nights and nights, I had dreamed of that first kiss which was to consecrate our engagement, and I knew not on what spot I should put my lips..."   Fiction/Classics Pages 240

The Art of Cross-Examination *by Francis L. Wellman*   ISBN: *1-59462-309-0*   **$26.95**
Written by a renowned trial lawyer, Wellman imparts his experience and uses case studies to explain how to use psychology to extract desired information through questioning.   How-to/Science/Reference Pages 408

Answered or Unanswered? *by Louisa Vaughan*   ISBN: *1-59462-248-5*   **$10.95**
Miracles of Faith in China   Religion Pages 112

The Edinburgh Lectures on Mental Science (1909) *by Thomas*   ISBN: *1-59462-008-3*   **$11.95**
This book contains the substance of a course of lectures recently given by the writer in the Queen Street Hall, Edinburgh. Its purpose is to indicate the Natural Principles governing the relation between Mental Action and Material Conditions...   New Age/Psychology Pages 148

Ayesha *by H. Rider Haggard*   ISBN: *1-59462-301-5*   **$24.95**
Verily and indeed it is the unexpected that happens! Probably if there was one person upon the earth from whom the Editor of this, and of a certain previous history, did not expect to hear again...   Classics Pages 380

Ayala's Angel *by Anthony Trollope*   ISBN: *1-59462-352-X*   **$29.95**
The two girls were both pretty, but Lucy who was twenty-one who supposed to be simple and comparatively unattractive, whereas Ayala was credited, as her Bombwhat romantic name might show, with poetic charm and a taste for romance. Ayala when her father died was nineteen...   Fiction Pages 484

The American Commonwealth *by James Bryce*   ISBN: *1-59462-286-8*   **$34.45**
An interpretation of American democratic political theory. It examines political mechanics and society from the perspective of Scotsman James Bryce   Politics Pages 572

Stories of the Pilgrims *by Margaret P. Pumphrey*   ISBN: *1-59462-116-0*   **$17.95**
This book explores pilgrims religious oppression in England as well as their escape to Holland and eventual crossing to America on the Mayflower, and their early days in New England...   History Pages 268

QTY

The Fasting Cure by *Sinclair Upton*   ISBN: *1-59462-222-1*   **$13.95**
In the Cosmopolitan Magazine for May, 1910, and in the Contemporary Review (London) for April, 1910, I published an article dealing with my experiences in fasting. I have written a great many magazine articles, but never one which attracted so much attention... New Age/Self Help/Health Pages 164

Hebrew Astrology by *Sepharial*   ISBN: *1-59462-308-2*   **$13.45**
In these days of advanced thinking it is a matter of common observation that we have left many of the old landmarks behind and that we are now pressing forward to greater heights and to a wider horizon than that which represented the mind-content of our progenitors... Astrology Pages 144

Thought Vibration or The Law of Attraction in the Thought World   ISBN: *1-59462-127-6*   **$12.95**

by *William Walker Atkinson*   Psychology/Religion Pages 144

Optimism by *Helen Keller*   ISBN: *1-59462-108-X*   **$15.95**
Helen Keller was blind, deaf, and mute since 19 months old, yet famously learned how to overcome these handicaps, communicate with the world, and spread her lectures promoting optimism. An inspiring read for everyone... Biographies/Inspirational Pages 84

Sara Crewe by *Frances Burnett*   ISBN: *1-59462-360-0*   **$9.45**
In the first place, Miss Minchin lived in London. Her home was a large, dull, tall one, in a large, dull square, where all the houses were alike, and all the sparrows were alike, and where all the door-knockers made the same heavy sound... Childrens/Classic Pages 88

The Autobiography of Benjamin Franklin by *Benjamin Franklin*   ISBN: *1-59462-135-7*   **$24.95**
The Autobiography of Benjamin Franklin has probably been more extensively read than any other American historical work, and no other book of its kind has had such ups and downs of fortune. Franklin lived for many years in England, where he was agent... Biographies/History Pages 332

Name	
Email	
Telephone	
Address	
City, State ZIP	

☐ **Credit Card**   ☐ **Check / Money Order**

Credit Card Number	
Expiration Date	
Signature	

Please Mail to: Book Jungle
                    PO Box 2226
                    Champaign, IL 61825
or Fax to: 630-214-0564

ORDERING INFORMATION

web: *www.bookjungle.com*
email: *sales@bookjungle.com*
fax: *630-214-0564*
mail: *Book Jungle PO Box 2226 Champaign, IL 61825*
or PayPal *to sales@bookjungle.com*

Please contact us for bulk discounts

DIRECT-ORDER TERMS

**20% Discount if You Order
Two or More Books**
Free Domestic Shipping!
Accepted: Master Card, Visa,
Discover, American Express